THE RESURRECTION CLUB

The year is 1827. In the dark recesses of a city famous for its learning and notorious for its low-life, its drinking dens and stinking graveyards, one man is consumed by his thirst for forbidden knowledge. For Alexander Brodie – maverick surgeon, medical showman and obsessive genius – no challenge is too great, no sacrifice too precious in the quest for scientific progress . . .

In present-day Edinburgh Charlie Kidd, rising PR star, is about to find himself outclassed in festival antics and carnival mischief by a new client, the decidedly devilish and strangely familiar Peter Dexter. Up in Edinburgh's ancient graveyards, he spreads out an inviting prospect before Charlie. But Charlie isn't the only one to think that this could all just be a show, a show dangerously out of control . . .

Edinburgh is a city in which many have cheated the grave, a city that has cultivated the arts of bodysnatching and of showmanship and the crafts of technological innovation and experiment. Now at the close of a century, the past and present collide with explosive consequences – resurrection and retribution.

CHRISTOPHER WALLACE is the author of one previous novel, *The Pied Piper's Poison*. He lives in Edinburgh.

THE
RESURRECTION
CLUB

Christopher Wallace

Flamingo
An Imprint of HarperCollins*Publishers*

F

Flamingo
An Imprint of HarperCollins*Publishers*
77–85 Fulham Palace Road,
Hammersmith, London w6 8JB
www.fireandwater.com

Published by Flamingo 1999

1 3 5 7 9 8 6 4 2

This novel is a work of fiction. The names, characters and incidents
portrayed in it are the work of the author's imagination.
Any resemblance to actual persons, living or dead, events or localities,
is entirely coincidental.

Photograph of Christopher Wallace and of woman
on pages 1 and 46 by Owen Edelsten.

ISBN 0 00 225857 9

Set in Postscript Linotype Janson by
Rowland Phototypesetting Ltd,
Bury St Edmunds, Suffolk

Printed and bound in Great Britain by
Clays Ltd, St Ives plc

For my mother and father, Caroline and Gill;
and for Marvin. Sleep well, little friend.

All creativity is good. You start with an empty page, a blank canvas, a silence; and you begin to fill the void. Where once was nothing, there is now expression, a light in the darkness.

All creativity is good, and all of us have different talents, different ways of filling the vacuum. Some will fashion objects, pictures and writings; for others the effort is less noticeable – the poetry is there in their everyday voice, the dance in the way they walk. All of us are artists, whether we care to acknowledge this or not.

My talent is for the situation, the definition of a circumstance with participants, parameters and point of disturbance, all feeding off the energy of each other. Set two fierce dogs on each other in an enclosed area – *a situation*, watch them fight. A cruelty? No, these beasts are artists, all creativity is good.

PIERSHILL CEMETERY. A large white marble stone towering above the other memorials, resting in the centre of a grassy mound. One of the first things Peter Dexter had taken me to see on this tour of Edinburgh – part of my initial briefing on the requirements of his account. We had been going for over an hour and I was yet to hear a mention of the gallery or the cultural programmes that would seduce the corporate sponsors. Rain. A dreech April morning, a spring day to gladden only a true Calvinist's heart. I had a vague, gnawing sensation of guilt; this was meant to be work, a constructive new business enterprise, but was surely a waste of time. I was wasting my time, or Dexter was wasting my time, or somehow we were both wasting my company's time. What about the gallery, what about the sponsors? Not a word. Dexter's spasm of uncontrollable enthusiasm had taken us off on another arcane, though undeniably compelling, tangent.

'Here . . . See, Charles? This is where he's meant to be . . . couldn't be . . . Every grave in Edinburgh is empty anyway, but you can see the impression he must have made for them to want to *erect* this for him when he'd only been here . . . what? . . . months.'

Peter Dexter is a small man with a commanding presence way out of proportion to his limited stature, and a voice that seems to bleat with whatever excitement there is in the moment, which usually as far as he is concerned, is more than plenty.

His hand probes forward to pet the cold stone, and I try not to notice the disgusting pot-bellied girth that is revealed as his coat is pulled open by this action. The man is a client. I'm trying to like him.

Where his fingers rest, I read the legend signed with a flourish – 'The Great Lafayette' – and below this a further dedication, 'In memory of my Dearest Beauty'.

3

'Peter, who was Beauty?'

'Beauty? Charlie, forget Beauty, that was just a fucking dog – given to him by Houdini though – but that's not the essential part of the story . . . not the important part at all.'

He spat the words out with urgency. It was obviously vital I absorbed the full implications of the Great Lafayette's sinister tale now.

'Just a fucking dog.' This from the man who would later take me to the most famous grave in Edinburgh, that of poor little Greyfriars Bobby, and recount with a tear in his eye how the faithful little terrier had followed his master's funeral procession and promptly stood by the graveside for the next fourteen years. An extraordinary act of loyalty, *'ex-tra-orr-din-arry'* Dexter would say. Still, he would add, rapidly composing himself, the mutt couldn't have been that clever or else he would have known that after the first night his master wasn't likely to be there. *'Ex-tra-orr-dinarily stu-pid.'*

But even this wasn't the essential part of the story that morning, not the important part at all. What was it he wanted me to take in?

The 'essential' part. The Great Lafayette was an American magician, born Sigmund Neuberger in 1873. In 1911 he was at the peak of his powers: thirty-eight years old, fit, charismatic, highly intelligent, and unfortunate enough to be performing in Edinburgh. His speciality was a dramatic illusion carried out during his stage show, 'The Man of Mystery', which had thrilled the capital's audiences at the Empire Theatre for several weeks before he decided to add a strange new feature, 'The Lion's Bride'.

On the evening of 11 May the packed house watched the show's climax in awe. Neuberger/Lafayette pranced around the stage set in his animal costume, astonishing the crowd with his athletic prowess, leaping cat-like among the elaborate Eastern scenery, seemingly clearing ten yards in a single bound. His prey, an attractive young showgirl, cowered helplessly as he moved in for the kill. Blood actually flowed as the beast's claws sank into the virginal white flesh and, for a diabolical instant, the creature was seen to physically devour its victim. Suddenly, all the stage lights surged in brightness and intensity as if overloaded with power. An electric wire leading

4

to a lantern fused. Darkness. A scream from the stalls, then more. A small flame licked up the scenery backdrop, and in seconds a large piece of jungle fern had caught fire as the blaze began to establish itself. The audience began to warm to this new experience, believing it to be part of the show they had paid to see. They gasped in delight as a sheet of flame roared across the footlights, narrowly missing the orchestra. Applause rang out as the safety curtain fell, taking the fire into the backstage area.

The lion stepped forward once more, tearing off his mask to reveal a handsome face. Lafayette's hands acknowledged the applause and then moved to silence the cheers. 'Please, ladies and gentlemen. In the interests of your own safety, leave in an orderly fashion.'

Yet nobody moved. He tried again, shaking his head at the absurdity. 'There is a fire, ladies and gentlemen. You must leave.'

At last some began to make their way to the exits, following the obviously shaken members of the orchestra, though the majority remained rooted, more terrified of missing the next part of the performance than the billowing conflagration. A scream, this time from backstage, halted Lafayette's fresh appeal. He darted back, vanishing into the thick smoke.

His final appearance came minutes later. He was clearly distressed, having failed in his search for a member of the company. A last anguished cry. 'For God's sake, save yourselves!'

At that moment, the main support beam for the stage ceiling collapsed. Lafayette disappeared for the last time from the stage, engulfed by the dark crackling void.

It took the fire brigade until three o'clock in the morning to control the blaze. Seven bodies were found, only four of which could be identified, the rest burnt beyond recognition. These were all taken to the police mortuary at the city's Cowgate where an identification process was undertaken by the Professor of Forensic Medicine. It was he who was able to advise which corpse was the Great Lafayette's, and he who was responsible for its removal to Glasgow for its final cremation.

Three days later, the charred ruins of the once proud theatre are being razed, and another body is found, this time in a hole where the stage had been. This body is also identified as Lafayette's by the large diamond ring on its right hand and double gold ring on the left. It is this body which was buried at Piershill Cemetery, next to that of Beauty, the magician's beloved dog who had died only the previous week.

The tremulous wobble which has returned to Dexter's voice tells me we have now reached the essential part of the story, or rather perhaps, the vital questions. Whose body lies in this grave – The Great Lafayette's or his stage double? Where does Sigmund Neuberger fit into all of this? Was Lafayette a tawdry role he invented for himself so he could waste his talents on the boards of endless provincial theatres or had he succeeded – once he had come to Edinburgh – in creating an entirely new character made real by the will of the audience?

Seven months on from the tragic blaze, rumours began to filter back to the city of a new 'Lion's Bride' being performed in America, although, in this new show, when the climax of the evening comes, the actor in the cat's skin does not remove his mask. Had the beast needed to be fed again? Had The Great Lafayette performed the greatest illusion of them all and cheated his own grave?

'A cheated grave . . .' laughed Dexter. 'As if there was only the one cheated grave in Edinburgh.'

He had relayed the tale with astonishing passion, lingering on every detail and as surprised as I was by each turn of events. The theatre scenes had verged on embarrassment as he had screamed and wailed his way through the melodrama; I was to be glad no one else was in earshot.

I listened in the drizzle for over an hour and there was still no mention of sponsors or how all this might lead to future business opportunities. I felt overwhelmed, more uncomfortable than ever by the time we turned and headed off towards the entrance gates. More guilt at wasting valuable business time, clocking up further unchargeable hours? No, that unpleasantness had been replaced by a more profound and disturbing one, one that had more to do with the way Dexter had told the story.

He told it as if he had actually been there.

TRANSCRIPT : TAPE 1

Transcript of interview recorded 5/7/99, with Daniel Lowes, the only respondent to the article which appeared in 'The Scene Setter' and who was reported to have left Scotland shortly afterwards. Currently, a 'Daniel Lowes' is being held in a Bangkok jail awaiting trial on drug trafficking charges. Although of similar nationality to the interviewee, it cannot yet be confirmed if this is the same man. A payment was made in return for participation in the interview, which took place in the hotel room of the interviewer. Lowes had arrived late for the scheduled appointment, looking tired and dressed shabbily, certainly older than his stated age (28). Throughout the session he would glance instinctively at his wrist – although he wasn't wearing a watch – and would scan the room to catch sight of one of the two clocks. He toyed repeatedly with his drink – a mineral water – endlessly topping up his glass despite drinking very little. These mannerisms seemed to belie the relaxed and easygoing impression he seemed, initially at least, eager to establish – although given the nature of his revelations over the course of the interview such a display of nervousness would be understandable. The heroin-related charges of the Thai court carry a death sentence, if the prisoner is convicted.

Voice of interviewer:
Please don't let this put you off . . . it's purely to help me remember, honestly. You'd soon get bored, believe me, if you had to wait for me to write everything down . . . okay?

Lowes:
It's up to you . . . I mean, I might ask you to switch it off for some things. Nothing personal . . . (voice becomes inaudible on recording) It's just . . . I might . . . you know?

Interviewer:
Whatever. Can I start . . . Can we start . . . by you talking us through how you first got involved in the show?

Lowes:
Got involved? Saw the ad in the paper – *Guardian*. That gave the number of the enquiry line, so I called that and it went from there.

Interviewer:
Sorry . . . had you heard of the show before then though? Did you have any idea what it might be all about?

Lowes:
I'd heard that something a bit . . . weird was taking place . . . or being planned. Nobody knew at the start whether it was all just hype though . . . happens all the time at the Festival . . . 'the most outrageous show ever!' kind of thing. There'll always be someone who'll condemn an act without even seeing it. Once you've got some councillor calling for your show to be banned, the box office goes bananas.

Interviewer:
So you had heard of it. How . . . and where?

Lowes:
I'd been to Edinburgh the year before, when I was a student. One of my friends at Oxford . . . his parents have a place here. So I'd seen how it all worked, and we'd had a great time. Last summer, after I'd lost my job, I thought I might as well come up on my own for the Festival. Seemed a good bet to make some contacts, enjoy a bit of *culture* (laughs), and I got this great flat in the Meadows.

Interviewer:
And what were you living on? Did you have money, were you working?

Lowes:
(pause) You want to switch that thing off?

8

Interviewer:
No . . . sorry . . . just go on.

Lowes:
And so I arrived for the start of the first week, and had a chance to read up on what was going on, and I knew where to hang out from the time before . . . the normal places. Gilded Balloon, Assembly Rooms and the like, but I actually preferred the more obscure places, for a number of reasons. I know it might sound strange, being a tourist myself, but you get sick pretty quickly of the obvious Festival types. You're here in this beautiful city, soaking up a different atmosphere, or trying to, and all you hear are these English bloody voices. Of course, half of them are Scottish, that's the strange thing. Edinburgh is full of Scots with Home Counties accents. They all get churned out of public school with the same voice, and all of Edinburgh's middle-class children go to these schools and the Festival is a very middle-class thing . . . or most of it is. Pseuds going to the workshops to see low-life reality dolled up for entertainment in *Trainspotting*. (affects accent) '. . . and this is how junkies actually live. How *marvellous*!' (affects look of distaste). So I preferred to go to the more obscure places. The Netherbow, The Stepping Stones, Leith Palace. More likely to meet my kind of people, do business with less . . . (pause) And also because I began to develop a taste for the shows that were more, *out there*. I went to see this Japanese performance of *Hamlet*, didn't understand a bloody word. Two hours of hysterical shrieking, but I had this sense that they . . . *meant it*, and then there was this dance troupe, Spanish. 'Dance Theatre of the Impossible', and their show was going to 'Explore the Impossible', and I thought – like anyone would – pretentious nonsense. But I found myself going anyway. One, because it was free, and two, because I knew it would be an *experience*. It was. Only four of us in the audience, and there's twelve of them on stage. And the girls – beautiful. Got their kit off four numbers in. I felt for them, really did, and so did the other three, probably in every sense of the word (laughs). Anyway, I wanted to see more of this, and to meet the people as well. Not that I'm a theatre groupie. I suppose I just got more into this whole thing of *performance* (laughs). Like I said, you can get into these things for

free if you are about just before they go on, if they've sold no tickets and they just want an audience. So I was that soldier, waiting at the bar of these places lunchtimes, afternoons and evenings, and that's when I got to hear about 'Proscribed'.

Interviewer:
What did you hear?

Lowes:
That somebody was putting on a show that was the ultimate in the avant garde, that nobody knew where it was but that was all part of it. The audience was by selection only and would be told the secret location only an hour beforehand. And of course it all worked, everyone was desperate to go, desperate not to miss out, determined to be one of the select few. The word was that the thing was so outrageous they only dared put it on twice during the Festival. In the end, of course, the first was also the last. It went out with a bang (laughs dryly), then lights out for ever. Sometimes I'm glad to have been there at the only showing – nobody can take away what I saw that night – and then sometimes I realise I'm cursed because of what I saw and how I can never escape it. Wish I'd never heard of the fucking thing, wish I'd never seen it advertised.

Interviewer:
You saw an ad in the press?

Lowes:
Couple of days after I'd first heard of it. Small ad, in the property section, under Rooms to Let. 'Proscribed accommodation. Edinburgh. Interested? Only a few places left. Must be discreet. Please call xxx.'

Interviewer:
And you did?

Lowes:
Well, I knew straight away that this had to be part of it. I called and I got an answer machine. Some girl with an impossibly breathy

voice, as if she was trying to sound desperately vampish. She came on the line, thanking you for calling *'Proscribed'*, and asking you to leave your address so that they could send you a questionnaire which would *'probe'* to see 'if you were suitable'.

Interviewer:
You received this? What was in it?

Lowes:
It came three days later. Printed on some kind of fake manuscript, meant to look old, antique. There was a brief note on the front: 'Pablo Dextrus invites you to his performance of *Proscribed*, a taste of taboo', or something like that. It then said that it had to test the compatibility of potential audience members against the artistic values of the performers and of Pablo himself. There were five questions after that, and you were invited to reply to them 'in as many words as necessary'.

Interviewer:
Can you remember the questions?

Lowes:
They were kind of bizarre, pointless in an open-ended sort of way. I can't remember them exactly, but there were things like 'What's the worst job for a midget?' 'Describe the tenacity of a fancy foot doctor.' Something about 'When can a concept not be conceived?' 'What's the very best kind of club to be in?' Can't remember the others.

Interviewer:
But you managed to answer them?

Lowes:
(pause) I was smoking a lot of dope (laughs). I must have come up with something they liked . . . To be honest I just crashed out the replies. Best thought first thought, you know? Anyhow, the thing reminded me of some kind of student fanzine. One of the questions I answered by writing a poem, another I tried to answer with some

phoney legal jargon, quoted the case, you know, Twat vs C.Unt, 1951. (laughs) Worst job for a midget? Basketball coach! (mimes enthusiastic writing motion) Best kind of club? An illegal one, a masonic one for the ritual and shared spoils but without the fucking police. And they bought it. Got my ticket a week later, and a note to phone for the address. (pause) Then one of the sections wasn't really a question at all. The last bit . . . it just said something like 'T is for Tarot but it also stands for Tourism', and the first time I read it I felt this . . . *pull* . . . an empathy. It was obvious nonsense but something that made a connection somewhere in my mind with the feeling that was growing in me, that the Festival could be something so good, so intimate on a grand scale, but that it's being squeezed by all the crass, the shit they know will sell . . . (mumbles) . . . 'Stands for Tarot but also for Tourism'. (clearer) Yes, I thought that this was just *made* for me. Should have been smarter, this was spooky . . . they were already inside my head.

OKAY. THE WORD ON EDINBURGH. What kind of job could you do with this bloody place? What would the brief be? Let's brainstorm in the best PR style:

Edinburgh. The Festival city. A city of unparalleled beauty and elegance. A refined city of culture and history. An overwhelming city. The Athens of the North.

All true, or at least based on part-truth. The pioneers in the black art of Public Relations certainly did their job here – every fault has become a charming eccentricity, a ghoulish past has been successfully repositioned as the kitsch of the present. A city where ghost tours wait for night to fall and the coachloads of gullible Americans to join. A professional job, worthy of an industry award if the culprits could be found. A presentation that misses, purposefully, the vital part.

Contrast this with *The Real Edinburgh*? A schizophrenic city, living on its own unique faultline, waiting for the earthquake to come. A city with an exterior allure and a rotten core. A city willing, able and waiting to deceive. Here, the graveyards are full – with headstones at least – of the fools and losers drawn by the promise of its captivating skyline. Headstones of the cheated. A city to break your heart.

So. Divided in two then, but by what? Where is the split? Between the old and new?

The Old. It's all 'old' but the oldest lies in the Old Town. The motley collection of medieval and baroque shanties tottering up the Royal Mile towards the Castle and down towards Grassmarket was once Europe's most notorious slum, built on a hill so the cobbled alleys and lanes leading off could function as free-flowing sewers. Of course the flaw in the design was that the gathering point for the tide of waste – including animal carcasses and, before they became a more precious commodity, corpses – was at the foot of that hill. The Nor' Loch below the castle. 'This 'Loch' was of course a cesspit, a fetid pool of excrement whose foul odours gave the city its first nickname before we PR men could get to work – 'Auld Reekie'. The language of Lowland Scots, not afraid to tell it like it was.

The 'New' came along when the men of the Enlightenment had the idea of draining the lake and thus opening up the land between the Castle and the Forth to the north, land that would be trans-formed into the network of Georgian symmetry and masonic squares that is the New Town. Designed by a twenty-three year old, James Craig, winner of the competition laid on by the city fathers to source a free plan. His prize? A place in the graveyard he laid at the centre of his scheme. Visitors welcome.

The bricks of the New Town were laid in the aftermath of the failure of Prince Charlie's rebellion of 1745, at a time when Edinburgh's genteel society was at pains to distance itself from the heathens of the highland clans whose behaviour – insurrection and then allowing themselves to be slaughtered – had disgraced the land. A time when Edinburgh society passed itself off as 'North British' rather than Scottish to emphasise the point. And to empha-sise this still further every street name in the New Town was a gushing endorsement of the victorious Hanoverian succession in the South; thus today we have Princes Street, Cumberland Street, Hanover Street, Frederick Street, Great King Street. What kind of agency would have the gall to come up with names like that nowadays?

The irony is that they need not have bothered. Within the next century the novels of Sir Walter Scott – whose monument of Gothic lego squats, gathering soot at the side of Princes Street – would make it fashionable to be Scottish again, through their trivialisation and romanticism of the highland clans who had previously been so despised. Thus today we have tartan shops still trading on a fraudu-lent version of history, waiting for the same coachload of Americans to finish their ghost tour and look up their ancestral cloth. 'Do you have an Eisenburger tartan?' 'Yes, of course, sir. The Eisenburgers are affiliated to the MacDonalds as in MacDonalds of Glencoe. The two go back a long way.'

The old and the new, reinventing themselves, reinventing the past, then as now. Where is the difference?

The high and the low is perhaps a more certain divide. The High leads us to the castle with its panoramic view, once so vital in its days as a garrison defending the city in the name of the King against the Jacobite mob below and now so attractive on a postcard. The other lofty spots reaching into the skies: to the east, Calton Hill with its miserable Parthenon; whilst opposite east is the spire of St Mary's; between them stands The Mound, home of bankers and flowers; and the flow from the Castle to The Mound cascades to the top of Leith Walk, before falling ever downwards to the bottom of the docks. And lastly, the brooding presence of Arthur's Seat, an empty prehistoric eruption of mountainous overhang which has seen all, everything in the city from its earliest pretensions, and will outlast every future pretension.

The Low? I'm afraid I was drawn to it from the start, pulled to it by a greater gravity, the hollows of low-life. The Grassmarket, today the location of beer halls, once a natural amphitheatre for the hangings which would attract thousands; Cowgate, lying in permanent shade of the Bridges above, once home of the morgue; Dean, the sleepy town beneath the city, cowering by the Water of Leith. There are more, many more, accidents of planning, flaws in the design.

Back to the brief though. *Concentrate*. These are the places, not the people, and surely it is Edinburgh's citizens who mark the divide; rich and poor, have's and have-not's? Perhaps. But the signs are more subtle. Visitors would be hard pushed to find the poor in Edinburgh. That is not to say they do not exist, rather that they are held at some distance so as not to spoil the views. The centre of the city, and the districts that surround it, are a middle-class ghetto. The poor have been excluded by the process of gentrification that gripped the streets this century, the process which, for example, saw the Colonies – cottages built for the workers who constructed the New Town – become the most highly-priced and sought-after address in the North side. No, not rich and poor. Resident and tourist, that might be a key. Yet by tourist I do not mean holidaymaker, although there seem so many of them. By tourist I do not mean visitor, some tourists have lived in Edinburgh for many years, some all their lives. Tourists are those still bewitched by the sights, slaves to the history. Residents are those who are blind to it, there is no time limit to their stay, only a sadness that the routine of living their lives has made them so immune to the canvas behind them each day. Tourists revel in the same backdrop. Peter Dexter is a tourist.

Resident and tourist, a reasonable analysis though the tourists can be sub-divided too, there are different levels for them; even the high and the low:

High tourists; shall we say, love the Festival, love walking the Royal Mile, take pictures, love Holyrood Palace, take more pictures, linger at the plaque marking the spot where Rizzio, Mary, Queen of Scots' secretary, was murdered, love Princess Street Gardens, love the Castle from every angle, take too many pictures.

Low tourists – they delight in the more sordid past, are familiar with the plaques on the Royal Mile marking the spots where criminals were publicly hanged, and they appreciate the irony of Europe's most bloodthirsty city posturing as an arts capital – but still love the Festival. Love the dead, the dead in the city's history, the dead in the cemeteries, the characters and villains of the past. Four hundred witches burned at the stake on the Castle Esplanade, the same spot where the coachloads celebrate the military kitsch of the Tattoo every year. Love the Festival. But then everyone loves the Festival. All the same really. A schizophrenic city. Believe me, even if I can't fully explain, I've thought about this so much – where I might fit in, which division I could call home. And then, on inspection, all categories start to merge into the same, don't they? And the only true divide is between history and the present, the living and the dead. No, a failed attempt. No brief. The bloody effort is beyond me. *The living and the dead*, a difference? Wrong, wrong again.

THERE was neither a sign nor a plaque on the door yet the old man knew he had found the correct address. The doctor had been very precise about where it was that he carried out his workings and experimentations, right down to the colours of his neighbours' wooden gates, down to the clanging sounds coming from the nearby blacksmith and ironmonger, down indeed to the stench emanating from the tanner's yard across the road. The old man wheezed as he recaptured his breath, a trembling hand reaching to his mouth. The hill had been steep. Even the horses pulling the wagons and carriages on the road behind him seemed to slow to a standstill as they made their tortuous progress up the incline.

The door opened almost as soon as he had finished knocking. It was a stern face that greeted him. The doctor was wearing his favourite dark suit, disconcertingly covered by a bloodstained apron.

'You are late.'

'Good day to you, sir, Dr Brodie. Please permit me to apologise for the delay in my anticipated arrival.'

The old man shuffled in and halted, looking for somewhere to hang his heavy hat. Brodie's abrupt closure of the door behind him had plunged the windowless room back into darkness. He watched the old man rub his tired eyes, waiting for his equilibrium to be restored, unaware of the tide of impatience surging within the mind of his host. Waiting, always waiting, thought Brodie. Waiting for others to follow their instruction. Leadership was a curse, but there were some skills he did not possess – specialist skills such as this old man's – and so he was reliant on others until he could find a better way.

'You have brought the machine?'

The old man sighed and raised his case in the air. Once more he looked for somewhere to place its contents. This time Brodie moved in swift sympathy, leading him smartly to the workbench and hastily clearing the required space amongst the anatomical drawings, sawdust and filings. The old man reached down to find, and then delicately place, his object onto the surface – a heavy velvet bag drawn at the top by a silk ribbon. Brodie stepped forward, moving his oil lamp closer before removing the object from its wrapping. A metal cylinder gleamed in the half-light. It was small, barely six inches long and an inch in diameter, small enough for Brodie, allowing himself at last a brief moment of pleasure to cradle in one hand.

'It fully matches my specifications?'

Brodie peered down the open end of the object, an almost solid concoction of cogs, wheels and levers meeting his eye, their minute intricacies holding a compelling beauty that he lingered over. The machine, his creation, a machine to marvel over, every detail the result of painstaking preparation, exacting consideration and meticulous execution. A machine that almost seemed to be taking him over, demanding endless sacrifices of time and effort. A machine with whom he now had a full physical and mental relationship, a lover's relationship, the machine being a cruel mistress. Yet any criticism of it was likely to be met with a flash of his increasingly fiery temper, any praise causing his heart to flutter like that of a besotted youth. Yes, an exquisite machine, he thought, the half-smile quivering on his lips. Too perfect for this world of ignorance and illiteracy. In a hundred years' time they would doubtless be in awe at what had been constructed with such primitive materials; they would be scientifically minded, ready to admire its unique qualities. But for this world, the squalid, grimy and dark winter of 1827, it remained too flawless, too pure to arouse anything other than suspicion.

Brodie eventually realised he had not received an answer to his question and lifted his gaze back to the old man. The old man was now wearing his specially-fashioned spectacles, heavily-framed with ludicrously thick lenses, glass thicker than the cobbles in the road outside, so thick that the old man's eyes now staring at Brodie loomed larger than a pair of boxer's fists. Blinking nervous eyes, though it had been Brodie who had been startled by their alien appearance and who had struggled to suppress a flinching reaction. Blindness, thought Brodie, the lifetime reward for every clockmaker of the age, the prize for years of diligence over the tiny details that the craft demanded. Perhaps it was better that he himself did not have these skills – what use a surgeon without his eyesight?

'There have been certain adjustments that were required, sir, deviations from the original plan to accommodate the wider realm of your demands, Dr Brodie. However, I must assure you, sir, that the overall scheme fits within yours, indeed . . . sir . . . what we have succeeded in achieving . . .'

'We?' Brodie's snapped interruption had the magnified eyes flickering ever more rapidly.

'I sought additional help, sir, in order to comply with your deadline. I had cause to doubt, sir, whether I, working alone, was capable –'

'Who?'

'A fine craftsman, sir. Recommended. An Englishman new to Edinburgh, sir – Mr Archibald Ervine. It was he who found the means of employing some of the more *unusual* aspects of your design, sir, even though he was somewhat . . . troubled by them.'

'I see. And doubtless the involvement of this fine craftsman requires a fine rise to my costs?'

'Unfortunately, sir, there will be an additional –'

'What did you tell him?'

'I told him nothing, sir, nothing.'

'And he did not ask about me, my methods, my needs?'

'Never, sir, and I myself never –'

'He did not enquire with regard to the necessity of the *unusual* elements to which end he had been employed?'

'Our conversations were entirely in order, sir. I took care that these were limited to prescient matters, that is to say –'

Brodie silenced the old man with a dismissive wave of his hand in his face, realising that the interrogation offered no respite from his rising anger. So, he thought, the costs were to be increased again. What was left in his house that could still be pawned? Perhaps his wife should be persuaded to part with another of her dresses – how many did she need anyway? They weren't active in Edinburgh society, at least not yet; that would follow later, once he was ready. Then there would be money enough. And what had the old man told of him to strangers? What did the old man know himself – had he copied his plans to his rivals? Would they even guess the purpose of the invention? No, genius was singular, that was the lesson he had learned. Genius made for a solitary life, for secrecy, and waiting, always waiting for others to catch up. He stroked the whiskers of his moustache, smoothing them down against his cheeks, taking a deep breath as he did so.

'Which *unusual* aspects troubled this Mr Ervine?'

'The heart, sir, the use of the rat's heart to pump the lubricant round the mechanism . . . the chamber where the organ itself is held in its pickled state . . . the mixture of the mechanical and the organic, sir. Mr Ervine wondered if it might be . . . *ungodly*, sir.'

'And you, you wonder the same?'

'I . . . I cannot say . . .'

The old man grimaced weakly as he floundered. Brodie studied him with contempt. Waiting, always waiting; the pitiful struggle for words was an answer in itself. If they thought his invention was iniquitous now what would they think when he asked them to create the mechanisms that would feed the final chamber to be appended to the device, once the last piece of tissue-matter was added? Delicate tissue. Human tissue. Human brain.

'Cease your damned vacillation! Although I resent having to utter any kind of assurance, let me remind you that I am a gentleman, and that my purpose is not "ungodly". You will understand that presently. They will all understand, even your Mr Ervine. I seek perfection and perfection is a testament to God. Can you understand? Why would so many be prepared to believe otherwise?'

Brodie realised he was shouting, and that his efforts to

convince were not entirely aimed at the petrified old man standing next to him. No, his opinion was of little importance; it was his own doubts that tormented him. Human brain. Living brain. Where was he to find the sample he needed? Brodie shuddered as he thought of the sacrifices that would still have to be made. Yet nothing was more certain than that they would be made. He had fashioned a cruel mistress indeed. He began to speak again, choosing both his words and tone carefully.

'Dear sir, this is not an *infernal* device. This is an invention that will enable the life of a man to be protected whilst he is under the surgeon's knife, a machine that will store his life during that, or other predicaments. Imagine the wondrous uses of such a mechanism – our soldiers in the battlefield will become invincible, our leaders immortal. The wisdom of our greatest preserved forever in this one contraption. Surely the Lord would be pleased with our endeavours in seeking to achieve such an ambition?'

His mellow demeanour had had its desired effect on the old man, whose reply was noticeably less reticent than his previous utterances.

'Aye, Dr Brodie. Very well. You will want to test the mechanism? We ... I ... have been surprised by the levels of vibration that are generated. It has been one of the greatest challenges to overcome, that the vibrations do not offset the winding balance, and I must issue a sincere warning on the thickness of the casing, sir. I am concerned that it is too thin, that the internal mechanisms are not sufficiently protected from external influences which may be brought to bear ...'

The thinness of the casing. As thin as foil rather than metal. As thin as a membrane. As thin as the design had specified. Did this old fool know what a membrane was? Brodie felt his ire rise anew as the babble poured out of the elderly mouth. How to close his ears to the impertinence that affronted him? His eyes lingered on the device standing proud on the workbench. Ungodly? Brodie felt a chill to his heart. Somehow it was as if his creation fed on his negative emotions. It was as if it were a living being, jealous of the attentions he gave others, capable of influencing him, and of casting its spell at a whim. A living being, yes that was the truth of it, that was what he was striving to create.

'Wind it up.'

'I beg your pardon, sir?'

'Wind it up, man. Let us see how your efforts perform, whether they are deserving of the apology you labour to make.'

The old man edged forward tentatively. On the bench was a myriad of plans and scrolls: circulatory schematics of the blood flow lifted from Da Vinci's early work; Chinese charts showing various points on the body with needles sticking into them; and scores of other plans featuring magnets and electric polarity. Brodie watched the halting gaze of the old man wander over them and wondered whether he should move to cover them from his prying. No, he thought, let him try to make sense of it, let us see whether he can retain his sanity in trying to amalgamate the knowledge of the world into six inches of thin steel. Would he want to wrestle with the torment and loneliness? Genius is pain, only the strong were equipped to bear it.

The old man's hands were shaking as he lifted the device and folded out its winding arm. His delicate touch as he wound it spoke of tenderness and respect. Brodie felt himself calm as he watched. A mechanical test. The second chamber was as yet empty but the exercise would still assist in setting the calibration. He longed for the day when the testing would all be done, even if this meant the second chamber would then have been filled.

Brodie wiped a hand across his forehead. He looked to his palm and saw it was thick with sweat. The nausea within him was swelling, nausea from the fumes of the oil lamps, from the smell of the old man, the lard in his hair, his noxious damp breath.

'Release it.'

The old man did as instructed and sat the device down erect on the surface. It quickly kicked into action, at first buzzing, then trembling and then gently gliding along the top as its inner mechanisms let forth their energies.

'You see, Dr Brodie, the vibrations . . . they cannot –'

'Stop it!'

'What? Dr –'

'Stop it shaking. Lift it and hold it, man!'

The old man gingerly extended an arm to pick up the pulsating contraption. It squirmed in his hand like a trapped rat.

'I said stop it, man! Grip it tight, damn you!'

Reluctantly, the old man obeyed, clutching with both hands, managing to halt the shaking in the machine. But the trembling had merely been transferred, he watched horrified as his forearms, then his shoulders and finally his whole body convulsed with the strange energy that passed through him.

'Dr Brodie, sir, I –'

'*Hold* it!'

'I –'

The old man was suddenly silenced, though this time not by Brodie's cry. It was the horrifying sight of his feet, which had been tapping the floor like those of a demented dancer, raising themselves from the ground of their own accord so that he found himself floating in the air. He seemed to climb with no effort, a few inches, than a clear yard, hanging there in the atmosphere despite the kicking and spasms that rippled across his bones, and his choked attempts to speak of the fear that gripped him. His eyes were now bigger than ever, filling every piece of glass beneath the enormous spectacle frames still clinging to his nose.

Then the crash, and the shattering of that glass, as he landed, the machine's energies spent. Brodie stepped forward, bending down to retrieve the device from the crumpled heap on the floor. He flicked open its base. The second chamber, still there, still vacant, a succession of gears and tiny levers still in motion regardless, like sets of insect legs, or drones busying themselves around the lair of the queen in the hive. It was time that this was filled. The machine demanded it.

The doctor awoke with a start. For a moment he thought that he might scream but managed to control himself, covering his mouth with his hands as he jerked upright in the bed. He left his hands where they were and let them smooth down the whiskers of his moustache. The body beside him did not stir as he eased himself back under the covers and his head down onto the pillow. He tried to close his ears to the sound of his wife snoring. It was time to think. Still dark outside, a winter's morning, five or six o'clock. What kind of day would he be facing? The disposal of the body need not be a problem; there were a variety of means open to him. He could sell the corpse for medical dissection, passing it back through the system that supplied him. The best method might be the one nearest the truth, to say that the man had come to see him in an attempt to sell him unwanted goods and had then collapsed, being in old age and ill health. Then there would be the matter of explaining the head injuries, though who would notice, or might these be the result of an unfortunate fall? Yes, there were choices, there were always choices for a mind like his. Genius meant choice.

Perhaps choice but not comfort; it was not the vision of the old man's lifeless body that had visited upon his dreams, terrifying him in the process. Brodie lay awake thinking of the spectre that had – the creation that was becoming a monster. He forced his mind to make the journey that he would have to make later that day, rehearsing his steps in the misty morning light to the row of workshops at the brow of the hill, imagining his hand unlocking the door, crossing the floor, the lighting of the lamps to reveal the form of the stiff carcass lying there, and, most disturbing of all, the dark velvet bag on the worktop containing the fruits of his secretive labours, the device, its second chamber now filled. Brodie's hands gripped his nightshirt as he contemplated winding the machine up to test its new power. What magic was it capable of now? Too perfect for this world. A harsh and demanding mistress. Ungodly. Perhaps he should destroy it before it was too late and the price to be paid for its creation became indefensible. Brodie's hands gripped his nightshirt tighter, wringing it with an urgency that threatened to tear the material. He knew he couldn't not go through with it now, too much had been sacrificed to bring the machine into being, a living being, there had to be a means of redeeming it from itself, saving it from its cruellest tendencies. Brodie twitched and snorted, the nausea had returned. The sound of the snoring would drive him insane – couldn't the damn woman be silent even in sleep? Ungodly. No, there had to be a way.

He looked to the window and saw a gentle light was rising outside. The day was coming whether he was ready or not. There had to be a way, his genius demanded that he provide a solution. A second chamber. Human brain. The light grew stronger. A third chamber. He would create a third chamber in the machine. With God's help he would bless the machine with a third chamber. He would create the perfect living being to contain the wisdom of men. A heart, a brain, and then a soul. He would fill the third chamber with a soul. All he had to do was to find one.

Interviewer:
So the next communication you had was to actually invite you to the performance?

Lowes:
The questionnaire went to a Box Number and after that I got the postcard telling me the date and time, saying that I would be informed of the venue immediately prior to that. 'Pablo Dextrus proudly invites Mr D. Lowes with pleasure.' Had to send them my driving licence or passport, back to the Box Number. We were to get these back on the day. 'A tiresome but necessary security measure to guard against infiltration of the show by those of a damaging and prurient nature. Pablo apologises.'

Interviewer:
You didn't think this odd?

Lowes:
(pause) I only thought about the show, that it must be pretty special to go to this extreme. I was more turned on by this than turned off. I guess it was the same for everybody else.

Interviewer:
And so you got the call telling you where to go?

Lowes:
The card had said Thursday 4th September, the last week of the Festival. A woman called at the flat that morning, about eleven. The performance was to start at three that afternoon. The address was somewhere on the south side of the city. She said it was off

South Clerk Street. Turned out to be a big house in the Grange, big stone villa, huge garden. I got there slightly late because of the bum directions. Went there via the High Street, had a few drinks at lunchtime and walked the rest of the way.

Interviewer:
What was the scene as you arrived?

Lowes:
The *scene*? (Sounds surprised at this choice of word. Begins to affect another accent.) The *scene* was hot, man . . . yes, sir, the scene was pretty hot that day (returns to normal voice). There was some kind of heatwave, must have been nearly eighty degrees . . . that's why it had taken me so long to walk down from the Old Town. I had my jacket over my shoulder and was wondering why I had brought it at all. Anyway, I followed my feet to the address I'd been given, and as it became apparent that this would be one of these big posh houses I began to wonder if it was all a wind-up. I was sweating; I had jeans and T-shirt on but it was still so fucking warm, and I could feel myself greasy under my clothes and didn't really fancy showing up at one of these doors for someone to look at me and decide *I* was the one putting on some kind of scam and calling for the police just in case. So it took me a while to decide I would go ahead and try. Then as I went through the garden gate and began to walk up the path, I began to hear the music . . . and smell something, not dope, not joss sticks but something . . . *alternative* . . . and I realised that this was the place.

Interviewer:
What was the music like?

Lowes:
Well, it kind of drifted over. I heard it better when I was led through to the back.

Interviewer:
Who led you?

Lowes:

I rang the doorbell and this girl appeared, not from inside, but from round the corner. Beautiful girl, in a full evening gown, striking . . . scarlet-coloured thing with the gloves that go up to the elbow. She had incredibly pale skin, dark hair done up in a bun. On a bright sunny day like that she was quite a vision – a blaze of technicolour in a black and white world, like she'd just stepped out of the cover of one of those magazines, *Tatler* or the like. And before she spoke she just smiled, so open, so friendly, and I felt such a slob. All I wanted to do was to go off, have a shower and come back in decent clothes. I went to dig out the card in the pocket of my jacket but she waved for me to stop. 'Daniel?' Her voice was something else too – BBC announcer, Radio Four, deep and rich, innocent and seductive all at the same time . . . And I nodded, so she smiles again and makes for me to follow her, which I did, her in front, crunching on the gravel. I think you can tell how rich the owner of the house is by the depth of the gravel and this was real wealth. I was sinking into it, fucking quicksand. This dress had two ties round the hips that formed into a big bow at the top of her arse, and I followed after, with my eyes fixed on it. I'm already thinking about her shape and how gorgeous she is and I almost want to ask out loud – I mean, these girls, are they for real? What does it take to have one of these girls? Is it a money thing, class? How do you get to meet them? (Shakes head ruefully) She was for real, she was live and kicking then. Never introduced herself to me. I heard the others calling her 'Clarinda', sometimes 'Claribel', then when I saw her picture in the paper later they had her down as Claire. Can't believe what's meant to have happened to her. What a fucking . . . waste . . . shit, you know? (pause)

Interviewer:

You mentioned music – was it designed to unsettle you?

Lowes:

(Sighs) Listen to me, will you, for fuck's sake. *Everything* was designed to unsettle . . . (calms down after pausing) Music? We went through another gate – there was a dividing wall between the front and back – and when we were inside the enclosed rear garden she announces me to the others – 'This is Daniel!' – and these people, about nine of them, applaud. And as I take this in, the music and the smell are suddenly so strong. They had the garden wired up with all these little speakers, like car stereo ones, tucked away under stones . . . flowers . . . everywhere. The music? I suddenly realised it was the guy's name (sings) 'Pablo Dextrus, Pablo Dextrus', going round and round in a loop, no instruments, just voices, like a chant . . . and they might have been singing something else . . . (sings) 'Pablo Dextrus muchos likus' . . . like it was all Latin, a Gregorian chant. And the smell? Well there was a barbecue set up, but they weren't cooking food, not then anyway . . . they had bunches of dried herbs, tied up and resting on the grate. Most extraordinary smell, like sandalwood being roasted with cinnamon. Exotic, you couldn't get close enough to it (inhales deeply).

Interviewer:
What were the others like?

Lowes:
Well, there was another guy in a dinner suit by the patio doors, talking to two girls. He was young, good-looking I suppose, and probably quite charming. The girls looked more normal. He was doing all the talking and they were friendly enough but awkward; you could tell they didn't know whether to let themselves go for it. To my left there's two men, student types, again younger than me, trendier, hair in ponytails, earnest-looking. And there was a wooden bench against the wall. Two other girls on that, one of them very gushy, blonde . . . and plump. Julia – she was introduced to me later – worked in public relations, kept insisting she'd give me her card . . . as if I fucking wanted it. Never did though, too pissed, or maybe she turned her attention on someone else. Had a voice like the one in the red dress . . . could have been her pal . . . already giggly and drinking very fast. I wondered if she really was a guest like me. Anyway, she was sitting next to this other woman – Sarah, the teacher – who was the oldest of the lot of us, not that she wasn't nice herself in a kind of elegant and mature way. She was the first one to sort of catch my eye and I went over to her. There was another man standing over her, and he and the blonde

seemed more interested in the younger one so I thought she would be approachable. I was just about to say this when the hostess arrives at my shoulder, carrying a bottle. They were all drinking from the same bottle, all of them. 'Now, Daniel, we've already explained the rules to the others. This one is your drink, compliments of Pablo Dextrus. Enjoy. Every time you hand myself or Ciaran an empty bottle, we will hand you one of Pablo's vouchers. Nobody is allowed inside to the show until they have three vouchers. Now we're watching you, so no cheating, you must drink every bottle. If you pour away Pablo's hospitality you are disqualified from the show. Enjoy!' And she hit me with another one of these smiles. This was a new one on me, a show where the performers insisted you were drunk before they would begin? It was a bottle of beer she'd given me, Damm, a Spanish designer beer, and I looked up and there was the other guy in the dinner suit waving at me – so he was Ciaran. I turned and faced Sarah for the second time. 'Cheers . . . any idea what this is all about?' She kind of laughed. 'Sorry, no. I'm Sarah . . . you?' 'Dan. How did you hear about this?' 'The piece in the *Festival Review*. I was intrigued . . . You?' I wondered what to say. She seemed very cultured and I didn't want to come over as some kind of letch, out for a cheap thrill. '. . . oh . . . friends, I suppose,' I said. 'I heard through friends . . . then I saw the advert.' She was wearing glasses and must have been about forty, classy with it though. Black frames . . . a sexy Nana Mouskouri, foxy, and she looked at me over the top of them, still sitting down, still giving me this icy distance thing. '. . . and what did your friends tell you to expect?' I thought for a moment. The same dilemma, back into the old interrogation blues. 'Nothing . . . Nothing and everything . . .' I was quite pleased with this but could see straight away it didn't impress. She took a big gulp and finished off her bottle, standing up, swallowing hard, waving to the bloke by the door. 'You'd better get a move on.' She nodded at my own beer. 'You've got some catching up to do.'

Interviewer:
Was everyone being forced to drink at a fast pace? Was there any kind of coercion involved?

Lowes:

Not really, no. It was unbelievably hot with absolutely no breeze in that garden. And the other thing I quickly became aware of was that nobody knew each other. We'd all come through the same selection and had turned up alone, and when you are in a situation like that I suppose you tend to drink faster . . . especially if it's free . . . (laughs) . . . Right from the start I wondered if some of the guests really were guests or were spying on us, setting us up, and I got the impression that others were looking at me thinking the same thing. 'What do you think will happen? I don't know, what about *you*?' We all moved around a bit, and after half an hour I'd spoken to just about everyone, including the one guy who was making a conscious effort to tab everyone. This guy comes to me and offers his hand in an awful nerdy way – 'I'm Colin' – (winces in sour distaste). Completely out of place . . . hated him from the start . . . Plus you just knew, like when you watch these old war films and you can tell which soldier isn't going to make it, who's going to get zapped . . . not that I had any idea of what was going to happen to the poor fucker . . . but I knew that he was going to draw the fire from whatever guns would be aimed at us. Knew to keep away from him somehow . . .

Interviewer:

Why?

Lowes:

I knew. Look, I know it's not exactly rational but my first thought was that every Colin I'd ever known before was a cunt. Then later when we were talking about ourselves and he said, 'I'm in law' and fucking blushes, I knew again that he was kidding himself on. He just didn't belong and this would all work out badly for him . . . I know they've said a lot about him to cover it all up, but to me he could have been a sick man well before Pablo's antics began. I'm no fucking mystic but you can read people's karma, their nervous energy, and he was all wrong. Eyes like a startled bird, talking to you and through you. I had to get away from him and made a note to distance him for the rest of the night. Just as well. So I wander over to Ciaran who'd handed me two bottles of beer but wouldn't

31

be drawn into chat. But the rest of us levelled out eventually. Drink is a great leveller; in fact as levellers go, there aren't many better (laughs).

Interviewer:
Did you catch up?

Lowes:
It wasn't a great problem, though I'd already been drinking before I'd even got there, so by the time I'd finished the prescription I must have been at least slightly drunk. And then when I was waiting for the rest to drink up, the girl knocks on the patio window and makes the great announcement. 'Ladies and Gentlemen. Pablo Dextrus has decided that since today's will be a *special* performance of "Proscribed", admittance will be granted to those with four vouchers only. Please see Ciaran for your extra bottle of delicious Damm which will qualify you for this requirement.' And then they turned the music up so it's just going round and round . . . (sings) . . . Dextrus Pablo Dextrus Pablo . . .

Interviewer:
What was the general response to this?

Lowes:
There was a groan, but everyone took it with a shrug. I don't think there was a question of anyone dropping out, not for the sake of another bottle of lager . . . Besides, it was good stuff. By then everyone had a taste for it (laughs).

Interviewer:
How would you describe the others?

Lowes:
Slightly nervous. Slightly drunk. No one outrageous . . .

Interviewer:
Sorry, I mean in terms of background, appearance . . . as well as behaviour at that point.

Lowes:

Well . . . there was Sarah . . . she was the oldest I'd say, and I was probably the oldest guy there. She was English . . . most of them were. No one foreign, but all visitors to the city for the Festival. Only one of the girls actually lived in Edinburgh. Can't remember her name . . . skinny girl, hair cropped really short like a lesbian, silver stud in her nose. Nice enough though. She said she was a nurse . . . one of them was, anyway. The guys? What would you expect? The one who went for it the most was called Steve, said he worked in advertising. Probably the kind of bloke you'd find an arsehole in any other circumstance but in a sunny garden on a beautiful day with free beer you could tolerate him fine, even if he tried to take every chance to dominate the proceedings . . . (smiles). The girl, the one in the red, and the bloke, Ciaran, they were wise to him though, sorted him out later. The blonde girl sat next to Sarah, she was full of herself too (affects accent). 'I'm Jules. I'm in PR.' Looked ready to roll though, desperate, desperate to throw herself at some guy and then hang on like grim death the way these hysterical women can. Had her eyes on Steve then. Leapt on him to swap agency-speak, talking in fucking code (quickly) 'I'm with KF and C. How long have you been at AB and C? Aren't they part of XY and Z? We're being bought out by Hype, Trite and Shite' (voice slows again) . . . The rest – just your average bunch. Pretty quiet, I guess, given we'd all jumped through bloody hoops to get here, and now we all just sat waiting for something to happen. Of course, the joke was, *we* were the fucking show.

Proscribed: **Cast Notes (1)**

In his seminal 1963 paper 'Intercourse, Alignment and Circumstance', the psychologist Dr Karl Harlam of the Geneva Institute
of Social Anthropology explored the migratory patterns of typical
participants at a number of interactive social events, tracking the
movements of subjects in what he termed a 'footfall' analysis of
individuals' minute journeys from group to sub-group at such large
gatherings as a wedding reception and an ex-postal workers' reunion
dance. Harlam was particularly concerned with isolating the effect
of the two base motivators behind an individual's circulatory
behaviour at such meetings – the desire for group 'acceptance', and
the anxiety of being mis-aligned with a socially unacceptable peer
group.

Although classified as an 'observatory' study, Harlam's team often
extended their roles beyond that of mere onlookers; disguised inves-
tigators would often play the role of particularly obstreperous party
guests, testing the limits of behavioural tolerance. In one memor-
able exercise a student member was filmed approaching shoppers
in the aisle of a large supermarket, asking where he could find what
were plainly non-plausible goods ('radioactive toast', 'an adaptable
orgasm', etc.), the objective being again to isolate the motivators
forcing the unwitting respondents' flight from Harlam's stooge. As
with all the previous exercises, different approaches and 'strengths'
of implementation were tested and the time taken for the rejection
response recorded. Harlam noted that this would often be dependent on 'circumstance' – whether other witnesses were there to
view the exchange, and the interest they took in the proceedings
between the respondent and the 'false' shopper.

The paper is a fascinating work, one that Dr Harlam sought

to further explore in a continuing series of proposed studies, his hypothesis being that of the two 'base motivators' the first – the need for acceptance – is the more active within the subconscious, and therefore the more powerful. Yet Dr Harlam's plans were never fulfilled. The good citizens of Geneva had voiced enough complaints at the intrusion into their mannered lives to make the provision of funds for a second stage out of the question.

It is natural that a scientist, having observed that his human subjects are as trapped by social convention and the expectations of their peers as a rat in a glass maze in pursuit of the exit that will grant it liberty, would want to follow through the line of enquiry by a logical probing of the hypothesis. What is surprising is that Dr Harlam did not realise that, as far as his team were concerned, the first set of experiments marked the end of the active stage of the investigation, that from then on his work would involve calculations, extrapolations, and strictly theoretical trials of his hypothesis.

Dr Harlam should have understood the limitations of his status, the boundaries of the laboratory; that only the *artist* has the licence to test to destruction.

OKAY. START AGAIN. Let's talk about me. Why not brain-storm? Yes, let's pretend there's the will and the wit to do just that.

Edinburgh.

I came to Edinburgh over two years ago, a fresh start.

Sometimes the sadness overwhelms me.

I think of everything that has happened since then and I would have to recognise that when I moved up I brought my faults with me; I had thought they belonged to London and could be left behind, but they couldn't.

I was sitting in the doctor's surgery trying to tell him – the job, the pressure, the debacles. He tried to be interested and, as I spoke, the impossibility of explaining it all and the sadness overwhelmed me so much that I was left sobbing like a speechless idiot. He prescribed tranquillisers, steered me out the door as soon as I had calmed down enough to co-ordinate my movements again, glad to get rid of me. I was in reception, then the street, tears still wet on my face, realising what a fool I looked.

And the sadness and the impossibility and the *absurdity* of it all overwhelmed me.

My name is Charles, Charles Kidd. An impossible name, think about it. 'Charles' is an absurd name. I cringe just hearing myself saying it – 'Hello, I'm Charles.' Bloody 'Charles'. Can you hear it? Pompous, mock-regal, but what is the alternative? 'Charlie'? That's a bloody bookie's name, or a Cockney bus driver's. I cannot think of any other name in the English language with such a polarity, toff or spiv, no in-between, and I'm stuck with it, part of my weakness. I should be able to deal with it, position it and build an image behind it, make the name represent what I want it to. Because this is my profession, this public relations thing. So why didn't I? Why have

I failed myself as a client? I'll tell you why, the whole thing, tell you about the client that failed me. Manipulation, something *I'm* meant to do? Sometimes the irony overwhelms me.

ROBERTS, BEGBY & LAWRIE W.S.,

MARY KING'S CLOSE, EDINBURGH.

FILE NOTE: CLAIRE LISTER, RECRUITMENT OF

She came to us at Roberts, Begby & Lawrie from
Walker Crighton, her references first-rate.
Intellectual Property being a departure from our
normal practice area, it was important to us to
recruit someone of the highest calibre, someone
with experience who could ensure ours was a credible
client service. She sat before us at interview and
we were impressed not only with her credentials in
areas of patent and copyright law, but her manner,
that the demeanour of this attractive, highly
competent young woman betrayed none of the
arrogance that might have been expected of one who
had achieved such early recognition of her abilities.
A quiet charm, a smile of elegant restraint, hands
clasped in concentration as if in prayer; we were
reminded perhaps of the politician's wife, stead-
fast and discreet. Of course now there are questions.
Did she change or had we been fooled from the beginning? Could we have done more to help? And how could
it be that such a delightful individual could have
fallen into such a ghastly mess?

Still, the simple matter is that she was made well
aware of the standards that have been set by the
founding partners and how she was expected to perform to them. Above all, we, as a firm, are not
ashamed to set such standards, nor are we afraid of
acting decisively when these are not met. When she
chose to flaunt them the outcome was inevitable,
tragically.

Our records show that she joined the payroll on
July 17th, eight weeks after the interview. We
stopped paying her the following March, by which
time her situation had become painfully obvious.
Some of us could believe that her tenure had been
longer, the sense of loss we feel caused by more
substantial duration of contact. But our records
are accurate – they have to be – proof that we did
what we could and <u>more</u>, more than might have been
expected.

FILE NOTE: CLAIRE LISTER, INITIAL PERFORMANCE OF

That there was a backlog of cases awaiting her when
she began was not due to incompetence or poor practice, merely a reflection of the fact that the partners had simply held on to work that they might have
referred elsewhere in the months leading up to her
appointment. Consequently, her initial weeks were a
hectic affair. She might have wished for a more
gentle start, a chance to build her own contacts
slowly. There are certainly those amongst us who
feel that events might have been somewhat different
had she been given time to properly settle into
Roberts, Begby & Lawrie rather than immediately
succumb to the frenetic rush which was there from
her commencement. Inherent in this comment, of course,
is the suggestion that if a proper pattern had been
established in the first instance, Roberts, Begby &
Lawrie might have been able to exercise a more sele-
ctive approach towards prospective clients, and
indeed might have been able to protect Claire from
her own enthusiasms – for many, the source of the
problem. However, this is to ignore the air of calm
efficiency which Claire exuded at the start. This
seemed a young woman who lived for her work, one of
our own. There had been concerns that intellectual
property was too dry an area for a young woman,
especially such an attractive young woman, yet the
individual and the practice sensibility seemed such
a good match. It is those apprehensions we should
have heeded, for here was a practice speciality that
may have satisfied such an employee's professional

aspirations but would always, we now concede, cause friction with the same person's more <u>sensual</u> ambitions.

There had been talk of an enagagement, broken just before she joined us, and not by mutual consent. And there was sonmething stoic about her early endeavours and high levels of commitment to her appointment. We never pry into the private affairs of our employees, although information like this always seems to surface despite our avowed lack of interest in such matters, and it is difficult to come to a collective view as to how it should be acted upon. Should concern be shown, guidance offered? A discreet monitoring of developments is our preferred option; intervention only when necessary.

This is difficult for us. Delicate. We would not wish to appear obstructive, but there are sound commercial reasons why we would choose not to divulge key elements of our business planning, nor would we wish to appear as if commenting in derogatory terms on our clients, to whom we afford the highest respect. Therefore, let our position be summarised thus: Any legal firm, any <u>progressive</u> firm, will always seek to diversify its sources of income. Today may be heralded as an era of unprecedented change but the actuality is that certain fiscal areas, even traditional ones, have always been prone to what the marketeers call a 'life cycle' whereby that area's importance in terms of revenue rises through growth until this slows down, leading to its expiry. Household conveyancing represents an example of a declining sector, intellectual property a rising one. The dynamic growth in the field of information technology is underpinned by a tide of entrepreneurial spirits mastering new techniques to harness its power. New computer machinery, new programs to make them work, new work practices to exploit them – all, if they are truly revolutionary, requiring the full protection of the law if their inventors are to be

41

justly rewarded. This was the image that fuelled
the vision at Roberts, Begby & Lawrie, the service
we saw ourselves delivering to the business community. And these are not words we are ashamed to
employ - service, community - the words behind our
vision.

Which is where Claire came in, and alas, she was not
alone. We believed she held faith in the sincerity
of our vision, yet quickly, under her management, it
became a tarnished thing, one more worthy of ridicule
than admiration. Were the clients unsuited to us, or
was it that we were unsuited to the clients? We
would be interested in the experience of others
venturing into this area. Did they find themselves
under siege from the inventors, eager to demonstrate
the genius behind their innovative contraptions -
new methods to take the cork from a bottle without
the use of hands, a fresh way to draw water from the
tap, a boardgame with universal appeal. All of them
fanciful, all of them frivolous, yet each with its
own inherent threat to our established order. These
inventors seek not representation, not registration
but an audience. Why is it that their efforts could
not be directed towards more worthwhile endeavours?
Alas, we at Roberts, Begby & Lawrie need no reminding
of who it is that finds work for such idle hands.

And we had left Claire at their mercy, unaware,
initially at least, of how the vision had become
sullied. One day, a creator arrived with something
astounding to show, a device with all the power of
the most addictive drug, one no woman could forget
once introduced to it. Was she interested? Could
Roberts, Begby & Lawrie act on its behalf? The device?
A tubular implement, leather and polished steel,
intricate and ingenious moving parts creating delicate yet strong vibrations at certain points of the
surface. The device? A sex aid. We are told it is
extraordinary.

So where did we get to? Nowhere. There's a surprise. So much for brainstorming as a route to new ideas and insights. Doesn't say a lot for my profession that this is the great tool of our trade. That's a use of the word 'profession' in its loosest sense, i.e. no bloody sense. 'Profession.' Who am I kidding?

I must admit I've had a few false starts, career-wise, I mean. You could say that about my life as well, that sometimes the failed opportunities overwhelm me. The first failure, school? No, I was happy enough at school, a boarder at Stuart's College for boys, a happy young chap in the braided uniform of a prefect. It was the exams I wasn't any good at, never really got to grips with them, hated the way they interfered with the routine. Always plenty to do, first-formers to round up and take to cricket or expeditions to the shops. Always someone telling you what to do, or rather someone telling you what to tell them to do. It took me until I was nineteen to leave Stuart's, that's the time it took me to scrape enough pass grades together to make the step up. I was the oldest scholar in the history of the place. They had to stretch the rules to keep me in. Then I was into university and the sudden independence overwhelmed me.

Today I can rationalise all this and label this difficulty 'institutionalisation'. Not my fault, the fault of my school for conditioning me to survive in just the one kind of existence. Back then though I didn't know such words and could only pass myself off as a sad inadequate. I lasted less than a year at university, doing the usual student things, drinking and not studying, then there's the gambling and the thieving. Not that I was thieving, no; people thieved from me, and I was a fool not to see it. Just the small things to start with – clothes, records, bits of cash. Then the larger things, larger bits of cash. Losing it, the time, the place, possessions – the whole game really, always losing it. There was a girl – she had an exam one morning – and she met this bloke the night before and slept with him, at her place. These things happen, not to me admittedly, but there seemed a lot of 'it' about on general offer. Anyway, she'd set the alarm so that she'd wake up in time. And when the clock went off the bloke went to it, to stop it ringing, but he felt frisky again, and so he started to canoodle. And she asked him the time and he lied. Lied so that he could have his way and she'd miss the exam – a dreadful, selfish thing to do. Thing was, this girl, she was meant to get me up for the exam, the same exam, and we both missed it because of this bloke. This kind of thing happened all the time. I lost it. Institutionalised victim or sad inadequate – take your pick.

A career history. Do you want the official CV or the real version? Try the first, first. Why not? Even after all I've been through, I can still thrill myself with the dark power at my disposal, marvel at how a few deft flicks of the pen can rewrite history, obliterating past shame and inventing former glories. To think that once people begged favours from witches in order to reincarnate, now there's a whole raft of agencies itching to take up the task, some at surprisingly competitive rates. Here's my own attempt; subject, me.

Charles Kidd, a thirty-one-year-old Public Relations professional with particular expertise in the area of financial services PR – support to banks, insurance companies, corporate institutions involved in flotation or merger, or acquisitions. My early experience in this sector was gained on the client side, in the City, as communications officer for the brokers Grevant Safety where I was responsible for the running of the external affairs office prior to and during their merger with Hastings Holmes. I moved from this position to the agency side, to Murray Millson PR where, as account manager, I held responsibility for the media relations programmes of a number of their blue-chip accounts. I moved to Edinburgh to take up my last role at KFC Communications, primarily to utilise my skills amongst the burgeoning financial scene in Scotland's capital, establishing a total marketing service for KFC's client base. Through this appointment I gained hands-on team-building experience, encouraging formerly reticent Scottish 'Life' companies to communicate in a meaningful and compelling way to their audiences. In this I was aided by the schooling I had received earlier in the testing environment of London, the knowledge of a harsher, more aggressive game standing me in good stead for this demanding position. I also attracted other clients to KFC, not all from the financial sphere. We presented credentials to key players from other industry sectors – whisky companies, transport operators, and the arts. The *arts*. Stop.

By this point I really am stretching the truth too far. Peter Dexter and his Experimental Gallery sort of selected KFC. In fact, they selected me. Selected and instructed and ruined me. Always there telling me what to do. Always running the *show*.

And I lost it, lost it all.

Proscribed —

The Experience
of a Lifetime WEEKS 1–3

(Venue and performances by invitation only)

Proscribed: Cast Notes (2)

Comedy is all about reaction. True comedy is organic, a spontaneous exchange between comedian and audience. Truly creative comedy is not about being funny: it is about setting up a situation where *all* the audience are comedians, when the audience does not know *how* to react.

True creative comedy is an art.

TRANSCRIPT : TAPE 3

Interviewer:
When did they finally let you into the house?

Lowes:
After five beers – they repeated the trick after we'd all had the fourth. Seemingly, Pablo *really* wanted us to appreciate the show and to give the performers time to reach their peak.

Interviewer:
Did anybody refuse?

Lowes:
No, it was still only about five o'clock. I was getting hungry but everyone was resigned to sitting it out, maybe even beginning to enjoy each other's company. We were all on the lawn, sprawled around, one big group by now, still waiting, still anticipating, digging the song (laughs), '. . . it's a grower . . .' – that's what one of the guys said. We tried to listen to the words. I was sure it was Latin but one of the girls swore it was French . . . (sings) 'Pablo Dextrus le plat de jour c'est moi . . .' I couldn't hear it though . . . everyone had their own theory, though you hear what you want to hear.

Interviewer:
They let you in after the last one had finished their fifth beer?

Lowes:
No! After all this fuss about tokens and proof and allocations the girl just disappears round the side and then comes out the house opening the doors. 'Pablo invites you into his house.' And we all look at each other and begin to drift across the grass and go inside.

Interviewer:
Then what?

Lowes:
Then we all queued for the bloody toilet . . . Then I had a piss. Want to know about that? (laughs) Actually . . . there was something about that. The bathroom and the toilet were a disgrace. Filthy, bar of soap covered in pubes . . . and these people were all so classy, the hosts, I mean, and they all seemed to live there. When I came out another one had appeared, guy in a dinner suit, quite famous bloke . . . seen him on television (pause) I'd tell you who it was but I don't fancy being sued. I'll just call him 'Eddie' for the moment . . . no proof, see? Unless any of the rest admitted to going there and that's unlikely, isn't it?

Interviewer:
Tell me later. What was the new host's . . . attitude?

Lowes:
Well, I'd say the same as the other pair except he wasn't as . . . polished. If you knew the guy from his shows you would know how he makes this thing of being a working-class bloody hero . . . and he was almost the same here, had the suit on but he looked . . . sleazy, I suppose. Stubble, cropped hair . . . chain-smoking . . . like a bouncer at some dive rather than a toff, but he had the accent. Definitely a case of downwardly mobile. I think he'd been born into higher things . . . For all that he was okay, didn't make a thing about being a *star*, very friendly in fact. There was an energy to him though, or an attitude . . . something that means you want to be on his side, no matter what. He's working the room, going round people, dishing out more beer – 'You alright?' (affects booming voice), and everyone is. 'Yeah!' (mimes large smile and hands enthusiastically taking hold of bottle) . . . Bastard.

Interviewer:
Did he take over the proceedings?

Lowes:

Not *officially*, but he had the strongest personality, and your eye just sort of went to him ... Yes, it was him that introduced the video.

Interviewer:

That's what happened next?

Lowes:

(in loud and confident voice again) 'Pablo has asked that you make yourselves comfortable and watch his short message which has been filmed with you in mind.' There were two sofas in the lounge, three-seaters. We crammed into them, onto the arms and stuff, the others on the floor, and watched while he stuffed the video in. And that's when we got our first view of Pablo, smiling out at us from the screen, false white beard and hair – like Father Christmas. Grinning like an idiot whilst the music blared. Same chant as before but this time as if sung by excited children. Then the camera pulls back and you can make out the pillars of Calton Hill behind him, and they've shot it to look like the Parthenon. That's what the beard is about, he's meant to be Zeus, except he's holding a bottle of beer in his hand; a Greek god with bad teeth, paunch and flaky eyes ... 'Greetings!' The voice was kind of thin and shaky (imitates a feeble intonation). 'My Greetings to you all! Welcome to *Proscribed*. Thank you for *daring* to come.' And then he swigs from his bottle. 'Let me also thank those kind people of Damm, the brewers of this fine refreshment, for their generosity in furnishing us with their product for nothing. However, I must state categorically, sponsorship of the arts is an issue I always maintain a firm stance against, even when the associated product is something as good as Damm.' He drinks again, face on camera. 'Yes, even a lager as good as this, as tasty, clear and distinctive is not something I would allow to be associated with my art. Even if its creamy cool flavour could delight the most jaundiced of palates, I would still refuse to bow to the notion that the ability of art to communicate directly with our very being can be hijacked by the silver of a patron's purse. So I must refuse Damm's offer, and their request for me to endorse their fine, fine lager – surely the best available in any reputable liquor establishment – for, as an artist, my favours belong to a higher realm. And to that realm, dear audience, is where we will travel right now. Your hosts will invite you to partake in a variety of pursuits, all designed to heighten your artistic perceptions and receptiveness. When you have completed these and entered a higher state of consciousness the performance will truly begin!' The music soared and then faded out. Once it had gone from the television it went from the room; they had switched it off outside. For the first time in about three hours, I didn't have this (sings wearily) 'Pablo Dextrus Pablo . . .' droning on in my ears.

Interviewer:
They wanted you to play games. Were you surprised by this?

Lowes:
When we were allowed in the house you could see there was no stage or even performing area. Surprised? No, too drunk. There was still the promise of some kind of act, and when the star had appeared maybe some of the others thought there might be a solo show. But we were all comfortable with each other, giggling at the video, commenting to each other . . . you know what it's like, a hatful of beers with someone and you are blood brothers. It would have been hard to shut us up by then if they *had* wanted to perform. They wanted us to play games and we were only too happy . . . In fact, we waited eagerly for our cue . . . Pigs fattening themselves up for the bacon slicer.

Interviewer:
What was the first then?

Lowes:
(sighs) A performance game, 'Taboo'. You can buy it in shops. You're given a card with a word on it – 'passion', say. Your team-mates have to guess what the word is by your prompts, but there is also a list of words that you are not allowed to use when giving clues – 'love, fervour, lust', for example. If you use them, that's taboo and you're disqualified. Eddie had us divided into a team on each sofa. Equal numbers of men and women. I had Sarah on mine

. . . Pissed she was, leaning right into me. You just rolled together on that kind of furniture, especially in that state . . . it's like gravity is stronger in the middle, and you're always fighting to stop falling together . . . or not, as the case might be.

Interviewer:
Was there anything unusual about the way you played the game?

Lowes:
(sighs) I wouldn't know, I'd never played it before. Unusual? Well, there was lots of shouting and cheering for everyone getting up to do their word, and that was before they – Ciaran, Claire in her red evening gown and Eddie especially – started cranking it up, either to give encouragement or just to inspire confidence. First up was Steve, insistent he was . . . can't remember the word, it was for the other side. I was up second. Believe it or not I did feel pressure, everyone had got theirs across up till then and I didn't want to be the first to fail . . . I'm looking into Sarah's eyes, begging her to get it. 'Lobster'. (laughs) You try putting that over without mentioning the sea, crabs or pincers . . . And she gets it, gives me a kiss and it's like I've just won the cup final (languidly punches air). Round each team twice and we were all square. It made you think . . . here we are, all civilised and intelligent people, and we've been in each other's company for hours so that the barriers are down, then this stupid game shows us all that none of us actually has any idea about how to . . . communicate with each other. We can't share ideas, can't really say what we want or hear it when others try to tell us. It's like we've suddenly hit into this need for a new language that can cut through all the crap so that we can just listen to each other without fucking suffocating because of the lack of meaningful words in the air. That's what I took it all to be about anyway, never got the chance to discuss it with the others . . . couldn't express it (laughs). So the moment went by and it was time for the second game, this time not quite so straightforward. This time they had to get Pablo back on the screen to explain it to us . . . This time he was dressed as the devil . . .

OKAY. START. CHARLES KIDD. What would they make of him?

The unauthorised Curriculum Vitae, for those in the know, those with insight, i.e. any bastard with half a brain who's ever met me.

Start again. Go. No stopping, no holding back, no avoidance of the facts. No more no's. So what's left? A series of lacklustre disappointments leading to one almighty catastrophe. School? You know about that. University too. After that, a period of drifting. Someone spoke to my family about the possibility of a new start in the army. It seemed a reasonable proposition so I killed a spring, summer and autumn waiting for an entrance exam into the officer academy which I then decided not to sit. I had this vision of me dishing out the orders to the troops, and the massed ranks turning sharply to a man in parade ground unison, telling me to fuck off. They would have seen through me just as I was beginning to. Me: 'Eyes right!' Them: 'No! Stick it up your arse, sir!'

Then there was the plan to travel and somehow *find* myself. I planned the journey in detail, never quite sure of where I might *be*. Planned several journeys in detail. Never actually went on any of them. I always found a reason to hang fire, look into things more closely, amend the itinerary. Europe then the Far East, then Australia. America then Australia. America, then Latin America. Hong Kong. No Hong Kong. And on and on. Or rather, not on and not on. Today I might describe this as 'a period of re-adjustment' for the 'weighing up of options'. Back then though I couldn't come up with such phrases and could only pass myself off as a listless inadequate.

My mother knew someone at Grevant Safety, brokers by appointment to Her Majesty. I think my mother had had a fling at some point in the distant past with someone in authority there, perhaps even Mr Safety himself. Funny? No, probably not. Obviously there was no 'Mr Safety', or even a Mr Grevant – he had long since died, having set up the firm over a hundred years ago. They had been brokers by appointment to Queen Victoria. Now they were brokers by appointment to those with no judgement. The firm was in the control of the Cameron family, and had been for about three generations, and it was one of them who owed my mother a favour.

The Camerons prided themselves on their integrity, which might have been a fair enough assessment of them as individuals. Perhaps it was just their firm that was totally bent. That's why it eventually went bust, not that you will have heard it put like that. You will have heard the story about *'tired assets'* and *'under-stimulated management procedures'* and how the merger with Everards was planned to *'marry'* the *'fine traditions'* and *'establishment values'* of the older firm with the *'youthful dynamism'* of the latter, and was not – and I must stress *not* – a rushed city cover-up of fraudulent accounting practices going back twenty-five years whose results had finally grown large enough to threaten the entire brokerage system. You will only have heard about the meeting of *'different though complementary'* business cultures which was *'applauded by analysts for its audacity'*.

Fine words all – my words. I discovered I could command the language of spin. I quote from my own press release. It was one of my final jobs for old Mr Cameron – after I'd failed in the roles of trainee broker, then trainee accountant, then administration assistant – to push an acceptable representation of the facts to the hacks whose lot it was to cover such momentous business events.

And they bought it, gave us press coverage to die for and all of it on my terms.

Success at last as the ship went down. I had found myself without ever having to leave London. I was a PR man. I was damned.

THE term 'Operating Theatre', or rather, the interesting use of the word *theatre* as the place of medical surgery, originates from the Edinburgh medical schools which pioneered the then brutal craft in the early Regency period. Operations and autopsies could be carried out by the star practitioners of the new discipline in front of packed benches, eager to learn the innermost secrets of the body. Competition for students, or more accurately their fees, meant that education became entertainment. The schools providing the best shows, with the most credible, charismatic performers, enjoyed the best fee-paying returns. In the very early days, Edinburgh University had dominated all teaching rivals, led by the brilliant father–son dynasty of Alexander Munro *Primus* (1697–1767) and Alexander Munro *Secundus* (1733–1817) who between them held the post of Professor of Anatomy in succession for seventy-eight years. Indeed, Munro *Secundus* was to be immortalised in medical circles with his discovery of the aperture in the brain known as 'the foramen of Munro'. By 1828, however, the prestige of the University was in sharp decline. Munro Secundus was followed in the chair of Anatomy by the third and final member of the dynasty, Munro *Tertius*. Lacking either his father's or grandfather's intellect and talent, the lectures of Munro Tertius became noteworthy only for their total absence of zeal and fervour, and their shameless use of guidance notes written by his predecessors decades earlier. Here was a Munro without the inventive spirit and gift for improvisation that had made his family name, using for illustration musty jars of the same pickled organs his father had once retrieved in the same hall. Bored students listening to his anaemic discourse would have

54

to look to his rivals for signs of where the next great discoveries might be made. It was the independent spirits who were not afraid to operate on real bodies, or to follow where their curiosity took them. Those who were not bound by academic convention were now leading the way.

Alexander Brodie seemed one such doctor, a dedicated man who sought, through the development of his surgical skills and the teaching of others, to establish himself at the forefront of this new science.

By 1827, Brodie's reputation was at its height, both as a surgeon of audacity and speed, and as a lecturer of authority and passion. Pupils flocked from all over Europe to attend the dissections he would perform in the operating 'theatre', narrating each incision as he went about his business, offering stinking cadaver organs to the open air for the education of the class. A good view was essential, both to enjoy the thrill of a fresh corpse being carved, and the charged rush of operations on live subjects, the latter being performed with unbelievable haste before the unfortunate patient's usually violent reaction to the pain being inflicted upon him rendered him inoperable. Amputations would pass in a blur, often taking with them the fingers and hands of the assisting staff trying to hold the subject down. Brodie, though, was an acknowledged master of the craft, never daunted by the struggles and squirming below his blade, eyes steadfastly fixed on the completion of the task.

But, colleagues noted, something began to change within Brodie. Perhaps a vanity had gradually outgrown his talent, or had his dealings with the criminal classes over the supply of graveyard corpses for his lectures eventually corrupted him? Whatever, Brodie's aspiration was seen to move from merely *understanding* the workings of God's creation to *proving* its perfection. He was no longer satisfied with extracting the body's standard organs, hacking out heart, lungs and liver for his class to identify. Now he wanted to find for himself the most elusive organ of them all. To some, Brodie spoke of a place in history beckoning him. He whispered about an invention which would transform the operating theatre, medicine and even life itself. He announced to chosen students that he would be the first doctor to surgically isolate the soul.

No surgeon of the modern age had ever claimed to have found this hidden, though surely vital, component of the human constitution, although the very earliest of doctors had thought that the brain itself was the soul and therefore should not be tampered with, in the living or the dead. Even the practitioners of the more modern science that Brodie led had reconciled themselves to never locating it. After all, was it not a fact that the soul departed the body after death and would therefore never be present in the bodies bought and brought for theatre?

For a fearless radical genius, however, there seemed only one possible way of succeeding – by performing an 'autopsy' on a living subject. The method would have to be an invasion of a swiftness fast enough to catch out the Almighty, a controlled search of the brain and torso, opening up everything for view within seconds if sighting was to be confirmed before the prize evaporated into the heavens above.

Brodie began to experiment, rehearsing an excavation of the skull with increasing rapidity and precision, each time memorising what there was to see within an ordinary corpse. When it came to enact the procedure in truth these were the items that had to be recognised and instantly discounted. What would be sought would be the new, the *unexpected*, and he had to be sure this would immediately stand out.

Brodie's activities kept the graverobbers busy. His commissions fulfilling either of two briefs, firstly the supply of bodies for the secretive rehearsals, and secondly the supply of corpses for the lectures by which Brodie could earn the monies required to pay for the first. The premium paid for fresh subjects understandably set off on an inflationary spiral as Brodie found himself bidding against rival schools for the best specimens. Yet this same competition that forced the price up also improved the quality of supply. Bodysnatching had become a lucrative trade for the criminal fraternity, indeed the only trade now exercising its finest minds. Here, they realised, was the perfect crime – the surgeons not only paid for the fruits of their evil deeds, but also disposed of the evidence. Soon, every felon within the city was working on one assignment or another, and rumours spread as to what could be behind this insatiable demand. It came as no surprise or insurmountable challenge when a third requirement was issued through the secretive channels – to find a corpse that breathed.

'Daft' Jamie Buchan had been born simple. Now an alcoholic vagrant in his twenties with a mental capacity of perhaps a third of his age, he was a moderately well-known figure in the city, sometimes seen begging at the Mercat Cross, sometimes heard pleading with his mother to take him back into the family home. After starting numerous fires and, during one of his childhood fits, toppling over the kitchen dresser with disastrous consequences for the family crockery, Daft Jamie was banished into exile. It was he who was persuaded to take the supporting role in Brodie's brave experiment. Daft Jamie would provide the raw material, having been reassured that Brodie's intention was to repair any damage done in the course of the exploratory probe into his cranium. Daft Jamie let himself dream of returning home to his mother, his reward in hand as his gift to her. He waited impatiently for his chance to redeem himself, dreamed as Brodie finalised his rehearsals, practising as he strove for perfection.

At last, Brodie was ready. The Great Hall in Surgeon's Square was booked, and a select group was invited to witness an historic occasion – the unveiling of a revolutionary advance in medicinal understanding. For this event, Brodie asked his peers to take the place of his students, to gather round closely as the operation commenced. What he sought to demonstrate could only be glimpsed briefly, but would leave none un-affected.

The moment came, the sacrifice prepared.

'Gentlemen, I beg your greatest powers of concentration on the procedure to be practised for the very first time tonight. To us falls the responsibility of reconciling the greatest achievements of our profession with the greatest achievement of our Lord. Gentlemen I begin with a rapid incision, necessarily deep and deliberate . . .'

Did he pause before bringing the hatchet to bear on Daft Jamie, who was blinking in a final vacant panic, gagged and strapped to the bench 'for his own good'? How much did the theatre assistants know of the nature of that night's operation? When did they realise a murder was taking place? Did they think to intervene, to halt this obscenity? Perhaps they too were transfixed, like the others, like Brodie himself, struggling to maintain his commentary. The first blow had been as decisive as he could have hoped, but the blood had squirted up in anger from the severed patutial artery with a force equal to that brought down upon it, causing Brodie a precious pause as he wiped his forehead to prevent it from running down into his eyes. Daft Jamie's desperate kicks and spasms made it difficult to prise open a greater cavity at the frontal lobes. Brodie was losing time. The butchery required had unnerved him. He began to speak again, as much to calm and remind himself of the validity of the exercise as to inform those around him.

'We find the frontal cerebellum . . . intact, shrunken by congenital deformity . . . intact . . . we . . .' He steadied his hands and pushed a pair of closed forceps into the cavity in his victim's scalp before giving a sharp pull to open them and lever the plates of bone apart. They gave to his exertions, cracking like a giant egg, spilling the contents out onto the wooden bench top. Once more, Brodie's voice struggled to keep pace with events. '. . . inner cortex, present . . . more quilutium fluid . . . neo-cortex . . .'

It was a mess. The vitality of his subject made the identification of items so difficult. Blood and fluid carried the evidence away on a ruby tide, something he was unprepared for, knowing only the dried stability of corpses.

And suddenly, amongst the red and grey-green at the core of the hole, an inviting sliver of silver – the prize itself. Brodie dropped his scalpel and rushed to clasp it with his bare hands. He dived to wrench the object free, its spongy tenacity and malleability making it seem like a starfish being hauled up from the bottom of some fabulous ocean. Both his hands tugged greedily at the entity, determinedly snatching at it for a moment's inspection before it could begin its journey to the heavens. The strength required to wrench it from its hiding place had lifted Daft Jamie's head clear from the bench so that it slid back with a sodden thud once released. Many in the audience had shielded their eyes from the lifeless body's petrified gaze. Brodie, however, was enraptured. The jewel was his.

'The soul, gentlemen. The soul!'

He stumbled forward, parading it to stunned silence.

Brodie did not want to let go, absorbing as much visual detail as he could before the heavens reclaimed it from his hands. As he paused in wonder at his achievement, the unease amongst the benches became increasingly audible. A voice rose from the rabble, a voice charged with indignity.

'What you have in your hand, sir, is the pineal gland. A gland which, like any other, will shrink through dehydration after death.' The voice had an authority which was at once recognised by those on the benches. This was the voice of Alexander Munro, Alexander Munro *Tertius*. His had been a cowed presence in the hall, but now he moved to make his outrage known.

'I cannot believe what I have just witnessed. The shame of it will linger with me forever. You are a fool, sir. A charlatan!'

Brodie looked to his bloodied hands. A gland. No, it was *new*. It had to be the soul. A gland which dehydrates, of course: he had been blinded to the simple fact. Was there time for another look? Could the real soul still be somewhere on the table? If he could summon the strength for another search, would they all be with him? No, the dream was over.

A dread silence hung over the stage, the realisation leaving him completely stupefied. His eyes were drawn to the carnage behind and he let out an insane laugh. It had all been for nothing. One experiment too many and the only thing he had proved was that the line between fame and infamy was so desperately thin.

Dumbfounded, realising they, too, had been party to an unspeakable act and struggling to cope with the shock, some of the audience began to join the laughter.

A situation, a *theatre*, an audience not knowing how to react. And thus the art of black comedy was born.

TRANSCRIPT : TAPE 4

Lowes:

Two minutes on 'Your favourite dead relative' without pausing or umming and ahhing or repetition. For every transgression during that time, an item of clothing must be removed. (Assumes feeble voice of Pablo Dextrus) 'Remember "F" stands for favourite and not for fake.' (Shakes head and returns to normal voice) He was all rouged up this time . . . lipstick and matching cape . . . Shot indoors, lots of smoke and the music much slower, a malevolent chant. Whilst we were watching the video they had drawn the curtains and lit candles. The music was all around again. I don't know how the others felt but there was a silence when it finished. For me, because of the phrase at the end – it reminded me of the thing on the application form and I felt a similar sort of chill as I had when I had first read it . . . feeling that sort of empathy for the *expression*, but not having a fucking clue what it actually meant. You've got to remember we had all gone from a state of high excitement – performing these words, getting caught up in the game – and then we sat down, squeezed up, told the game is going to get darker, naughtier. Take our clothes off? Who would back out? Did anyone want to spoil the party, be seen as impossibly square? Might it all be fun, an *experience*, the one we'd all come for? Eddie is pushing out more beers . . . yes, a *beer*-pusher (laughs, and assumes assertive tone). 'You all heard the man . . . two minutes, each of you. Who's going first?' While the others hesitated, I found myself volunteering. Get it over with, nothing worse than waiting. (Adopts voice again) 'Aha! Brave man! Good for you, Dan. The floor is yours . . . your time starts . . . Now!' Two minutes is a bloody long time, especially with ten pairs of eyes on you. Still, I thought I could just make it up, so I started, the plan being just to follow my own mind . . . (closes eyes). 'My favourite dead relative,

61

the one I love more than all the others, the one I adore most of all with a special place in my heart ... (Mumbles 'repetition') ... was my Uncle Stanley because when he was alive he was seven feet tall, taller than ...' (Assumes other voice) 'Stop! We said F stands for favourite not for fake. Penalty of two items of clothing for deliberate invention. Pablo knows when you are lying ...' (Back to normal voice) Pablo wouldn't have had to be a genius to work out I was lying, unless he believed I came from a family of giants, and that was never on because I'm only five-seven. I could have kicked myself for being so stupid, so blatant, and wondered how the hell I would get through the rest of the time ... but this wasn't an immediate problem. I had a chance to work something out: every time you were stopped you went back to the end of the list, and when you were up again the clock was meant to start from where you had left, so every try was for a theoretically shorter period. My shoes didn't count as an item of clothing, but the socks did. I listened to the next shot, barefoot ... every time you would have less and less on ... My favourite dead relative? I began to try conjuring up the memory of real ones. Pablo knew if we were lying ...

Interviewer:
So no one had pulled out at this stage? Nobody refused to participate?

Lowes:
(pause) Maybe people think that they can pass the test, that they are smarter than the rest. The problem then is making sure you will do it. Stripping off is not an issue because you've already told yourself you'll succeed where the others have failed. We are also playing for a team that we've ... *bonded with* ... whilst playing Taboo for the last hour ... and once I began there was no way out for any of the others. I can see that now.

Interviewer:
How did the others perform?

Lowes:

About the same. Most would get about thirty seconds into it before drying up. Some of them began to copy previous tries and were bounced straight out back to the start, minus whatever they were taking off. Then there would be arguments about what constituted a piece of clothing and what didn't . . . Fun boy Colin was very concerned about rules – shouldn't a man's shirt be considered two garments since the fucking girls were wearing bra's. Honestly! Actually, I'd taken him for another Edinburgh plum when he'd introduced himself at first, but when he spoke about his dear Uncle Cameron and how they tossed fucking cabers together or some shit, it turns out he's a Highlander from some whisky puddle north of Inverness. Funny how some accents can throw you in the wrong direction. Anyway, all clothes count the same, so it was handy to be wearing socks, or a waistcoat . . . that is, if modesty was what mattered to you at that moment (pauses).

Interviewer:

You are implying that it didn't to some . . . Were there those who perhaps needed little encouragement to strip?

Lowes:

True for some . . . one of the girls . . . the fat one. Always the ones with the most to be modest about. (Shakes head) But no, that's not what I meant. The thing is revolving round so fast, you see. One minute you are out, shirt to take off and one minute ten seconds to kill next time, and then you are back on again . . . there's cheering and whistling as everyone else is peeling down and then handclaps for starting you up again. 'And my favourite dead relative is . . .' – whilst remembering that F stands for fucking Fake. So Steve, poor bloody Steve, he opens up about his *real* favourite dead relative. (Adopts voice trembling with emotion) 'My father died in 1988. I was in my final year at university, packing in as much partying as I could before I would settle down to some nine-to-five somewhere, earning a real living. My father had had cancer for some time, stomach cancer, and he'd got worse without us really noticing. We knew it was terminal but had grown used to this fact, and for months and months it had just seemed like he would hang on

63

forever. Then my mother called and said he was fading – could I make it down that night? It was a Thursday, late licence at the union bar – I didn't want to go home. And the next night would be Friday, the big party time. Would I miss that? He'd last; I'd had these calls before – he'd pull through. No. Can't make it, studying for my finals. Oh, I . . . *we* understand, son. You come on Saturday, come when you can . . . He died on the Friday morning. Everyone else was there. I missed it for the sake of a piss-up and I've never had the guts to admit it to her. I . . .' (Pauses before resuming normal voice) So then he cracks up, crying, shoulders heaving, the lot. And they're shouting, 'Penalty pause! One item of clothing. Twenty seconds to go next round. Next!' How could they be serious? The guy's in real distress. So it's Zoe on next and she looks confused, and Eddie's roaring at her, 'Go Go Go, Zo!' so she starts, but doesn't get very far because the others are trying to comfort sobbing boy and she stalls. 'That's a penalty pause, Zoe. We'll have something off, please.' She looks at Eddie as if she's going to cry, or tell him to fuck off, or both, but he faces it down. 'Come on. We thought you were more fun than *that* now!' Course, the other thing is that Zoe – she'd be early twenties, civil servant I think, so hardly used to this amount of booze, as well as being quiet and not as sharp as the others . . . the thing is that she's obviously already been fucking hopeless at this game and doesn't really have a lot left to take off . . . had on this cotton sort of bodice, just a light thing, white. She looks at Eddie and undoes it at the back, pulls her arms out and there she is, tits to the world. Eddie cheers, Ciaran cheers, even the vision of beauty in red – classy Claire – joins in. 'My favourite dead relative . . .' And she's still got over a minute to go . . .

Interviewer:
What effect did this have on the others? Were they shocked?

Lowes:
We must have all known it would reach a point where someone would be asked to . . . so, no, not really. Did stop Steve from crying though, until he had to do his last few seconds . . . then it's a virtual repeat. Some of the others went the same way, followed him, talking

about aunts and mothers and brothers, all the shit, and then falling down. Left sitting there in knickers and bra's . . . left sitting there, naked.

Interviewer:
What about you?

Lowes:
I was okay. I . . . concentrated. Thought of a real one, a cousin who went in a hit and run when I was about ten, and how I'd got his presents that year because it had been close to Christmas and they had already been bought . . . but I didn't lose it. I wasn't going to let that happen. I didn't like how the whole thing had changed . . . The most distraught were the ones with the least clothes on, and I couldn't see how they would let this happen. You've got to understand, taking your clothes off for a dare is nothing . . . it was this *performance* that stripped you of your dignity . . . Yes, I began to see what Pablo was up to.

Interviewer:
Didn't you want to leave?

Lowes:
No . . . I *had* to stay . . . Had to stay for the show, wasn't going to miss anything now. (Laughs and smiles ruefully) I thought I could just go undercover and watch.

It must have been somewhere between nine and ten o'clock, still light outside but going fast . . . Hot and clammy outside. You can hear the echoes in the air of the insects in a thousand neat little gardens, clicking and hissing like Edinburgh is downtown Rio at four a.m. And I thought of the places in the city centre, the best bars – The Bank, The Barony, The Bow Bar, Abbotsford and Cafe Royal – all gearing up for another night, a Festival night, for the beautiful people that would go on until the early hours. We are in Grange, downhill and down wind from Princes Street and the castle. The heat and the noise of the city has spilled down from the top, sitting right on us . . . and I felt jealous of the people up there in those bars right then, the ones buying in the rounds and cracking jokes, the ones with the girlfriends and the money to burn and the guide books ... all the Festival accessories ... the stories to tell about last night's show. Well, soon I would have a story to tell, one that would entertain the listener and damn me as I told it, because *I* had sought this out ... Yes, that was what I hated the most, I had *looked* for this and come on my own – the outsider, lured by the bait.

Interviewer:
It seems to bother you that you had to tell the truth to pass the test.

Lowes:
I wanted to make it up to maintain some kind of ... *privacy*. They had us bringing up cherished memories for entertainment ... for mockery ... and I was one of the few not shaken by the telling, but even that was a failure. You see, I just couldn't think of anyone I had loved who is now dead, and again I suddenly had this sense of being so removed from the others, jealous in a strange kind of way ... Steve talking about his father, undeniably moving. My father? No; still very much alive, never a favourite. He was seventeen when I was born. Can you imagine that? Didn't marry my mother until I was eight, and then it only lasted two years and he was off again, out of my life ... didn't reappear until I was at university. I'm cooking a meal in the campus flat one Friday night and one of the guys comes through and says there's someone at the door looking for me, and I go and there's my dear father with a holdall and a sleeping bag, come to share the action with his son. Of course everyone was enormously impressed: he's a good-looking guy, could have passed for being in his twenties, a charmer, relaxed and cool, apart from the flared jeans and embroidered denim shirt ... and no one can believe he's my dad, sat there rolling a joint, asking if any girls are coming over. No? Well why not? Why don't we have a party? A family reunion! Sure, dad, sure ... I was nineteen. I would have been as impressionable as the rest of them. Going to Oxford was the first time I had been away from home and I'd only been there three weeks. It was all new to me, this; sharing a flat with four other cunts. And these were an alright

66

bunch of lads . . . clever . . . some ex-public school, but generous and interesting all the same, and we would have got on fine . . . but then dad arrives and soon we're all under his wing. He's the one setting the agenda and he's not even a student. I think of it now, a practically middle-aged man, crashing out in a hall of residence with five other green recruits. It must have been so bloody easy for him, and the fact that he was obviously hiding from someone, or something, made it all the more glamorous to us. Nobody ever asked what it was for fear of spoiling the illusion. So he took me, us, to places we might never have gone, brought us into touch with people we might not ordinarily have . . . sought out. And that was the picture for the rest of that first year – him being with us, one of the lads . . . Most people would take us for brothers, except he is called Dan as well. He would be, wouldn't he? And when we talked it would never be in any sort of father and son way; the opposite, in fact – him egging me on, distracting me, rubbishing my studies (Let's get out, for Christ's sake!) and I never mentioned the past because somehow it was clear that this wasn't part of the deal. At the end of the third term somebody grassed him up to the Hall staff. The porters came looking to see if we were putting up a lodger. They saw his stuff and we all got a warning, told to clear him out or else. He wanted to laugh it off but the others were really pissed with the whole thing by then. It was the dealing, you see. Everybody was cool about him getting hold of a little grass for us all to try – all part of being a student, yeah? – but then you've got these people showing up at the door, looking for 'Dan'. Bikers, rastas, punks . . . some of them turning nasty when what they get is me. It's no wonder that the others had had enough of it. The wonder is that it didn't come sooner. So Pater is persuaded to sling his hook, and I could tell that they wanted me to beat it too. I only saw him the once after that, bumped into him drinking. We chatted but he was joined by some heavy types. I left him to it . . . The day after, I was arrested. Spent seven weeks in remand, waiting for the imbecile police to realise they had pulled the wrong man. Seven bloody weeks . . . missed the year's finals, got thrown off the course. I didn't tell them it was actually my dad they were after. I thought, for some stupid reason, that I owed him that. Too young to realise how he'd used me in every way, left me with nothing . . . Seven weeks inside. You got family? Would you do that to them? 'Favourite dead relative'? Just '*dead* relative' would be good enough.

Interviewer:
Next?

Lowes:
Next, I began to lose my head. I became worried, increasingly worried, that we were being filmed, or watched . . . looking into the mirror above the fireplace and wondering if it could be a two-way number. If it wasn't, where was the deal – in the ceiling? Paranoia. *Justified* paranoia? You tell me. You really not heard from anyone else that night? How do you know this is for real? How do I know it's for real? How did I know it was for real then? Never known anything like it – a lot of people shaken up by what they had heard themselves saying. Those that weren't shaken up were shaken up by the sight of how badly shaken those that went for it were. Follow me? Yes, we were all feeding off each other. Lesson number one, we had bonded as a group, a losers' group. I could tell, and that's why I was even more scared when the next video came on. Pablo's next greeting of joy . . .

Interviewer:
Why did this message scare you? What was he dressed as this time?

Lowes:
I can't remember what he was wearing exactly, sort of seventeenth-century gear – powdered wig, buckled hat and black coat. A pilgrim father. (laughs). No, what unnerved me was the way I had kind of felt I knew what he was going to say, where we were headed next. He began to talk about clubs. Edinburgh clubs, not dance places but associations, illegal associations, that they had tried to eradicate throughout the city's history. Edinburgh has always had its clubs, he says, some of them still revered like the 'Easy Club', so-called because it was easy to join and was basically just a drinking club for would-be drunks. But the important point was that it had a proper membership and accounts, and stations of office – chairman, treasurer and the rest. What does that say about the Scots? asks

Pablo. The Easy Club was big until late last century, and there were others in a similar vein ... Then, he says with a smile, then there were those of a darker persuasion. In the late 1700s, the largest Hell-Fire Club in Europe was in Edinburgh. This club existed for the express purpose of arranging wild orgies where nothing was too debased to be tried ... Just think, Pablo says, a club which elected one of its members to the post of honorary devil. Outlawed groups like this refused to be confined by society's rules and norms. They lived by their own ... like the Sweating Club which met in the city's taverns; young men, sons of the city's great and good intent on mischief ... They would drink their fill and spill out onto the streets and set upon that night's victim, the first bystander that they happened upon, who would be chased and then beaten to death, after his exertions had caused a good enough harvest of perspiration – the merry band's calling card. By the mid-eighteenth century, the city streets were no longer considered safe. The town guard had to advise visitors to stay indoors to avoid marauding, murderous gangs like these. And then there was the Surgeon's Club whose members would stalk and then pounce on a victim in a similar fashion before setting about them with the cleavers and hatchets that were the doctor's tools ... The rumour of the time was that these were the antics of drunken students of the medical schools, eager to try out their techniques. But let's not talk about surgeons or doctors, says Pablo. Let's just admire the way they challenged the establishment by creating their own establishment ... What kind of club do we want to be in? A *friendly* club. Why don't we all introduce ourselves properly? There is incredible strength in unity, we will see ... We will see.

Interviewer:
So when this video finished what did you all do?

Lowes:
We played 'Twister'.

Interviewer:
Are you serious?

Lowes:
Am I? Were they? Yes . . . A 'group' activity, fun for all. Music back on, volume turned up, and it's the same number but in a jazzified, sort of Benny Hill style. Ciaran and Eddie are smoothing out this mat on the floor. Claire has an elegant hand on the spin board. 'Come on. Pablo forbids anyone to be miserable at his parties. Twister the name, Twister the game, boys versus girls. We want a captain for each side. Volunteers now!' And she caught sight of me, or had I been looking for her, looking to prove I wasn't as pathetic as miserable Steve – a stronger man me. (laughs quietly) Yes, I'll be captain of the boys! Never been a team leader in my life. Sarah's the other captain, geeing up the girls. Come on, Andy. Smarten up, for Chrissake! I must have been so drunk . . . Simple rules for drunks – one player added with each spin until there are four on the mat, then the opposition keeps calling the spin until the whole lot topples over. The Captain decides which one of the participants has to make the move prescribed by the spin of the board. One other rule – no one gets to put their clothes back on from last time. There *had* to be cameras watching us.

Interviewer:
Did everybody play? Nobody sought to leave at this stage?

Lowes:
They all got into it . . . got each other into it. The girls dry their tears and spin the dial . . . it says 'hand to blue, foot to red' and I'm shouting at one of ours to stretch to reach, and the girls are squealing because the boys are squeezed onto each other, sweating, pressed up. Disgusting . . . then the girls . . . some of them podgy . . . bellies hanging out over a pantyline, splaying themselves, every grimy hairy corner on show. We win one, they win one. Each new game more important than the last – shouting louder, pushing harder. Eddie, with his beer bottle erect at his crotch, jeering and leering . . . the school bully watching the younger lads squirm in the dorm. I can't believe we did it for them, yet we did . . . teams believing that it *mattered*, the two captains belting out instructions . . . two sets of otherwise healthy heterosexual boys and girls slavering over each other. You see, some didn't seem to mind, 'all in the

70

spirit of the party', stuffing your head into some stranger's armpit, or cunt . . . as long as we win . . . Strength in unity? We were one big ball of arms and legs and everything. One big fucked-up ball with no energy left for the next outrage . . . That's why it was time for Pablo's pick-me-up . . .

Interviewer:
Another game?

Lowes:
(snorts derisively) More of a dare.

Interviewer:
Can you explain?

Lowes:
The girl in the red ball-gown, *Claire* . . . beautiful Claire . . . what on earth could she get out of it? She had disappeared during the last bouts of Twister. Then I saw her coming back in, carrying silver trays and laying them on the dining table at the far end of the room. I thought it had to be food; we'd been there seven hours, drinking all the time . . . *had* to be food . . . although there was no smell . . . (shakes head) It wasn't . . .

Interviewer:
What was it?

Lowes:
We're all sat down, or rolling on the floor, whatever . . . No one can see what's on the actual table because it's so flat. But Eddie – he knows what it is. Smiles that Cheshire bloody grin of his . . . 'A *tonic*. How excellent, how generous of Pablo.' Then he's got hold of a straw, bends over the table, finger to one nostril, snorts it up really loudly. Kind of laughs and coughs in one as he straightens up . . . and you can see his eyes are gone, but only further than they were before. He's already been on it – that's where the super-bloody-confidence comes from . . . (clears throat). 'Friends! As guests of Pablo you are invited to partake in some of Pablo's invigor-

ating herbal tonic . . . an elixir of unparalleled excellence. Just what is required in this modern age of hectic lifestyles.' And then Eddie cuts up – a fit of the giggles. He's been reading this crap from a piece of card the girl – Claire – is holding for him. She takes over. 'Come on down!' (claps hands) And she's looking round, after volunteers again. 'Captains first!' I wonder what the fuck to do, but the other captain has already stood up, over at the table, like it's another challenge. 'That's right. One big sniff . . . right up the line . . . try not to sneeze . . . *hold* it . . .' Jesus Christ, she's a school-teacher.

Interviewer:
So the drug – could you tell what it was?

Lowes:
Not by just fucking looking at it, no. White powder? Cocaine . . . heroin . . . amphetamine, a mixture? And you couldn't tell either by the immediate reaction of those taking it. When it came to my turn I peered real close at it – small crystals, like salt. Some coke in there . . . fine powder . . . I hoped that would be speed not smack. Had to be. After all, had he not said a 'pick-me-up', and you don't pick anyone up with smack (dry laugh). And then the powder could have been dipped with acid, spiked with whatever hallucinogen they thought appropriate. I said it was a dare, not a game? No, it was a game alright. He's got us playing roulette, Russian fucking roulette. Price of admission – your mind.

Interviewer:
And everyone partook?

Lowes:
Everyone.

Interviewer:
How long did that take?

Lowes:
Fuck knows.

Interviewer:
How did . . . whatever you took affect you?

Lowes:
Badly.

Interviewer:
In what respect?

Lowes:
(in low voice) In every fucking respect.

Interviewer:
Could you speak up?

Lowes:
I'm through. Finished. End of chat . . . Money, please and I'll split
. . . been here too long already . . .

Interviewer:
But you haven't finished. What happened next? You said there was
one final game . . .

Lowes:
Give me the money now so I can see it. Then I'll tell you, if you
can believe it . . . tell you what old Pablo had cut the drug with . . .
now . . .

Interviewer:
(pause as something is handed over) Right?

Lowes:
Yeah. (takes deep breath) What had he cut it with – smack, acid,
speed? All and more. The power of expectation . . . and then some
. . . something to top the lot . . .

Interviewer:
And what was that?

Lowes:
(incredulous) Ghost. Fucking ghost ... and that's what really freaked everyone out.

OKAY. KFC. Let's think about KFC and where they fit in. Someone has to.

KFC had a smart set-up in the West End, at Drumsheugh Gardens. Four storeys of Regency terrace, filled with eager young things; these are the kamikaze shock troop elite of Public Relations. It looked like an office but was in fact a war zone: stripped wooden floors, garish modern art hanging on the walls, palm plants growing berserk on every landing, the pungent smell of fresh coffee – the works. I took it all in.

The obergruppenführer himself, Nick Kennedy – the 'K' in Kennedy Fraser Communications – interviewed me in the boardroom on the ground floor. He had paid for me to fly up for the meeting but didn't seem inclined to sell me his company. He must have known there was no need to. They were called KFC then, a consumer and trade relations specialist agency. That was after they had been Forthright Relations – before Nick and Pete Fraser bought out their own agencies, but before Nick joined Pete and we re-launched as Kennedy Fraser Media Management Group to specialise in corporate affairs. KFMMG was notionally the parent company to KFC itself, which was, of course, the same people just wearing different hats. I can't honestly remember how it all really worked, or how we were meant to sell it. Names come and go so fast in communications. Waiting in reception for Nick to come down that day, I heard the harassed girl on the telephone answer twenty-odd calls, each with a different greeting: 'Good morning, KFC'; 'Hello, Kennedy Services Group'; 'Ferris Kennedy'; 'PM Group'; 'PMT'. Endless, the response depending on which number you dialled, unaware it was all coming into the same switchboard, the same company.

The interview itself was dominated by calls – Nick sitting down, apologising, then leaping back up to take another urgent one when he would mutter important-sounding contributions into the receiver. 'Yes, that's the short term. What about the long term? But don't forget the medium term.' He sounded the part – 'Mmnnn . . . that's an end-game scenario . . . let's map out the parameters . . .' – and looked it too, every oily inch; dark suit with heavy shoulders, hairs from his chest reaching out just over his collar and loud tie, the thinning hairs on his head cropped aggressively tight, a stern, hard face daring you to disagree with him. He used the word 'quite' quite a lot, not in a way I'd heard it used before. He would employ it as if to demonstrate that you had just caught up with him. You would remark it was raining outside and he would reply deadpan, 'Quite.' A word and sentence in one to show how he'd already got there first. This was something you could really listen to, enjoy for its own sake whether you understood any of it or not. The essential part was the heartless conviction with which it was all conveyed. A full-on guy. It was overwhelming.

'Sorry about that. Pete, Pete Fraser should be with us shortly. Listen, you been offered a coffee?'

I couldn't remember. I'd been sat there so long I'd forgotten what it was I was meant to be there for.

'Yes . . .' I thought I might have been at some stage and didn't want to drop anyone in it if I hadn't.

'Can't be persuaded then?' Nick Kennedy stared at me, as if he was disappointed at my lack of thirst.

'No . . . Well, yes then.'

I thought I'd failed the interview before it had even started, having proved myself so weak-willed I couldn't even abstain from a hot drink without prevaricating. Time to reinvent myself, rapidly. From here onwards it would have to be Charles Kidd the decisive.

'Milk?'

'No thank you.'

He opened the door, bellowing instructions to no one in particular – 'Two coffees . . . black!' – and returned to confront me across the table. I decided to dive straight in, to tell him what I thought he might want to hear. Why bother waiting for the questions? Be decisive and pro-active in one bold swoop, even if they were the same thing anyway.

'Seems a busy set-up here, Nick. Obviously a lot going down. Makes me wonder how I might fit in. I've always enjoyed that kind of atmosphere, found it stimulating. It's what I've been used to at Hastings Holmes – and Grevant Safety before that. I'd like to think that the kind of experience I have gained there would be of value here. You might have a team that is enthusiastic but perhaps lacking in direction. I could bring that . . . and then there is the specific financial public relations know-how that could be of direct benefit to your existing client base.'

'What about our *future* client base?'

His eyes had narrowed. He could be a sharp one, a nasty piece of business. Okay, I think, here comes a comment. 'Decisiveness', I remind myself.

'*Quite.*'

What an answer. I knew straight away I'd scored a direct hit. A smile crept onto his face as the coffee arrived. I'd shown I spoke his language – literally – and he obviously thought he'd found his man, a communications professional, recognising a fellow black belt in the midst of combat. After a satisfied pause he went on to explain the company's philosophy, how none of them were frightened of hard work, how staff were encouraged to put 'their balls on the line'. I nodded thoughtfully, wondering what the hell he meant. It was a testing manifesto, dependent on a team that 'knew their arse from their elbow'. I felt my buttocks clench tight as my body offered instinctive reassurance that it could make the distinction.

Then, after my decisiveness came my silence; I'd made my impression and could now only dilute this. I knew I didn't have another response in me that could match my previous score for either technical merit or artistic interpretation. I concentrated on keeping my mouth shut.

Pete Fraser never joined us, not then, not ever. Did he ever really exist or was he a figment of Nick's imagination? No, he must have been around at some stage to have been immortalised on the KFC headed notepaper but no one ever mentioned him, as if he'd succumbed to some unspeakable vice or disease. Nick was the driving force, the one with more balls on the line than any of us. What he said went, and he had decided he liked me.

A month later I was there, the new employee who had promised an immediate contribution, the latest employee to live in fear of Nick Kennedy's dark moods and sharp tongue. A lost soul, feeling the pressure to establish myself, to pull in the new clients. The silence tactic had outlived its shelf-life and I had nothing to replace it. I had talked my way into this. Could I talk my way through it, be a success for once? That had been the plan. It was meant to be easier in Edinburgh yet here I was, twitching at a desk on the second floor, trying to look busy, flicking through a contacts index file, wondering who to call, feeling cheated but somehow relieved when I'd be told they were on holiday or had left their company. And every day I would dread the shadow of Nick Kennedy appearing over my papers and Mickey Mouse coffee cup. In a month he'd gone from a daily exchange about how I was settling into the city, or into my flat, to a more direct and brutal daily inquisition into what I was doing there and if it was any use to him. 'Any leads? Any progress?' he'd grunt, the sub-text always being: can you justify working here, justify your salary, the cost of the electricity you are using, the wear and tear on the chair you occupy so unproductively? All I had to answer back was name, rank and serial number.

I was vulnerable. Desperate for a friendly face in a cold place. Meanwhile, the rest of them scurried about, kept on their toes by the odd strategical sacking.

There was Carol, a chain-smoking, early-forties ex-hack who may or may not have been Nick's occasional bedmate when the mood took him; Julia, a determinedly up-beat late-twenties redhead who tended to wear the same two-piece, blue-cream Armani copy suit all the time, and who called herself 'Jules' when in flirting mood, which was too bloody often; and Andrew, nominally my account executive assistant but clearly superior to his superior on any professional measure.

Andy was the baby of the floor, having joined the previous summer from university. His parents were of Italian stock – his surname was Adriano. He had the lithe hips, grumpy charm and long eye-lashes of a pizza house waiter, the type all the girls would fancy or grow to fancy the more he ignored them. He intrigued me, always so well turned out, despite being paid, presumably, a pittance; never flustered despite whatever shit Nick was throwing. He was a graduate, had a good degree – didn't he wonder what he was doing throwing his noble youth away in the company of inadequates, in a company *for* inadequates? Never exactly unfriendly, he didn't go out of his way to extend a hand of friendship to me. He never, for instance, invited me out for a drink after work, and would repeatedly turn down my offers of the same. If I showed interest in anything he was doing – work or social – he would fend off my attention, swearing loudly at a jammed photocopier or darting off to grab the stuttering output of the fax machine. I told myself that this was the Scottish way, that his reserve would eventually thaw. But I would hear myself becoming more obviously desperate, and him more obviously rude, and my attempts more transparent to the rest of them. Yes, I wanted to get close to him – what's wrong with that? He was so much better at it than me, better at everything; work, friendship, life. Perhaps I had the scent of the drowning man about me from the off. They must have seen it all before, and as a result I worked in an atmosphere of sinister quarantine, the date when I was to be humanely put down writ large above my cage for all to see, except me.

There was eventually the one exception. One Sunday morning my pager rang: it was Julia, desperate for me to contact her. I couldn't imagine what the emergency could be – all KFC staff had pagers, not because of frequent crises but because Nick liked to tell all clients that we had them – and when the damn thing started bleeping the shock had nearly killed me. Julia, however, only wanted to know what I was up to.

There's a walk, a circular route that starts in the West End of town and has you striding out to the Gallery of Modern Art. You can stop there, of course, but it's better to head for the path at the back of the building that leads steeply down the grassy bank to the gently flowing Water of Leith. Walking along the bank leads through to the village of Dean, nestling under Queensferry Bridge which towers above as if belonging to a different world. Such a strange situation – so many cities claim to have pockets of country-side within them, but how many have a secret garden of it *under-neath*? As you continue, the trees and brush grow thicker again before clearing when you finally emerge at Stockbridge, the Green-wich Village of Edinburgh with its own concentration of cosmic

79

offerings to the new age traveller. The choice then is to head further out from town towards the park and boating pond at Inverleith or to cut back to the centre through Raeburn Place and Frederick Street. The latter will take you to the doorstep of The Bailie, consistently named in the guidebooks as one of the city's best pubs.

This was the route and destination Julia and I found that Sunday, once the walk had tired her and she began the transformation into 'Jules', aided by a production line of large gin and tonics.

'Bloody Monday again tomorrow . . . I just can't believe it . . . I'm so bloody busy . . . the days just evaporate before me.'

'Busy.' The word was enough to make my heart pang with guilt. How could she complain about being 'busy', the lucky bitch.

'What have you got on?'

She cringed and took a gulp of gin to ease the pain. 'Bloody New Town Photocopiers . . . the launch of Diamond Gold Maintenance Service . . . or is it Gold Diamond . . . Gold Diamond Emerald . . . usual shit anyway . . .'

'You seem happy enough when you are there, Julia. What's going to be different about tomorrow?'

This triggered another cringe and another swallowed mouthful. 'Oh come on, you don't think I get turned on writing bloody releases on fax machine maintenance or how your photocopier can be fixed free of charge after someone tried to Xerox their arse on it, do you? *Diamond Gold Maintenance* – naff, isn't it? Know who thought it up? Nick, telling them how to rip off their clients, adding an unnecessary service level to the one we launched last year as the "ultimate" . . . and then we'll add another and that will be the ultimate ultimate and which poor bloody sod will have to write up the crud for that? Bloody muggins here, me, explaining that the last one was actually the penultimate ultimate. Having another?'

Julia eased off her stool to lift her bag up from the floor. She hadn't waited for an answer but as it happened I didn't think that writing releases for Diamond Gold copier services would turn her on, but then would anything? It said everything about Nick's influence, and her impressionability, that she would adopt his phrases so willingly, without a pause to think how ridiculous they might sound coming from her own lips. I wondered if she was about to tell me that she had had to put her balls on the line. It was curious that someone whose chosen profession involved the careful development of statements and announcements should be so carefree with words when speaking, not only just now, when she was tending towards drunkenness, but all the time, and often spectacularly. She had a great habit of mixing up metaphors and sayings.

We were at the bar, a large circular mahogany effort that had drawn quite a congregation since we arrived an hour or so before. The set-up had more than a touch of an agreeably smoky speakeasy to it that Sunday – dark decor and limited daylight, antique wood and painted mirrors absorbing the muted chatter of the punters. This was the full-on authentic Edinburgh Sunday pub experience.

Julia paid up and headed for the toilet. I watched her push her way through, plump legs squeezed into an ill-advised pair of Armani jeans still muddy from our earlier hike. My eyes fixed on a diminutive figure, struggling to make her way in the opposite direction. It was a girl, exceptionally short, about three feet tall – a midget trying to take her share of pleasure that the rest of us took for granted in a world permanently stacked against – and above – her. I know that the drink had affected me a little, but as I looked at her with her stunted features and cruel lack of height I felt an empathy, as if here was a fellow outsider – a physical dwarf moving unknowingly towards a social dwarf. The thought stayed with me as Julia wedged herself back into her seat.

'Where were we? Not in a hurry, are you? Those toilets are a disgrace, I tell you . . .'

She stopped; a tiny hand had appeared, tapping the back of her shoulder. Julia turned and shrieked out loud as if reacting to some hideous fiend in a horror film. It was my midget-girl, trying to reach the bar, asking if Jules would let her through. The mite looked overwhelmed with confusion and hurt for a second before regaining her composure. She gave an embarrassed smile which Julia returned in a shaky way before turning back to me.

'Bloody hell . . .' she muttered, patting her heart. 'Bit of a shock, you'd think she could have warned me . . .'

Julia picked up where she'd left off – what about that time she'd saved Carol's bacon and redrafted the credentials document that was all wrong? Had anyone thanked her? No. And that other time – I must have noticed it – and the one before that. She was in her stride and drew closer as she spoke, placing her arm on my forearm. We were co-conspirators now, she taking my silence for under-standing and sympathy. I found myself switching off, and wondering what kind of warning she would have had the tiny troll make before asking to squeeze by her. 'Okay. Turn around slowly now. Let's take it nice and easy, stay cool and no one need get hurt. Ready, okay? *I'm a dwarf.*' Communications professionals, both of us. Per-haps, for a modest fee, we could have advised the poor unfortunate what to say in future, what language to employ and how and when to say it so as to be received in the most favourable light and for her minuscule body to give the least offence. Perhaps we could devise a continuous programme that would allow her to hold her head high. Professionals offering professional advice. Useful advice. Perhaps not.

Jules whinged on, only now she'd moved onto the let-downs in her personal life. I had a feeling she was on the verge of yet another one as I felt the needle on my own internal Jules-ometer tilt into the red danger-zone area. Somewhere in my brain a light was flashing yet nothing could halt the flow. It was overwhelming. What about the bastard that had slept with her and said he'd call. He hadn't. He'd given her a number she could call and after a whole week's waiting she'd swallowed her pride and called – just to see where she stood, mind – and somebody answered and it was a bloody Chinese carry-out shop. He was a bastard. Why would he do that? Another bastard boyfriend had nagged at her to change, and when she had he left. Why? 'You're not the same.' A bastard. Why did all men treat her so badly? I didn't offer anything but thought there had to be something telling in the consistency with which they were all bastards. Poor Jules. Maybe she had mentioned she liked Chinese food and the guy thought he was doing her a favour. She was drunk now and would probably regret sharing all this with me. Her hand gripped tighter, a drowning woman. I had had her all wrong. Perhaps I had everyone wrong, all of us just a step away from the most awful self-loathing and loneliness.

'Anyway, Charlie, you're always so nice, so balanced. Why don't you have a girlfriend?'

Her face was close to mine. She'd been trying to speak right into my ear so that no one else would hear whilst maintaining full eye contact, a struggle that involved muttering out the side of her small mouth like an agitated horse chewing on its bit. Her eyes had the trusting innocence of a cute animal too. How could these men have found it so easy to dump her? As my gaze looked back on hers I noticed the freckles that our earlier walk had brought out already on her delicate skin. I shrugged. No, no girlfriend. Time for another?

'Charlie . . .' she purred, blinking in exaggerated disappointment before asking what she presumed to be a rhetorical question. 'Is the bear a Catholic?'

I got them in. The interruption seemed to have shaken her off the previous line of enquiry. By the time we were settled again she was on a different tack – Andy.

'Bit stand-offish, isn't he? Don't know why Nick bothers with him. Keeps threatening that he should join you in the new business effort – would you enjoy that?'

Would I? I managed to hide my shock that Jules found it necessary to ask. Does the Pope like to shit in the woods?

I shrugged, embarrassed at the thought that she might be able to read my mind. Was I so transparent? The taste of the beer was still in my mouth, curiously delicious. I wondered whether enjoying it so much was some kind of symptom, and began to feel a vague guilt about taking pleasure from it. Jules pulled close for one more whispered question.

'Charlie . . . Can I ask you, you know, something? Are you gay?'

This time I was the one who felt like shrieking. And the answer came out before I could even think about it.

'I . . . I've never been gay in my whole life!'

A dry laughter rose up to strangle her throat as she creased up at my burning embarrassment. For a moment she was left riveting like some kind of alcoholic frog, all watery eyes and lurching on the water lily of her barstool.

'That's another thing I just love about you, Charlie . . . You're *so* bloody funny!'

ROBERTS, BEGBY & LAWRIE W.S.,

MARY KING'S CLOSE, EDINBURGH.

FILE NOTE: CLAIRE LISTER, PAUL DEXTRUS, INITIAL
           MEETING WITH

He loitered in our reception: an old, oily-skinned
character, one who had perhaps endured too much time
in the open air. Badly dressed, garish tie and dark
shirt. An eccentric, perhaps a contrived eccentric,
but an eccentric all the same. We are too polite a
firm to throw anyone out merely because of the suspicion their appearance might generate, though in
this case more than one of us wishes we had. The
straggling grey hair tied in some sort of ridiculous
strand at the back, an obvious clue, as were his
crooked teeth. There was nothing unclean about him
per se, yet there was an undeniable sense of relief
amongst the rest of our staff that they were not
going to have to deal with him, and the discomfort of
our receptionists was plainly apparent through the
glass shields of the meeting lobby.

He took an inordinate amount of time signing himself
into our visitor's log - Paul Dextrus the name used.
We were not to know whether this was a false one or
not - how typical that was, to invent a name to suit.
Then the despicable behaviour - the vision of him
leering over the desk down onto our girls would haunt
us still. His trick was the excruciating attempt to
be charming; an old seducer, he would have us all
believe. 'Do you mind me saying, I hope you won't
mind me saying...but what an exquisite scent it is
that you wear... so... so floral... isn't it?' He
would say the word as if describing the most

intimate thing yet finding some sort of powerful
beauty where others would be repelled. And though
there was more than a whiff of the insane about him
he would be using this to his advantage, intimidat-
ing the girls with it. '...yes, dahlias it is, my
dear...no! Lobelia ... fresh lo-belia...that's it,
most definitely.'

A ham performance yet an effective one which could
transmit the shame onto the innocent party. Claire's
meeting notes show that he had come to discuss their
'personal massager', though anyone who looked at it
would have had no doubt as to its suitability to
massage anything other than a crevice. It has to be
wondered just how he had the gall to sit there at
our table, in our office, drinking our coffee, talking to our staff like that. A deviant, a calculating
deviant and charlatan, new to us though in many ways
the heir to the crooks we used to represent. This is
where we might have helped her; when dealing with
this sort of person, it must be demonstrated from
the start who exactly is setting the agenda, who is
in charge. This situation had been engineered so
that the embarrassment was hers, outmanoeuvred in
her own office by a seedy stranger assuming the role
of the naive. '...and some say the relief can come in
waves, from minoris to majora and back in again...'
Licking his lips and staring intently into her eyes.
'...can you imagine what that can do for today's
overstressed young professionals without the time to
pursue a satisfactory private life? Can you imagine
how many women are in need of this relief?' So the
mortification is hers, ours, Begby, Roberts &
Lawrie's ...as if we have something to prove, that
we are sufficiently open-minded to be alert to this
ghastly device's commercial potential, which we are.
And yet there is a point where the line has to be
drawn and we cannot forgive Claire for not drawing
it there, in those first few minutes of the meeting
when her chance to control it all ebbed away. Did we
not tell her? Were we not explicit in our instructions and orders? Claire, the errant will always be
found out. Claire, the errant will always be punish-
ed. We had no choice. Claire, how could you do this
to us?

Dean Cemetery, Late June. I'm okay, although I'm having a sense of déjà vu all over again as Peter Dexter talks me though the tale of another headstone, except this time the story is more preposterous than the last. A voice which I never liked that much to start with has grown in its irritating properties to such an extent that I find myself concentrating, in preference, on the sounds of the traffic on Queensferry Bridge. It's either that or my head will explode with the exasperation of it all. It was overwhelming. Every second I have ever spent with this man has been a waste of time, and every second passing now amplifies the mistake.

'. . . by then he was acknowledged as a master of modern warfare, a genius . . . but that's not the vital part . . . no, no, not at all . . . want to know what the essential part is?'

As it happens, I don't, and Dexter knows my concentration has been wavering. I couldn't be less interested. The vague promise of new business leads coming through this man has never seemed more remote; the notion that he might be in some kind of position to arrange introductions had never seemed more absurd. The thought enters my head to just leave him to his rantings, let him find some other inadequate to lecture to. I will head back to my office on Drumsheugh Terrace, to my desk, my contacts book, and begin to work through the list again. Make some killer calls, sound as if I really mean business – yes, sir, you will be sorry if you don't give Charlie Kidd the chance to come round and outline just what KFC public relations can achieve for your business. Yes, Andy Adriano and bloody Jules will hear a different story today when their ears tune in. Yes, yes, yes!

Or will they? Why will nobody give me the opportunity to at least begin to explain? I feel clammy under my clothes. Going back means facing Nick Kennedy.

'Look . . . *Peter* . . . I don't know . . . Can we talk? This is very interesting but I must be back at the office by . . . well, *soon* . . . and we said we would discuss the plan to launch the appeal for the pre-festival exhibition.'

'*Pre*-festival?'

'As we agreed . . . *pre* to take advantage of the build-up of hype when everybody's in a state of anticipation before it begins. A lot of events start up a week or so before for this very reason, in week minus one. I told you Mr . . . *Peter*; it's part of our plan.'

'But surely if things start *before* the festival, and you are saying many do, doesn't that mean they satisfy this mass craving for the arts before it has had its chance to begin? Or does it just mean that there is an unofficial opening a week before, a pre-festival festival? Or a fringe fringe . . . Mnnn . . . what about a post-pre-festival that takes place during the official festival? Only problem would be what to call it, but that's your speciality, isn't it, Charles?'

This is a blatant attempt to wind me up, a punishment for trying to rush him. If Dexter thinks I'm going to fall for something like this he is very much accurate.

'You can call it the post-early-for-bloody-Christmas pre-menstrual-tension festival for all *I* bloody care. All I know is that once a year the city swells up with slavering idiots desperate to see something so they can tell their bloody mates they've been touched by culture, and since by and large they'll watch any rubbish it might as well be our rubbish *if* we can ever get round to talking about what that might *actually* be.'

Dexter sizes me up as if I'm about to hit him, his face a mixture of hurt and knowingness. He blinks, slowly, almost disdainfully. His lips pout somewhere beneath the twitching moustache and goatee, and at last he's ready to express himself. My apology for soiling the atmosphere remains unspoken but these gestures tell me it has been graciously accepted.

'The vital part is *understanding*. Understanding is everything, Charles. If you *understand* you will be better able to *persuade*. And if you can persuade you will achieve what it is that you want.'

It's that simple, of course. And the way he tells it, I *am* persuaded that this is a vital point. Peter Dexter can speak with an authority that carries the listener, an enviable talent and one not dependent on volume or barely concealed aggression like Nick Kennedy. Dexter simply has presence. Fat, short, ageing and badly dressed, he still has it to turn on and off when he chooses and I want some. Would it work over the telephone?

No, that is not the way of it. You have to be there, to see it for yourself. Small stature, big presence, that's Dexter's thing. When I first encountered him he had his back to me, sitting at a bar, and I could still tell he was listening to me, even though he was a complete stranger with his head stuck between the broadsheet pages of *The Scotsman*. This was in Indigo Yard, a West End haunt of ageing insurance salesmen passing themselves off as financial advisers and advertising space hawkers posing as media operators. A reptile enclosure where the ersatz jazz tunes hover above the chinking sounds of identity bracelets and groaning gussets straining at the bulge and insincerity of the cunts behind them. A favourite hostelry of mine, as you will have guessed. And we were there, and Dexter was tuning in.

I say 'we', meaning the Edinburgh Publicity Forum – an informal gathering of communications industry worthies whose 'Third Thursday' meeting this was. Theoretically, the Publicity Forum included both agency people and *real* people – clients – and was intended as an informal meet-up whereby industry-wide issues could be discussed in a friendly and open way by like-minded pro-fessionals. This was why Nick Kennedy suggested I attend each painful meeting. In practice, a client turn-out was as rare as a good outfit in this place – this was my third third Thursday and I was yet to see one – none of them willing to risk the sycophantic slavering that would follow them once the pack got the scent of client blood, an absence that left the disappointed PR sharks to circle only each other.

To be fair to the eavesdropping Dexter, Indigo Yard, with its colour-washed stone walls and harsh slate floor, has the acoustics of an amphitheatre. That and the open spaces of a minimalist stage design which one of his avant performance groups would doubtless admire. There are no hiding places and everything is heard, torture for a drowning man like me trying to fit in with an increasingly raucous crowd of hoorays whilst remaining its least animated and most ignored member. I don't know what was worse, loitering in silence pretending to be part of a conversation that continually passed me by – 'Heard the latest? You remember that *awful* client, Mr Take-my-brief? Yes, *him* ... Well you know where *he* went? *Yes*, that's right ... *them*!' – or talking up my own pitiful game – 'Charles ... Charlie Kidd ... just joined K F C, up from London ... what am I working on? Just *now*? Couple of projects ... irons in the fire sort of thing.'

The drowning man/me heard a voice over his shoulder as his life flashed before him like another fizzing tray of gin and tonics. Musing absentmindedly on the prominent panty-line of an overweight peroxide's quasi-military two-piece squeeze, it took a while for him/me to realise that the echoing warble wasn't part of the abstract jazz soundtrack but was in fact addressed in my direction. I turned and the fat man at the bar had lowered his newspaper. His hand mimed a drinking gesture, an action that was definitely aimed at me – would I have a drink? What was this about? Was he trying to pick me up? He was old enough to be my father, but had a hopelessly dated hippyish air to him, white goatee and handlebar moustache, straggly pony tail, collarless white shirt and cravat – Christ, a cravat! Dirty old man. Was this really that kind of place? How was I going to begin to explain, and in front of the full congregation of the Edinburgh Publicity Forum? I would never live this down.

'Did I hear you say you are in public relations?'

Me, and twenty others. I couldn't deny it.

'Then you might be in a position to help me out. Can you spare me five minutes? What will you have?'

And my introduction to the world of Peter Dexter and his Experimental Gallery – The East Coast Collective Art Experimental Gallery, to give it its full dues – began. Dexter explained so that I might understand, and if I understood then I might be able to persuade the better. Dexter explained about his work within the city, his patronage of artists whose endeavours would enrich Edinburgh, financially and creatively, now and for future generations. Did I believe in the power of the arts to enrich the environment? Yes, I did. I did right then because he was explaining it so well that I understood and was persuaded. Could I help him take that message to those in a position of influence, those with the means to support the arts? And I of course would know that the corporate pocket is deeper than the personal one, and that this was where the message had to be heard. Could I, a *professional*, tell him how to make the banks, the life assurance companies, the insurance houses and the fund managers listen? There were artists – important artists – and exhibitions – important exhibitions – that needed, and deserved, support. Would they at least grant him an audience? Of course, I must know these people, or know of them. Perhaps together we could learn more about them, maybe the whole process could open some doors for me. That way I might establish my own reputation and my own relationships. It was just a thought. Would I have another?

No, I said. I'll get these. What will *you* have?

Dexter took a drink, and all my attention. The Publicity Forum moved onto another bar, a better bar – Ryans – but I stayed where I was, with the man who would take me to graveyards so that I might understand.

There would be an exhibition. An exhibition about graveyards – Edinburgh's desecrated graveyards, unique in the whole world. The artists and their work would tell of the past, of Auld Reekie's sins, and challenge the romantic view of the city's mysterious history in a compelling way. Did I *want* to understand about that? If I didn't then I was free to walk away. 'I don't want to waste *my* time either, Charlie,' Dexter said.

Quite. I'm sorry. Please continue, I said. Tell me the vital part. First in a bar, now in a graveyard. Go on, tell me.

Dexter didn't look too convinced, but the invitation to perform was there and the tale was obviously bubbling inside him ready to erupt. A pity it was so ludicrous.

To reach Dean Cemetery you take the road from the West End of town that sweeps out of the city towards the bridges across the River Forth. You walk past the Parisienne-styled tree-lined avenues of lawyers' town-house terraced flats that line either side of the street. You ignore the swarms of giggling schoolchildren in scarlet and black blazers and turn left off the road before you reach their school and you are there. The corner of it where we were stood was tucked away behind a miniature forest of green holly and ancient yews in the furthest spot from the entrance, a secret plot within a cemetery that itself could rank as a hidden burial ground on the border of the New Town. There is something Masonic about the atmosphere there – the pyramids on top of the main gates, the diagonal symmetry of the paths, the dark green obelisk that Dexter turned to admire.

'Beautiful, crafted . . . what does it tell us? It reminds us of his triumphs in the Orient. A handsome man.'

Peter Dexter leaned over and stroked the face of the bronze bust which had been casting its impressive profile towards us. Underneath, the headstone read 'Major General Sir Hector MacDonald, 1853–1903'. Fresh battle ribbons had been attached to the torso of the piece, delicate cotton tartans resting on the stern metal chest. I had been led to the grave of 'Fighting Mac'. A military genius, Dexter told me with total conviction. MacDonald had been born the son of a Highland crofter and had enlisted in the army at its lowest rank, a private in the 2nd Battalion of the Gordon Highlanders. His talent had been quickly spotted and he soon became a colour sergeant, the highest level a soldier of his social class could expect to achieve in Queen Victoria's forces. However, MacDonald's spectacular acts of leadership and bravery in the Afghan campaigns of 1875 could not go unnoticed and eventually he was offered a choice of glory or career – a Victoria Cross or an officer's commission. Despite the financial hardship he would have to endure – given the expense of life in an officer's mess – MacDonald followed his vocation and thus began an equally meteoric rise through the officer ranks which included service in the British-controlled Egyptian army and action in the Sudan. On 2 September 1898 the fanatical Dervishes are put to the sword amongst scenes of unimaginable carnage at the Battle of Omdurman as the British reclaim the land and avenge the fall of Khartoum the year before. This was MacDonald's triumph, one inscribed on the side of the plinth before me. It had been his courage and masterly deployment of superior weaponry that had saved the Imperial cause from disaster that day. He would use these skills again against the Boers in South Africa. It was here that more great moments would lead to his downfall. MacDonald's decisive leadership served to ensure ultimate victory, but also highlighted the weaknesses of those around him, thus earning him some powerful and influential enemies – including the future General Kitchener. Two years later, whilst on duty in Ceylon, MacDonald was accused of indulging in vile homosexual acts with junior officers and holding unnatural influence over his coterie of native servants. The validity of the charges was dubious, but the scandal meant MacDonald was ruined, and he knew it. On his way to London to answer the case against him he booked into a Paris hotel where he was later found dead, shot in the head – apparently suicide. In conditions of great secrecy, even the hooves of the horses pulling his coffin were muffled to ensure their silence, his body was brought to Dean Cemetery here in Edinburgh for a night burial. A sad and lonely end for a broken man. And yet, said Dexter, stabbing the air in excitement, this is not the essential part of the story.

By curious coincidence, MacDonald had a cousin, a German serving in the Prussian army – Colonel von Mackensen – who died in a Berlin military hospital the very same day.

Stranger still, some months afterwards it was announced that a ghastly mistake had been made: Colonel von Mackensen was not dead after all, but had in fact only been seriously ill. He was now recovering but had lost his memory, and spoke German with the greatest difficulty.

In the years that followed, von Mackensen gained both renewed control of his mother tongue and new – extraordinary – military acumen. By the end of the Great War he had risen to the rank of field marshal and then commander in chief of all German and Austrian forces on the Eastern Front. Rumours abounded in Edinburgh that von Mackensen was MacDonald, that the suicide in Paris was a hoax, the coffin buried at Dean carried only stones, that MacDonald was too strong a man to allow his enemies such an easy victory and had vowed to face them on the battlefield.

Could it really be true? Dexter smiled as he considered his own question.

Film of the 1936 Olympics shows an elderly soldier sitting to Hitler's right during the opening ceremony in the Berlin stadium. A distinguished old soldier bearing a remarkable similarity to Sir Hector MacDonald. Documentary proof, the evidence overwhelming. For Dexter, the facts were undeniable; for me, unbelievable. The stories were becoming wilder and wilder. How could I believe this man's word on anything?

I made a mental note of the name on the headstone. This was Dexter's last chance. I would check out the real facts – whatever details the National Library could yield on this old soldier. I would find out the truth and use it as final proof that I was wasting my time, that I was dealing with a deluded fantasist.

I visited the library on South Bridge three days later – Thursday – and the assistant directed me to three texts: Turnbull's *Guide*, Willsher's *Understanding Edinburgh Graveyards* and Boyle and Dickson's *Edinburgh Heritage*. MacDonald was mentioned in each, as were the doubts over the authenticity of his suicide and suspicions of a new life in Germany. I had a fleeting moment of nauseous panic. Another cheated grave. What was it Dexter *really* wanted me to understand?

LAUGHTER upon laughter, joke upon joke. The audience was almost cheering. Where could the performance go now?

Unless he could think of something they would arrest him there that night. And even that might be preferable to being left to the mercy of the mob that was sure to gather once word of his actions spread. He realised he had to take command of the situation now, or be forever lost. What was there that could be done? If he declared that his patient had been dead all along, would they believe him, or should he just fall to his knees and plead for clemency? He took a deep breath to steady himself. Courage, discipline. The answer had to lie in believing in the potency of his own genius.

His deliberate stride to the back of the stage did not betray his faltering nerve. He reached into his case, bloodied hands staining the soft leather pockets inside. The object he sought was a small one, a slim cylinder, elegant and smooth like a large cigar but metallic and less tapered – a stretched bullet. He turned his back on the stalls and studied the device in his hands, pulling the delicate lever mechanism out from its side. He rotated its thin arm through an anti-clockwise motion, repeating the movement at speed whilst trying to take care not to snap the fragile apparatus. A good charge was essential.

He turned, still shielding the device as he did so, and approached the body once more, making first for the straps that had bound the arms to the table. He let them loose. A smile as he lifted the head, and slipped the probe into the cranium from the rear. He did not look down but could feel the size of the cavity his earlier efforts had created. This was far larger than he had ever envisaged attempting to work with.

Inwardly, he cursed his earlier enthusiasm. How could he expect this to work in these circumstances? He pressed on. He had no choice.

'Gentlemen, may I ask you to please leave in an orderly fashion. My patient and I require privacy to complete tonight's work.'

Gradually the laugher subsided, the audience's stupefaction almost tangible. What new outrage was he inferring now? Was he insane?

He waited until he was sure that all eyes were concentrating upon him once more in search of an answer. He stared back with an intensity bordering on defiance.

Unblinking, he released the catch restraining the wind-up mechanism at the base of the probe. Immediately he could hear its whirring sound as the energy was let loose. As the vibrations spread, the tremors began in the remaining facial tissue. These were soon joined by the reaction of the crowd to the jerky motions of the arms that the body now contrived to make. The gasps and shouts from the audience easily drowned any noise coming from the operating table. When Daft Jamie coughed and retched there was bedlam.

Brodie knew the charge would wear off in an instant. The illusion could only be carried for a short time. He had to get them out now.

'No murder, gentlemen! As you can see, there has been no murder. And now, I must ask you to leave as your presence is unsettling to my patient and it is *I* who will hold *you* responsible for his welfare. I thank you please, good night.'

Brodie ordered his assistants to extinguish the theatre's lights. The audience departed in the uneasy darkness.

NICK INSISTED that Andy and I work closely together over the general publicity for the 'Resurrectionist Expression' events, and especially for the press conference which would kick the whole thing off. I pretended to be put out somewhat by this, and gave it the best 'what do I need the kid for when he can only slow me down' act I could come up with. Was this Nick's way of showing his lack of faith in my ability to manage the thing alone? I went a bit too far in asking this because obviously it was, Nick's squirming silence telling me as much. Inwardly though, I was thrilled. Working together meant some kind of bonding might take place, surely, and that Andy would have to drop his reserve with me. With a show of reluctance I promised Nick I'd keep an eye on him, a promise I knew I would keep in every sense. Okay, Nick, *okay*.

I remember introducing Andy to Dexter, hoping for some strange reason that Dexter would like him, and then being alarmed that maybe Dexter would like him too much, and then hoping that Dexter wouldn't make it too obvious that he was making up the whole thing – our PR plan, strategy and tactics – as he went along, that Dexter knew my game depended on him being deferential to me. I was meant to be in charge and Andy was here to help me exercise control so that things would run to KFC standards. In the end the meeting was uneventful. Dexter was on his best behaviour and didn't even mention graveyards. He did, however, throw a bit of a stop over my insistence at some kind of formality for the launch – rows of chairs rather than free-standing for the hacks, name badges, tea and coffee on offer – which wasn't part of his 'concept' of how it should be. I dug my heels in and thus showed the handsome Andy how I could tame this volatile artist-type and be as strong-willed as any of them.

Andy wanted to know why we were pressing ahead with a press

call when to date we had no sponsors and, presumably, the event itself was in some doubt. A good question from a bright boy, one which caused me more anxiety than I cared to let on. I took him in my confident gaze. Well, *Andy*, I guess it comes down to how likely you think it is that we are going to tempt the sponsors. Do we think, on the one hand, that the big corporations will want to be in on this from the start when they can help get it off the ground, or do the corporate egos dictate that they can only become involved in something once it is already known to be a success? My guess, Andy – *do you know how good-looking you are? Do you find it opens doors for you, helps you get on?* – is that we wouldn't even be seen by the key companies until there's at least some recognisable identity and momentum to the thing. That's why we're doing it this way, Andy – *I guess you've never known life any other way. Can you imagine what it is to be ugly, a dwarf, a drowning man?* – so that these people can't not back us in case their rivals do and get the credit for it. It's a game of bluff, but experience dictates that perhaps it has to be.

Experience. Whose experience? You've done this before?

Well, Andy – *when did you become 'Andy'? Whose choice was it? Were you ever Andrew? Not the same, is it, I can't imagine you as an 'Andrew'* – it's how I feel we should play it this time.

But you said 'experience', like you'd tried this somewhere else.

It was Andy's turn to be difficult, just when I thought I had explained the plan with such conviction and clarity that he would be persuaded. Listen, Andy, it's the way it's done in the London agencies – *please believe me. Don't give me a hard time over this. It's harder for me than you, I was born into a loser's caste* – and I can see it working here.

Before he could line up another question I was saved by my pager, its urgent bleep telling me Jules was in a state of crisis again and in need of my help. Silly cow, thank God for her.

THE SURGEON awoke long before dawn. He reached for his boots. His wife did not stir, long used to his nocturnal wanderings; she was not to know he was never to return, that she would wake to widowhood. Perhaps she would take to it. He crossed into the hall in absolute silence. The last of the midnight carriages had left Royal Crescent hours ago. Everything was in darkness: he moved by memory, not daring to light a lamp. His son's bedroom door was ajar and he deliberated whether to visit a farewell kiss upon him. The child's cough put paid to the notion.

The stairs creaked as his bare feet found their way to take him down. Then into the scullery where his suit and greatcoat hung waiting. He dressed quickly, over his nightshirt. This would save him carrying an extra item as well as providing protection from the bitter wind blowing in from the Forth. The boots went on, followed by a thick pair of woollen stockings over them to muffle his footsteps on the icy cobblestones outside. His last look around the room where he had eaten for the previous eleven years. To his surprise, he felt little emotion; he had to get on, there was too much to do if the procedure was to be well executed. It was important that the procedure was well executed.

The keys to his workshop jangled in his pocket as he walked. He found he could only silence the noise by carrying them tightly in his hand. The wind attacked him in random gusts, pushing his hat back, breaking any momentum to his progress. He cursed the cold, knowing that there would be a longer walk to the docks at Leith should everything go to plan. At least he would have some respite from the elements once he reached his premises, a rest too, even if it would be better if his time there was short. That depended on Rennie sticking to his agreement, the one part of the plan outwith his control. No one else was in sight; not another soul was out on the streets.

He reached the end of Royal Crescent. As he headed into the descent, the light faded behind him, the gas streetlamps stopping at the brow of the hill. He welcomed the darkness. Somewhere inside came a nagging reminder that this would be the last time he would make a walk that had been routine for so many years. He sought to ignore deliberations and to concentrate on the procedure. No musings on the past, no farewell to his wife or kiss for his son; what use were they now to him? Neither were part of the plan. These were cruel times. The rewards of the new scientific age were only there for those with the discipline to adhere to planned process; those that couldn't were damned to be its casualties. How hard he had worked to discover new advances, to his great personal cost. It would have to be worth it all some day. He would show them all, he thought. No kiss for his son.

On Leith Street the wind was right against him, blowing the stinging hail straight onto his face. The socks over his boots had become sodden and made a squelching sound as he progressed. He stopped and peeled them off, throwing them over a hedge. His eyes lingered on them, troubled not so much by his discarding of potential clues as by the simple fact of the waste. He pressed on. He wondered if the foul weather would have kept the drinking dens quiet that night and whether this would make it impossible for Rennie to fulfil his last commission. Up ahead, to his right, the High Street; was there less light, less noise than usual? It was not for him to worry over this. Either Rennie would or wouldn't succeed; he could not influence the outcome. All he could do was to stick to the agreed plan.

He crossed over as the Street bent left and turned into Calton Road. Almost there. He felt for the keys, hands so cold he could barely feel them in his palm. His workshop was the sixth door along in the terraced row of carpenters' and masons' yards. A hive of industry during daylight, the gloom of the winter night now gave them the malevolent air of a ghost town. He turned the two locks as soon as he reached the doorstep.

Inside, shelter from the gale at last. He fumbled with his matches as he toiled to light the paraffin lamp on the work top, fingers frozen stiff from their exposure. He took out his watch; three-thirty – what was left to be done? The cupboard key was in his waistcoat pocket. He walked over and unlocked the iron doors that kept the tools of his trade – the saws, the pliers and drills that he had customised himself – safe from prying eyes, hoping one day to patent his own proven range of medical apparatus. But he could not take them all with him; his choice had already been made. The pride of the crop was already inside the leather case by the door, including the static-charging penetrator to which he had devoted so much of the last two years, and the chisels with which he had sought to perfect the rapid lobotomy. These he would take with him to the next life. He would have to hope for better appreciation there. He lost himself in a moment's bitter reflection: the mechanical soul – how close had he come to its realisation before the experiment had been aborted? All that effort for just the one trial, even that reduced to a showman's stunt as he had been forced to use the device as a means of escape, setting it to deliver a deliberate overload.

The whisky bottle stood on the bottom shelf. He took it and unscrewed the top, sniffing the contents to check that it could still pass without suspicion. The smell seemed alright, but he was not a regular drinker; the empty bottles scattered around the floor had been collected for show, to add substance to the scene he hoped to create. He carried the bottle over to the worktop and reached for the small yellow phial sitting there, pouring another inch of the musty oil into his bottle of malt. He fixed the cap back on and shook it to mix the two liquids. The whisky had already been laced with enough laudanum to do the job but it seemed prudent to add a further measure just in case. It was important the plan was well executed. Now he would pour a glass and wait.

An hour later, the knock at the door.

'Mr Brodie . . . ye there?'

He jerked to his feet, almost startled. Rennie's voice was instantly recognisable. He unlocked the door and the weasel face confronted him from out of the darkness like a macabre apparition – bony forehead, sallow chin, greasy grey whiskers shining in the moonlight. There were two others behind him, one propped up by the other's strenuous efforts. This was not part of the plan but he let them in anyway; he had no choice.

As they entered, he saw that Rennie's accomplice was young, a teenager, and that the prize they carried was either already dead or unconscious. They laid him on the floor.

'Where did you get him?'

'Tollcross, Mr Brodie, up by Bennet's Bar. Alex here cracked him guid an proper, aye.'

Brodie bent down to examine what evidence there was that the lout had indeed done this, worried that too obvious an injury might arouse suspicion. He was dealing with amateurs. The best of their trade used suffocation as a preferred method of killing, in the knowledge that the receiving doctors would then always be able to pass the death as by natural causes. He prodded the skull with a pair of forceps, preferring not to touch it yet with his hands. The hair behind the victim's left ear was matted with blood, but the bleeding had stopped some time ago. There was no obvious fracture.

'Is he guid enough, Mr Brodie?'

Good enough? He would have to be. Brodie was already thinking how the feature might be used to his advantage. If he could lay a heavy bar across the skull it might look as if a rafter or beam had dropped from the ceiling and stunned him, preventing his escape. It could add to the tragedy.

Rennie's brief had been for a male in his early forties, five foot eight. This one was at least ten years older and two inches shorter, the difference in height being the more significant. Still, if he didn't use this body what else could he use it for, and when would a better match become available? Good enough, Brodie nodded, determined to enter as limited a conversation as possible with the low-life Rennie.

'Guid enough, aye, Mr Brodie. Ah telt Alex it'll be guid enough . . . ken aye.'

Brodie peered momentarily at Rennie's half-wit companion, a young urchin in the same filthy rags as his elder. Could he be relied upon to remain quiet, or would he also have to be persuaded to share a whisky? Another risk that would have to be taken; time was running out. Brodie turned his back to them and pulled out his wallet from a pocket inside the lining in his waistcoat. He handed over the notes that the illiterate Rennie took an age to count.

'Five poun, Mr Brodie. Ye said ten.'

'I'll give you the rest tomorrow. Come back then.'

Rennie's face showed no enthusiasm for the proposal. 'Five poun, ken, Mr Brodie.'

'As I said, I'll give you the rest tomorrow . . . Here, man, have a dram, no hard feelings. Have I ever let you down? Always kept my part of the bargain, haven't I?'

Rennie still scowled sourly but took the glass all the same, downing its contents in a succession of small gulps. He wiped his lips with the back of his grimy hand when he finished.

Brodie refilled the glass immediately. 'One for the laddie?'

The boy drank unenthusiastically, probably accepting because of a reflex which told him to take anything that was offered for nothing. Brodie was again relieved to see the glass drained. What would it be like to be born poor? Could one rise above it? To be poor . . . it had to be fascinating, an underclass, an underworld of deviants living by their wits and cunning. Perhaps he would have taken to it.

'Here, my fellow,' he said, turning cheerily to Rennie. 'Take the bottle . . . unless you fancy another before you head off?'

Rennie eyed Brodie with what the latter took to be mistrust. Why the sudden friendliness? Brodie tried to hide his unease, pouring another measure. To his relief, Rennie lifted the glass from his hand once more.

'Aye . . . it's a cauld night . . . an this'll keep me gaun.'

Brodie smiled. Keep him going? It would almost certainly stop him going forever. In five minutes, once he had staggered half a mile into the wind, the drowsiness would be overwhelming. Once he stopped, the hypothermia would finish him off in the next half hour; the boy as well. Even if they survived the cold, both had taken enough laudanum for their memories of this particular night to be lost to the elements like the last heat from their breath in the frozen air.

'Now, gentlemen, if you please. I have work to do.'

Brodie clapped his hands and shepherded the pair to the door.

'Five poun . . .' Rennie's voice had turned to a barely audible mumble. How much ground would he be able to make once he left? Would it be far enough from his workshop? Brodie pushed him out impatiently. 'Tomorrow, I promise. Please, I must get on.'

The two stumbled out, stooping and drooling, like sleep-walkers heading off towards an eternal slumber. Good enough, thought Brodie, bolting the door behind them. *Guid enough*.

He turned to the body on the floor, addressing it in a whisper as he exhaled, squatting down beside it.

'And you, sir, are you . . .' He touched the skin at the top of the throat directly under the chin: it was stone cold with no trace of any pulse. '. . . dead? Yes, I'm afraid you are, sir. Excellent. Your hands, sir?' Brodie lifted the right hand. It was smaller and thinner than his own. He took off his signet ring and placed it on the hand of the corpse, then lifted its left hand and put his wedding ring on its third finger. 'Never been married, sir? Can't say I would recommend it. Still, never too late.' There was no problem in manoeuvring the rings on the appropriate fingers: death had been so recent that the hands were still pliable. Brodie opened the man's jacket. 'You don't wear a waistcoat, sir. Damn . . .' Brodie paused for a moment and considered the practicalities of undressing the body and putting his own waistcoat on it. Too much of a nuisance, too much of a waste. He took out his watch and laid it on the chest of the corpse; the flames and heat would surely see to the rest of the task. Almost done, he glanced over to the glass paraffin canister – was it time to go? He looked at the face of the man who had been bought to replace him. Another brute – how many of these animals had he carved in search of the secrets of nobler creatures like himself? Did the poor have souls? Perhaps that was where he had gone wrong, not questioning this assumption. What if the poor were made differently to the rich? What if they really were another species? Then everything he knew was useless, and everything the bastard Munros had built their reputation upon too. It was an inviting notion.

He was about to stand when he had another thought, this time one he could not ignore. He had almost forgotten the final part of the procedure. He lifted a gauze cloth from the floor and pushed it into the inert figure's mouth. 'Open wide for me please, sir, just need one look . . . Damn you, sir.'

The sight had been enough to drain him of any jaunty enthusiasm he had tried to convey to the corpse. Brodie sighed. Damn you to hell. Here was a problem, one that might take some fixing. He had the tools to do it, but it was the time it would take in the process that caused him to curse. His tongue worked its way around his mouth as he pondered the situation, feeling his own teeth which were, unfortunately, almost perfect by comparison with the cadaver's. He felt for his watch, forgetting he had already removed it and placed it on the chest of the body. It was still balanced there, now showing almost five-thirty.

The set of pliers he required were locked up beside the rest of his soon to be discarded kit. He brought them to the offending mouth and knelt down alongside. What next? Where to start? Somehow he could not bring himself to begin. He stood up again and raced over to the work top. There were two rags lying there which had been used as tourniquets: both he now grabbed and stuffed into his pocket. The spare teeth were in the top drawer. It made sense to locate them before extractions commenced, if only to reassure himself that the grim effort was worthwhile. He was almost disappointed to find them, wrapped in a soft green cloth under his equipment ledger. He returned to the floor beside his alter ego, sizing up the scale of the dentures against the gums of their final home. Another waste. They were a fine pair, wood and enamel, and had been over sixteen guineas, a cost almost as high as that of the body itself. Brodie levered the jaws of the patient apart and fed the medium pliers into the cavity that yawned open before him. He checked the lower, then the upper plates. The teeth that were there were in a pitiful state, decayed and isolated: three front upper, two upper molars and pre-molars, one lower molar on either side and one lower canine. All would have to go. They could never be taken for those of a gentleman like Brodie. They would have to be replaced by the false set and when the body was found word would spread that behind the smile of Mr Brodie the surgeon – the disgraced surgeon whose scandalous attempt to push forward the frontiers of medicine had brought him recent infamy – yes, behind his smile there lurked a sinister falsehood, his teeth. This would be an even greater scandal. What would the smug Munro have said against him for that? Brodie clamped the pliers hard on the first canine, twisting and pulling as he held down the dead man's face with his other hand, breathing through lips pursed tight, whistling as he inhaled, almost as if in sympathy. The tooth took some persuading to leave, roots cracking and snapping as it clung tenaciously to the very last. Brodie panted, placing it on the cloth beside the dentures, the thick blood from its tentacle strands staining the fabric on first contact. One down, eight to go, to go with him all the way to Leith lest they be found later and confuse those who would later find the whole charred scene. Brodie gripped the next in line, clenching it tightly, too tightly, his sense of urgency giving him a new strength. The tooth itself splintered quickly under the force of the metal grip crushing down, causing Brodie's hand to shoot upwards as the resistance against it vanished. The sudden jerk pushed Brodie off balance, and he lurched over the prostrate body, landing sideways on top of it, his face brushing the cold cheek of the dead man. He raised himself up in disgust. The sleeve of his shirt was now wet and dripping with the syrup-like blood. Brodie struggled to compose himself. Are you happy now, Munro? I swear I shall live to extract your smile from your smug countenance forever, I swear it, Sir, and it will be your soul – yours alone – that I clasp in my forceps to prove the validity of my theory. The second tooth gave way as the anger surged through his veins. Brodie stopped and sighed again.

The teeth slowly relented to his exertions. Within the half hour only a few stumps remained in the mouth whilst the green cloth had turned scarlet and now held a collection, a strange collection, that its former owner would have had no conception of when he set out on his evening's drinking all those hours ago. Hours ago? When would he have started – nine o'clock? Six hours ago, yet also a lifetime ago. Brodie wedged the dentures into the newly vacant mouth, slotting them unceremoniously into the gap.

The final act of the plan beckoned and once more he stopped to pause and consider. This was the room where he had rehearsed his triumph, now he was to leave in a smoky cloud of deceit. If he could make his exit undetected it would be a victory of sorts, but one he would only be at liberty to enjoy himself. Not long to go now. He must calm himself down: it was important the procedure was well executed.

THEY ARE always going to be unbelievably hostile. The only thing to do is to prepare yourself for it and assume every one of the bastards is going to be at their hateful best, otherwise it can be overwhelming.

You could be arranging the thing to announce something really positive, something so good it speaks for itself with no need for any 'management' at all – a new cure for cancer, an end to war, blessings for everyone. And what would the reaction be? – Why wasn't this done before? Why did we have to wait so long? Who is responsible for the delay and how much did it cost? What's the real agenda, *what are you hiding?*

What are you hiding?

That's where the story is for these people. You can look on journalists as fellow professionals, there to help the communication process and enable the message to be spread, but they are not interested in that. Instead they shuffle into these conferences in their appalling gear – crumpled suits, rustling nylon overcoats, dandruff – light up a fag, sneer at the release inside the info pack that you and your colleagues have spent all night writing, printing and collating, and then they will start writing sarcastic notes to themselves as soon as you start speaking. I could imagine what was being scrawled: 'a major multi-site exhibition' – *couldn't afford a proper gallery*; 'showcase for new talent' – read *no talent*; 'an attempt to portray the city's past as its enduring future' – *lost me there, old boy.*

I had almost looked forward to this one, not because it meant working with Andy, although that might have been part of it, rather that, for once, Dexter's refusal to play by the rules might be a useful weapon against those with the power to hurt. What were we trying to sell here – something tacky, self-serving? No. What *was* our hidden agenda – something sleazy, scandalous? No. All we were trying to do was set up our exhibition, the 'Resurrectionist Expression'. Sure, we might have been putting a degree of gloss on the thing, perhaps giving the impression that it was all a bit more finalised and more supported than it actually was at that stage, but if the hacks dug deep, surely all they would find was the inner core of sincerity behind it all? Dexter was doing this for the good of the arts, in the belief that this would in turn be good for the city. Was this too novel a concept for the press to grasp? What are we trying to hide? *Nothing*. Can't they get that? Shame on you. Give it to them, Dexter. Explain so that they understand.

I think it must have been a sign of how confused I was that day that I actually mixed up sincerity and Public Relations. This was the first of many mistakes in the sixty minutes of chaos that followed. Everything that happened was upside down, everything opposite to the way it should have been, as if we had all somehow strayed into a parallel universe where our other cosmic selves behaved in a way alien and inverse to normality. Dexter had an off day and failed to perform. We had the beating of them all right. It was me that was the weapon, it was *that* bizarre.

Dexter had negotiated access to a real gallery for the launch – the Collective Gallery on Cockburn Street – a beautiful space on a twisting cobbled path winding down from the High Street to the foot of The Mound. A privilege to be there normally, but that day had the makings of a trial. A real gallery; that meant real pieces of art on display, none of which were in *our* exhibition. How many times do you think I'd had to explain that? 'No, we're only borrowing this area for today. It's not part of what we will be talking about . . . no, a different project . . . yes, it's nice but it's from a different event . . . as in not fucking ours, dick-brain . . . comprendez . . . understand?'

Confusion. Dexter had organised name plates to sit in front of us on the table top of the stage we had created. They had been drawn up by one of his people, all swirls and blue inks, a flowing script imbued with a grace way beyond the functional requirement. Dazzling really. Except the names on them failed to match the people. Peter Dexter sat behind one stating 'Pablo Dextrus'. I only noticed with minutes to go. He'd also pulled in a celebrity backer,

Edward Dix-Beaton, sometime presenter of televisions's 'Glass Labyrinth' action show. There he was, looking as stoned as ever and not saying much except, 'Art is an experience, a reaction.' Where had he come from? It was infuriating. If I'd known we could pull someone like him in I'd have perhaps tried to make better use of him. I'd at least have made sure he was briefed on what it was we were trying to push, and that he had a better name plate than 'Eddie Famous'. What was the point? And yet even his badge was better than mine. I had to do without a name. I had to sit like a fool behind a moniker with only initials – 'KFC'. Yes, 'Mr KFC' to the giggling hacks and Andy's curious gaze. I was mortified.

The name plates had appeared late, as had Dexter and his guest. By then the room was already filling up with members of the press, Dexter's office having faxed my invitation out to its list of correspondents and arts commentators. This was two weeks before the Festival kicked off and the arts freelancers were in town, hungry for stories, glancing urgently at their watches, but not because of any imminent copy deadline, more probably because they had to keep tabs on when the babysitter was meant to clock off. Women, loads of them. Every chair was taken, Mr Bloody KFC was facing an army of them.

Then. Then a strange sensation that goes with the moment when a PR person is on parade like this, a feeling of anti-climax, of not giving a damn when the starting bell finally rings after all those rounds of sparring in preparation for the bout. Andy and I had laboured all night to prepare the packs now being disassembled by the hacks. Some bits of it were being junked after a second's glance, others turned and shuffled to the back, or folded and stuffed into the tatty cases and satchels of the horde. What were these offerings? Various carefully crafted items to help the flow of information – a biography of Dexter (supplied by him, but now only of use if those receiving it realised that the man sitting behind the 'Dextrus' name plate was one and the same), notes on the period of history covered by the proposed exhibition (Andy's bit), a schedule of proposed events, contact lists, colour copies of Dexter's initial inspirational sketches for the show which the other Collective artists were now going to interpret, a list of potential photo-opportunities (none mentioning 'Eddie Famous' who may actually have been of use here) and a brief plug for KFC (my bit). All bound together in a simple but attractive glossy white folder pinched from the office and over-stamped with the kooky motif Dexter had supplied – a sort of opening door or opening coffin lid with the legend 'Club Resurrection' running underneath.

I sat under our audience's semi-expectant eyes. Time to kick off the speaking bit, things were stalling somewhat. I looked to Dexter: he looked unusually sombre, and beyond him the famous Eddie looked aggressively vacant. They both looked at me and I realised I didn't have a plan.

'When you are ready, please . . . ladies and gentlemen. Whenever you are ready we can start . . . If we could possibly begin . . .'

I ranted on like a music hall stooge, knowing I had to think of something to follow my phoney plea and to stop myself from shouting 'Order! Order!' because, of course, there already was perfect order except for everyone wondering what the hell I was on about. They had all shut up once the first words had left my mouth and now gawped at me like I was some kind of idiot for straining to quell a rabble which was in fact perfectly silent.

'WILL YOU BE BLOODY QUIET!'

The voice drowning my own had a distinctly posh tone that made the jokey irony all the funnier. Eddie thumped his desk in indignant frustration and puckered his face in disgust. It drew a big laugh and he held the expression, unblinking. His eyes were glazed: he was obviously 'on' something and I couldn't decide whether to despise or envy him. The thought bubble of arrogance above me had suddenly gone, zapped by the searing rays of panic now being emitted by my brain. What the hell to say?

'Ladies and gentlemen . . . I present Peter . . . Pabo . . . Dex . . .' As my arm waved in his direction I couldn't help fixing on his name plate – why had he changed it?

'Here he is . . .'

I don't pretend there haven't been better introductions, but what else could I do? The famous shit, Eddie, raised another titter as he knotted his eyebrows in alarm. I could imagine the front rows beginning to blister under the intense energy beaming out from my scarlet face. Speak, Dextrus. For God's sake, speak!

But Dexter was, for once, apparently reluctant to grasp the baton

I had been trying to pass to him. It took an agonising wait before his voice revved up into an audible gear.

'. . . Pablo Dextrus . . . Dexterous . . . Dexter . . . you will know Eddie from his televisual activities . . . a supporter of the Arts Collective . . . and Mr Kidd of . . . Kidd . . . Financial Communications.'

I hadn't made all of it out except for another wrong name. What was I to say? Should I correct the title of my company? Had it registered out there or would I merely draw more attention to it if I mentioned it now? What would Andy be thinking – would this all be relayed back to Nick at HQ? Who would take the blame for the state of anarchy erupting at a KFC press call? Anarchy, total chaos, only one man could retrieve this situation, if only I could find him. Okay, steady now, here he comes. Let's hear it for Charles Kidd the decisive, returning for a one-off special guest appearance.

'Thank you . . . And thank you all for attending today's announcement. I'm sure you will have guessed by now that this is intended as an informal briefing, whilst we have a few things to say about the launch of the Resurrectionist Expression. These are already summarised in your press packs and let me know, or one of my staff, if you want any more pack information . . . rather, the bare bones so to speak of what we have to say is encapsulated within the releases but we are happy to add to that in the question and answer session . . .'

I ended with a smile, a purposeful smile, or rather the most purposeful smile I could conjure. I suppose I must have looked like a scout master trying to face down accusations of molesting the cubs. Silence. I wasn't surprised, I could barely follow what I'd said myself but at least the ball was on the other side of the net.

A voice from the crowd, sounding equally puzzled, emerged from the stalls.

'When is that?'

'What?'

Same voice, same puzzled tone: 'The question and answer session.'

'Well, now . . . Any questions?'

Another voice came out from the murmurings.

'Yes, I have a question.'

A chap in a waxed jacket and glasses pointed his chin at me from the second row.

I tried to sound helpful. 'Yes . . .'

'What on earth is this all about?'

'GOOD QUESTION!' Smug Eddie's interjection followed so close on the heels of anorak-man that it was impossible to tell who had drawn the laugh that followed. Time to show grace, purposeful grace. I looked sternly to Dexter.

'Well, Peter . . . Pablo . . . any words you want to give?'

Evidently there were not, the folding of his arms telling us all as much. Deep breath. It was back to me, time for another deep, purposeful breath.

'In that case what I think we would say is that it is all about art. Art for the city, art informed by the city and informative about its past. Our exhibition title refers to a period rich in terms of mystery and intrigue and also of great importance in terms of the development of the image by which we all know Edinburgh today. A period which has proved sufficiently rich enough to fire the imaginations of the artists in the Experimental Art Collective Group to commence some vivid and exciting new works which will be unveiled within the duration of the Resurrectionist Expression during the Festival.'

'Can we have some detail of that?'

'Sorry?'

'Where are these works on show? Where can we see them?'

This was another voice – female, strident.

'BLOODY GOOD QUESTION!'

The laughs now were undoubtably Eddie's. He was getting off on this, playing Mr bloody Punch to my squealing Judy.

'In your pack.'

'I'm sorry, it's not. Five pages of stuff here but not anything about where.'

Nods of agreement all round. The bitch *was* speaking for everyone.

'My understanding . . . The precise location details will be confirmed once we near the actual launch.'

'You *don't* have some sort of gallery space booked *now*?'

The shrill crone had scented blood – a story angle. What sort of exhibition is it when you can't see it? I had wanted to present some kind of façade that everything was about to fall into place, a constructive angle on all of this. I hadn't realised how hostile it would all be. Only one learned colleague on the bench beside me saw fit to offer any kind of support and even then his was questionable in the extreme.

'OBJECTION! NOT A QUESTION!'

I waved Eddie down with no attempt to cover my irritation.

'Our press pack does make clear that we are proposing something quite radical. We are proposing that the business community joins with the arts community . . .'

'And pays for your self-selected group of artists to indulge themselves . . .'

'OBJECTION! OBJECTION! LEADING THE WITNESS!'

A sarcastic riposte to a sarcastic assertion. The bolshie cow deserved it. What did they have to be so angry about? What had I ever done to her? Where did all this contempt come from? I stared at her, a forty-year-old grey-haired frump in some kind of Laura Ashley farmer's wife floral balloon disaster. Andy stood directly behind her; he had his head in his hands. Who was she?

'Who are you?'

'Sorry?'

She had heard me of course but pretended not to, or perhaps not to have understood the question, which did, admittedly, break the convention. The convention was that the shit could only fly in one direction. I offered no reply. I wasn't going to grace her obvious stalling with anything other than an impatient stare.

'Stephanie Maxwell. *The Herald.*'

I had the name. She was now going to get the full treatment.

'Well, Stephanie, has anyone mentioned "indulging" themselves? "Indulging" themselves – isn't that what artists are supposed to do? You bring this up as if there is something distasteful about what we are trying to achieve, something underhand that we are trying to sneak through without it being noticed. Is there? I don't know, is it distasteful or indulgent to let artists express themselves and to bring that work to public attention . . .'

'HEAR, HEAR!'

I had been in mid-flow, nerves turning into a genuine anger. I was practically punching the air when Dexter's celebrity friend saw fit to intervene again. I turned instinctively.

'Shut up, can't you?'

The applause took me by surprise. Again I couldn't judge if there was an irony in play here that I was missing. Eddie placed a large hand across a contrite mouth. They all looked expectantly towards me but I couldn't figure out where to start again. *The Herald*'s arch critic kick-started me.

'Resurrectionists though . . . it's all such a cliché, all this grave-robbing stuff. Been done to death, surely? Isn't the only real audience for this the tourists doing their history tour?'

'And this is the question, Stephanie, that your readers demand an answer to? I don't know. I'm sorry. You tell me when this was last done, or can anyone tell me when the last exhibition on this subject took place?'

It went quiet as the room waited for someone to step forward with the necessary knowledge. I considered the silence some sort of triumph and continued. 'You see, I have lived here for just a short while – under a year – but have found Edinburgh such a beautiful and resonant place to be. A compelling city, and what makes it this way for me at least is the sense of history, the past all around us, everywhere, in the tenements and cobbled street right outside. And the more I learn about that past the more I relate to it and understand my place within the present. Am I wrong to think that it could be the same for anyone else if they had the opportunity to stop and think about these things? We asked ourselves how we could make more people *understand* more, enjoy more. How? Through art, ladies and gentlemen. Making the city and its history more immediate and intimate and accessible through art. Because the danger is that without work like this we will take all the culture that surrounds us for granted and become immune to it, leave it for the tourists. Shouldn't we *all* be tourists in this city? We are all here for such a short while, our lives are too short not to appreciate the beauty around us. So has it been done before? Who knows, who cares? Let's do it this time for us, for now!'

Where had all of this come from? I was beginning to sound as if I was addressing a mass fascist rally. In front of me the heads were all down, guiding thirty-odd pens and pencils through a bout of frantic notetaking. Some of this might make tomorrow's editions, I thought. How pompous would it look in cold print?

A question came from a head to my left, a scribbler injecting a shot of realism to my new-found demonic passion.

'But you can't say where the exhibits will actually *be* on show?'

'No, we can't. That will depend on the help we get.'

'You mean sponsorship? Have you failed so far in your efforts to find backing?'

Of course we had. I had. I hadn't even managed to get into a position to ask. Why not admit as much?

'We haven't asked anyone yet, nor will we. We would be grateful to look at any offers. What we would like to do is work with those who support us, firstly, to source locations where we can show our exhibits and, secondly, perhaps to cover some of the physical costs of putting the show together. But one doesn't always have to follow the other. We think of the spaces that the banks, the insurance houses occupy or own, spaces that are already open to the public and that could be donated as a form of sponsorship. We mean the foyers of main offices, shop windows and gardens. All are spaces that we could use if asked. But we won't be asking. It is up to these companies in the forefront of the city's commercial life to ask themselves if they are doing enough to support its cultural life. If they are happy that they are then they shouldn't approach us.'

I must admit, this sounded convincing to me though I knew the bluff would only work if the writers listening to it took it upon themselves to hound those being spoken about. For that moment, I could see that it might just work. They might just have believed me. I might just have won.

It was time to get out, I had made my impression and could only foul it up by speaking longer and diluting it. I stood up.

'Thank you, ladies and gentlemen. I'm afraid we have run over schedule. Please excuse me. Any further enquiries can be directed to Andy Adriano of KFC.'

And with that, I was off, striding confidently into the glare of the high noon sun hanging over the Old Town. It had been the performance of my lifetime.

TRANSCRIPT : TAPE 5

Interviewer:
What do you mean, 'He'd cut it with ghost'?

Lowes:
'Snuff', Pablo called it, once we got to meet him in the flesh. (Adopts tremulous tone) 'Did you all enjoy your measure of Pablo's snuff? An original blend of invigorating spices mixed with the powdered bones of some of Edinburgh's finest, harvested to give you a taste of the past . . . Nothing beats a good snort, straight into the bloodstream, Pablo says.'

Interviewer:
Do you think he really meant it, that he had used powdered bones as part of the mix?

Lowes:
(impatiently) Yes, yes, yes and yes . . . When he said it I could tell. I went to blow my nose which now felt disgusting, like it was bunged up with soot or something. I looked at what came out on my sleeve, it was like the inside of a fucking Hoover bag.

Interviewer:
So this is when you were face to face with Dextrus, not a video performance. How had he made his entrance?

Lowes:
Eddie had guided us upstairs, Ciaran bringing up the rear. Pitch black. Couldn't see a thing, but the music was louder and louder the higher you went, loud enough to drown out the sound of feet scuffing on the steps . . . feet of zombies. Then we are in an attic,

a large one, blacked out so we are all feeling along the wall. They had another sort of sound system, better than the one in the garden, or the one downstairs, far louder, crisper . . . more real. My eyes are still trying to become accustomed to the lack of light when there's this flash . . . explosion of noise and light, music pumping. (Sings, thumping his chest) 'PABLO PABLO DEXTRUS DEXTRUS'. Smell of burnt gunpowder, a theatrical flash, and there he is, the man himself, right in front of us – Pablo Dextrus, smiling like a lunatic.

Interviewer:
Can you describe him? Was he as he was earlier in his videos, and what effect did his actual presence have on the others?

Lowes:
Like nothing I'd ever seen before in my life. Grotesque . . . compelling . . . whoever did his make-up deserves a fucking Oscar. Totally white face mask, rouged cheeks, black lipstick, pompadour wig . . . a kind of oily sheen to all of him . . . a short guy packing a lot into his fat frame. Did I say what he had on? Unbelievable . . . a waistcoat on top, no shirt, his arms and belly covered in the same white slime . . . the waistcoat has got mirror badges on it, hundreds of them . . . he moves and you can see yourself . . . and the others . . . and then under that he's got white oily legs poured into a pair of women's suspenders and garter belt. His dick and balls . . . hanging out to the world, and they've had the black lipstick treatment too . . . He had (laughs) he had this silvery vibrator in his hand and he would wave it around like some kind of magic wand, never kept it still for a second.

Interviewer:
Did he announce himself, or make any introduction?

Lowes:
He smiled, just smiled for fucking ages, and no one thought to talk to him. That's the measure of . . . of how fucked up we all were, how intimidated, stoned, tired, whatever. No one was ready to laugh or to challenge him for frightening the shit out of us . . . No,

we would have done anything he wanted . . . and he knew it, that's what the evening had been building up to.

Interviewer:
And the last game?

Lowes:
A show. A show by individuals to demonstrate their appreciation of the evening's hospitality . . . a fine Scottish tradition, the 'party piece' whereby guests entertain their hosts to thank them.

Interviewer:
Pablo Dextrus explained this?

Lowes:
No, he was still to speak. Eddie had re-entered, shouting above the noise of the music, now looking absolutely dangerous, face caked in the same powdery dust, eyes flashing like a coiled fucking cobra. The dinner suit was gone. He had a cape on, impossible to tell just then what was underneath. Claire was behind him, had the same gear . . . still beautiful with it though . . . I drifted . . . couldn't tell any more what was real, what was happening or why I was there. Again I'm worrying that we are being filmed, victims of a joke . . . and my mind is approaching overload with these questions going round in a loop, round and round like a mantra . . . is this happening or am I hallucinating? Is there a punchline to this where the lights suddenly come on? What do our hosts possibly get out of this? Where are they taking us or are they just seeing how far we will let ourselves go?

Interviewer:
Would you say you know now?

Lowes:
Every time I think about it . . . it changes . . . (I'll) see it all in a different way. In many ways that night was as clear as it got . . .

Interviewer:
Have you talked about the events with anyone else, or anyone who was there?

Lowes:
Never. Tried to put it all behind me (sighs). I'm telling you all this as it happened, how I think it happened. I'm maybe not emphasising enough how unsettling the whole thing was, how *soiled* the whole experience left me, must have left us all . . . And the terrifying thing that's still with me, is that the whole *knowing* air that Pablo had was for real, that he really did understand us, was *inside* us . . .

Interviewer:
So you performed for them?

Lowes:
Didn't come to that, for me. I missed something, selection of another 'volunteer' . . . no, because Eddie and Claire were dancing, circling each other, swirling around, cackling, stoned, flashes of white flesh as the capes rode up on the spin of a turn. Pablo started speaking, commentating (in voice) 'Couple number three are two young professionals with the world at their feet. *He* is in communications whilst *she* is into law.' Not the same reedy voice as before, this time fuller, coming out of the same speakers as the music but in phase, one box slightly lagging behind the next so the enunciation flowed through the room with an echo that spun your head . . . or was this an effect of the drug as well? (Resumes voice) 'But tonight they are keen to display their gratitude with an *unashamed* display,' and they opened their capes and flapped at each other, naked . . . steps to take them face to face and then backwards. I'm looking on. We all were – are they going to do it? Are we expected to do it? Pablo is striding between them and then out as they close, droning on, the noise is deafening. 'Tonight we have raided the graves of Edinburgh to cut loose the spirits you have helped us *celebrate*. Your favourite dead relatives are here watching on . . . we have revived and *imbibed* them, we have inhaled of their ashes . . . Burke and Hare are here, watching on . . . teaching us to love one another . . .' He says this and the two come together, wrap the

cloaks over each other as she hops up onto him. Are they doing it? Can't tell in the dark . . . Pablo smiles and snatches the coverings off them . . . a flourish of his hand, unveiling the new exhibit . . . seems they are . . . the volunteer is being led towards them. Steve naked and erect, looking so pink against the chalked skin of the others . . . lucky Steve . . . what about the rest of us? Who will back out? Who do the girls get to fuck? What about Pablo, what does he get out of this? And then the man himself ups the stakes. 'We are *vampires*, ladies and gentlemen, friendly *vampires*, and we ask you to join us, show your gratitude and affection and join our immortal number . . .' And I'm watching this, hearing this, thinking about this . . . he's serious . . . he is a vampire and they are feeding off us. Pablo has his hand on Steve's pecker and he's leading him to Claire, guiding him in . . . 'One taste is all that is required. *Join* with us!' He's shouting at us to gather, come and get a closer look. We trudge forward like the zombies we are, peeling off what's left of our clothes for the ultimate game of Twister.

Interviewer:
And you would have done this? You said earlier that you were going along with it all just to watch what happened next. 'Undercover' was how you had put it.

Lowes:
Well . . . I still was, to an extent, not as stoned as they maybe thought I was, and I was looking out for Sarah. I thought if this is it, and we are all going to do it, I might as well be first in with her.

Interviewer:
But this was what they wanted you to do.

Lowes:
(sarcastically) I know . . . but it was also what *I* wanted to do . . . It was the main reason I'd hung around all night . . .

Interviewer:
To indulge in an orgy?

Lowes:

(perplexed) To see where it was leading and then make my *own* choice about whether I would indulge.

Interviewer:

And that was it then, so you were happy?

Lowes:

No, that wasn't it, at least not for me. It was for those who chose to cop out at that stage, because Pablo gave them the choice. These two are screwing behind him and fooling with Steve, and Eddie's giving the fat one a major grope when Pablo starts to wander around us, smiling and the like. At first I think he's looking to crash someone else's action, which would have been a problem for me because I just didn't fancy him enough for him to be part of a fucking threesome, but then he starts his chat and because he's still miked up his voice just booms. I mean, they must have been able to hear him in fucking Glasgow.

Interviewer:

What did he say?

Lowes:

(pauses) He says thank you for coming, that we were to enjoy the fruits of the night . . . that we had made up our own little Hellfire Club and he was honoured to be its devil. He looked at me, and then he seemed to want to catch everyone in the eye, no matter what they were doing (laughs quietly) so that he can say, 'This is where we end, for those of you who do not want to go any further along our journey of self-discovery. This is our special "members' night" but it is for one night only. You will never have an opportunity like this again in your lifetime. You have the choice, but for those who would choose to go with us to the furthest extreme there is one more step we would ask of you . . . and one more question – Dare you follow us?'

Interviewer:

Was everyone listening at this point?

Lowes:

Oh yes, we were tuned in. Every time he spoke, every time he mentioned 'choice' our ears pricked, a conditioned reflex by now, like Pavlov's fucking dogs. You see . . . this 'for one night only' thing, he'd set it up so that we could go as far as we ever would. We were different people there, no one knew us. We could all disappear back to where we came from and no one would know we had ever been there, and with him and his people jumping around it was as if they were just as guilty and had as much to hide. Endless dares, always just one step more attached, come out and see how dark you can be, for one night only, and then run back to reality . . . That's what a dealer offers, isn't it? That is *the deal* . . . Take this pill, this line, this injection, and I'll show you a part of you that you never knew existed, and you can put it back in its box afterwards and revisit it as often or not as you like. And nobody ever turns down the deal, nobody . . . take it from me . . . doesn't matter how many casualties. We all want to know what's in the box, *our* box.

Interviewer:

Do you think he was evil, or a charlatan, or a harmless eccentric?

Lowes:

(pause) Yeah . . . Everything and anything . . . A manipulator. Just like the rest of us.

Interviewer:

Do you think he was murdered? Was it premeditated?

Lowes:

(inhales, sighs audibly) That's a question you'd have to pay a lot more than this for me to answer.

Interviewer:

But you have an opinion on this based on what you saw?

Lowes:

I have an opinion all right. Others may choose not to believe it but I know what I saw.

Interviewer:

So what was his final dare?

Lowes:

(adopts feeble voice) We are a special club, a club that believes in love and unity. An escape club, an ex-tra-ord-in-ary escape club ... Will you help us rescue someone?

THE FIRST SIGN that following Thursday that this would be no ordinary day. A call. The telephone rang. An outside call: you could tell by the ring tone. Okay, here comes a moment.

'Mr Kidd? Elizabeth Malcolm here, secretary to Henry Hughes, Communications Manager of Standard Mutual. He asked if I could arrange an appointment for you to come and see him regarding your . . . Resurrectionist . . . Expression.'

I was nodding silently. Could this be a hoax? I certainly didn't recognise the voice and looked around to see who might be tuning in to the call. There was no sign of anything untoward. Jules, Andy, Carol and the others were flying around, droning like killer bees searching for pollen amongst the hive of cables, printers, computer screens, cold cups of coffee and ashtrays that made for normality. It was business as usual. I edged forward to my desk.

'When would suit Mr Hughes?'

'Let me see, I guess you need things organised pretty quickly . . . how are you for next Tuesday?'

I looked at next week's pages in my diary, all completely empty.

'I think I could manage something in the afternoon.'

'Ah . . . You couldn't make it in the morning, could you?'

'Yes.'

'Can we say ten o'clock?'

We certainly could, although I didn't want to admit to this too readily as well. What would she be thinking?

'I've got a couple of things to rearrange first but that should be alright. I'll call you if it becomes a problem, otherwise let's stick to that. Can you give me a number?'

She gave me one and that was that, almost. I rang it straight back.

'Good morning. Standard Mutual.'

'Can you tell me the name of Henry Hughes's secretary, please?'

'Mrs Malcolm. Can I put you through to her?'

I hung up, almost too excited to continue. It was for real. This was a result. I could hardly believe it and scampered over towards Andy. He was moaning at the temp who had jammed the photocopier by filling it with the wrong paper.

'For fuck's sake, you're sure no one told you how to use this thing?'

Andy took the frightened silence for a yes and ploughed on. 'Then why did you dive right in and wreck the thing without asking anyone?'

The poor girl seemed ready for tears. This was only her second day and Andy was giving it the full latin machismo bit, the matador of the office, hands on hips, shirt sleeves rolled up to reveal surprisingly delicate hands and impossibly hairy forearms. Perhaps she thought her chances with him were blown for good, perhaps she just thought he was being a horrible bastard or perhaps, if she was like Jules, she was thinking a bit of both. Whatever, it was too beautiful a day for such considerations. I had a result, life was wonderful, P R worked.

'Andy . . . Andy, can I interrupt? I've just taken a call from Standard Mutual . . . fixed an appointment. Henry Hughes. Ever heard of him?'

He brightened up momentarily, eyebrows raised to the heavens, a growing smile below and eyes full on mine. He offered me his hand.

'Charlie! My man, the man with the plan . . . Good show. They must have seen the piece in *The Herald*.'

'What piece?'

'You haven't seen it? This morning's paper – arts pages. Jules will have it.'

Much as I was tempted to stay and complete the bonding experience right then the deeper need was to discover just what had been written about our launch of the exhibition. Jules was on one of her 'But why' phone calls, and hardly noticed me rummaging through the top of her desk for the publication in question.

My hands tore through the pages to the arts section and there we were, even though there was no picture or visual reference to guide me eye to it, I knew straight away which piece was ours, the words 'Resurrectionist', 'moving exhibition' and 'Art Collective' leaping out at me from the page, dazzling in their jewel-like brilliance. I could feel my pulse quicken and stomach tighten. A write-up – they had fallen for it, or had they?

I was so keen to absorb the gist of the article that I found I had to force myself to actually read it rather than scan over and over, looking desperately for positive – or particularly bad – words. These weren't immediately apparent it has to be said, nor indeed was any clear meaning. The problem was that the writer – my fat friend in the floral tent, Stephanie Maxwell – had obviously filed what she thought was a particularly clever piece, one that perhaps her editor also enjoyed, but which remained impenetrable to the rest of the reading population. Even the headline 'A Serious Launch For No-Show Show – Arts Event Launches Non-Event' had me paralysed in bafflement. What line was being taken here? Why should Standard Mutual get so excited by this that they had chased me for an appointment? I read again, breathing deeply.

The good news? It *was* a positive piece. But it was about the launch rather than the actual exhibition, which was relegated in importance to a sideshow. The writer seemed to think that this had been deliberate on our – by which she meant my – part. She congratulated us on having organised Edinburgh's first – and possibly the first *anywhere* – 'post-modern' press conference and our achievement in leaving an indelible mark on our audience. The launch had been an artistic statement in its own right, passing a judgement and expression on – here she really lost me – 'the impending media overload', 'the caustic inertia of the Scottish arts establishment' and the 'continuing revolting evolution' of 'history into kitsch into history'. As simple as that. How else, she argued, to explain a journalist's briefing at which no information was given on when whatever we were launching was meant to happen, or where, or why a television celebrity had been brought along to endorse, well, something he wasn't sure of exactly either. Dexter had a mention, or rather 'Dextrus', again for his refusal to say anything at all at his own news gathering, and then there was me, the star of the show. Catch this next time, she said, for the spellbinding anomaly, a straight-talking P R man. 'Mr C. Kidd, a communications guru', had seemingly set the scribes into a flurry of self-analysis with his 'passionate interjections' and 'bulls-eye direct' commentary. What exactly *did* big business do for the arts anyway except feed 'leech-like' from its energies? Isn't it right to subject our 'lazy' acceptance of cultural baggage to 'ruthless testing through re-expression'?

So many questions to which I immediately added two more of my own: firstly, had I actually said any of this?; secondly, was the article meant to be ironic, and therefore an attack on me, or had they assumed *we* had been ironic? The latter was the key to the piece being either a good or bad review, but how to tell? It seemed to depend on how you read it. I found that when I stood up and went through it quickly I could be rather proud of what was being said. The problem only came when I sat and really studied it.

Still, the man from Standard Mutual had obviously taken it on the hoof, and I could only hope that others would do the same. Another phone call – this time from Scottish Provincial – seemed to indicate this was the case. They also asked for an appointment. This time I didn't bother checking to see if it could be a wind-up; by now I knew I didn't have to worry about that.

And then, after that, the phone rang again, this time a different tone telling me that it was an internal call. It was a message from Nick. Could I go and see him – now. I felt my heart instinctively drop and my whole body sag with dread at the thought of another inquisition. What could he hit me with now, though? I was a star, a straight-talking PR man, and there weren't too many of them around. Courage, I told myself, decisiveness; I had appointments. I still felt sick.

Downstairs Nick's PA – another temp of very recent vintage, the last one having left suddenly following what Jules would only teasingly describe as 'an incident' – waved me through the anteroom straight into the lair of the beast. Nick fixed me a reptile smile.

'Grab a pew, Charlie.'

He sounded downbeat, tired. The blinds behind his desk were drawn and things did not look cosy in the forced gloom – piles of files stacked on the floor, pictures down and leaning in reverse against the walls they once adorned, papers on every other flat surface. Symptoms of media overload perhaps, or maybe he was in a spectacularly shitty mood and had just trashed his office. There was certainly a morning-after air to him, face lined and hangover-grey eyes, hiding behind little round glasses I'd never seen him in before. Perhaps it was all meant to be post-modern. He came straight to the point.

'When you meet clients, do you introduce the company as Kennedy Fraser Communications or KFC?'

Shit. He was going to have a serious pop at me over the conference name plate nonsense. Time to stall.

'Depends.'

His face warmed up a bit with contempt. I would have had to admit it was a resolutely lame answer. '*What?*'

Okay, he had me. Time for some of my famed straight talk.

'KFC ... mainly.'

I still couldn't resist hedging my bets, especially as he seemed on the verge of an epic tantrum.

'What ... *Why?*'

'Snappier ... to the point.'

'Think so?'

'Definitely.'

This appeared to be along the lines of what he wanted to hear. He hummed almost contentedly in agreement before continuing.

'And this is what our clients would prefer?'

'Quite.' I couldn't claim to be answering on behalf of any particular clients, except perhaps the two potential ones who had just called me up. Still, this technicality didn't seem to bother Nick as he mused on my words.

'*Snappier* ... yes ...'

'Why do you ask?' I was fishing to see if there was any kind of charge against me, to see if I could relax and let my stomach settle back down nearer my kidneys than my throat. The mood had seemed to be ripe for this, but my question changed that. Nick jerked his head back like a cobra and brought his hands slowly together, knuckle to knuckle. The silence that followed nearly overwhelmed me. He conjured up another stare, a don't-tell-anyone-this-on-pain-of-death stare.

'Pete Fraser has left.'

'I see.'

It took a major effort to maintain a suitably glum front whilst inwardly jumping cartwheels of joy. The court martial was over. So Nick's business partner was off – there had probably been another 'incident'. So what? So one of our firm's founding principals had been fired, or jumped ship. Who cared? So it was all-change, with the agency pitched into chaos. When was it ever different? What mattered, crucially, was that it wasn't my fault. Time for an official statement: 'Nothing to do with me!' says communications guru.

Time to appear solemn.

'Will he be taking any clients with him?'

'Maybe . . . doubt it. He'll be taking his fucking name with him though, won't he?'

Would he? I didn't know. Normally these things were tied up in whatever agreement the partners had made for this contingency when founding the business.

'Don't you two have a contract preventing that?'

I had strayed onto a particularly sore point. Nick squeezed his hands together with an audible crunch of bones. He leant forward like a nightclub bouncer about to explain which part of the establishment's door policy it was that dictated that you would have to be beaten up.

'Of course we have a fucking contract covering that and fucking everything . . . and he won't be able to operate as "Fraser" fucking anything, or tap any of our existing clients, or go to the toilet without telling us . . . if I buy out his share of the operation at the agreed price written in the fucking contract.'

He finished with a smile of sorts, an idiot's smile pulled on me as if to say 'Understand now?' I did, and offered back a smile of my own, a 'Sorry, I get the picture now' kind of grimace, although it might have come across as more of a nervous twitch.

'So will we change our name then?'

'No! For christ's sake, no!' He screamed in frustration. '*We* don't change our name to anything. We keep to what our clients know us as.'

At last, a second of insight penetrated the quivering blancmange of my mind.

'KFC?'

'Kennedy *Financial* Communications. Our letterhead, logo and listings all lead with the initials. We just drop the "Fraser" as the stocks are exhausted. We don't have to change anything else. Think it would work?'

An ingenious scheme, how blind of me not to spot it. We had changed so many times when all the key personnel were in place, it stood to reason that the only time we would be constant was when they left. Agreement was in order – it was what Nick wanted to hear. It was why I had been summoned.

'It's great. All we need are some heavyweight financial clients to back it up.'

The nightclub heavy pushed his brutal face close up to mine, his words hissing with the promise of barely suppressed violence.

'That, Charlie, is meant to be why you're fucking here.'

FILE NOTE: CLAIRE LISTER & PETER DEXTER, RESPØNSE TO

The partnership would always prefer not to intercede
except in cases of obvious imperative and need. We
have long-established criteria to help us establish
if this is indeed the case, but even such a trusted
and time-honoured procedure can be found wanting by
the most extreme circumstances such as we found ourselves in during this most unfortunate instance.
Certainly, the kind of intervention we were forced to
make was one that had never before been envisaged, one
that, although eventually decisive, threatened our
own methods of operation as much as the intended
miscreant's.

Initially, when the first contact between the 'Dexter'
character and Roberts, Begby & Lawrie was made, the
consensus was that a subtle evasion would suffice; a
gentle steering away from the problem by a guiding
hand. That the employee herself, for whatever reason,
chose to pursue some kind of intellectual liaison
with the new 'client' despite our best advice, was
disappointing, but a disappointment we would have
coped with, even if it meant losing the services of
Claire, of whom we had such high hopes. Then it became apparent that there was a hidden danger as well
as an obvious irritation in everything this man stood
for, and also that we would have to re-examine our
criteria for supplication for here was someone who
posed danger not only to the general moral well-being
of a member of our staff, but also to the service
Roberts, Begby & Lawrie provided its clients – and
indeed to the establishment itself. The partnership
realised that whilst we were not alone in being under

assailment it might fall <u>indubitably</u> to our perhaps
unique <u>puissance</u> to <u>exculpate</u> the very body we hold
in such deep <u>veneration</u>. We can put it no simpler
than that.

And why would we feel so honoured to take up such a
burden? Because, frankly, that is the mission that
Roberts,Begby & Lawrie had in mind from our very
inception as writers to the signet, one that we have
striven so as to have the power to undertake. Today,
over one hundred and fifty years since our own forma-
tion, it is a matter of considerable pride to the
partners that we can consider ourselves guardians of
the establishment that others would seek to undermine.
Sadly, such 'others' may have at one stage included
our own employee, Claire. We can see that it is
feasible she was misguided, led by 'Dexter' to believe
that the 'establishment' was, and is, no more than
a cabal, operating a policy of exclusion so that
whatever wealth and benefits circulate amongst society are the automatic preserve of the chosen few –
who are themselves chosen on the basis of class,
creed or vested interest. Is this what was told to
her, that in the establishment we have a self-app-
ointed caste, continually overseeing a 'carve-up'
of public assets in favour of the few? It is difficult to ascertain which 'establishment' the protag-
onists of this thesis refer to when they lambast it.
Is it the local i.e. Edinburgh 'establishment', or
the national 'Scottish' one? Or indeed the world-
wide conspiracy, the 'Established' establishment?

Such questions do not concern us. We are proud to
consider ourselves members of the <u>establishment</u>,
but only as we see it, and we do not see it as
some elite. We can only stress exactly what it is
we stand for. We stand for an establishment which
represents the essential <u>faith</u> that keeps our world
in order. Like some of our partners, our establishment has no physical presence, it cannot be located
on a street map or directory. It can only exist in
our consciousness. Thus, its detractors, in the
unlikely event that they are blessed with sufficient
intellect, would be aware of the irony by which their

denunciations <u>actually</u> confirm its <u>actuality</u>. The
establishment will die only when society ceases to
be comforted by the notion of its being; it should
be made clear though that our establishment exists
as a <u>faith</u>, a faith in the <u>professions</u>.

We have that faith as a tenet that has helped us
achieve the remarkable. Faith conquers all. We know
this better than most – the very durability of
Roberts, Begby & Lawrie is testimony to that. We
have faith in the law and its practitioners, as we
do in accountancy, management consultancy and even
the less 'professional' of the new professions –
marketing, advertising, public relations. We have
faith in these more modern arrivals because, like
their predecessors, they provide worthwhile endea-
vour for otherwise idle hands and minds. Yes, we
would freely admit, none of these occupations has
any tangible value. Would any be deemed essential to
the future of our society? Would any future genera-
tion invent them should they not have existed already?
Obviously not, but that does not stop livelihoods
being made and esteem being bestowed upon the best
of their ilk. Through the professions, those who
would otherwise be lost are given a sense of purpose,
and so our educated classes do not descend into
anarchy. Individually, there are those who will have
their temporary dilemma over the validity of what
they do; this is only natural when what they do do
can only be judged to be ultimately worthless. Some
will drop out of the roles and structures into which
they have ingrained themselves, but collectively the
system moves on. This widespread faith requires
guardianship. Occasionally, however, it also requires
a ruthless cull of its denigrators. Which is why the
arrival of 'Dexter' and his obscene device sparked
alarm amongst us. In many ways we were to be thankful
he had chosen to engage us, out of all the possibilities open to him, for <u>we</u> knew that this could only
be interpreted as a direct challenge. As keepers of
the faith we had to respond. In ourselves, he had
met his match, and this we could state with an absolute
and dread conviction.

DID I KNOW he was going to do it? No, nobody did. Nobody was supposed to; the whole point was that it was planned to be spontaneous. 'A spontaneous exhibition of thanks and progress toward the Resurrectionist display. Honour to our patrons, praise to our artists!'

I only heard about it when one of the hacks he'd invited faxed his fatuous words over to me at KFC with twenty minutes to go. She wanted to know what the hell was going on. She wasn't the only one.

I'd kept Dexter informed of progress as the news had come in: four major corporate backers would donate reception space and potential purchase/leaseback deals on the works themselves if the individual costs were below ten grand a piece; three further lesser sponsors – trading houses, specialist fund management groups – were determined to get in on the act. I'd been a busy boy, out there meeting the people, making the deals in a way I could have only dreamt of months earlier. The prince of the city. I could call Sheila Clements of Scottish Provincial, Henry Hughes of Standard Mutual, Mike Walker of Greenwood Investors, *any* of them, *anyone* and *expect* to be put through. They *listened* to me, thought my opinion on the news management of their company's largesse worthwhile. Some even showed signs of interest in what KFC could do for them on a permanent, consultancy retainer basis. But the more I told Dexter this the less attention he paid to me. Where was my thanks for these efforts on his behalf? Where was my notification of this event?

This time we were in Class and Thompson, a delicatessen halfway down Dundas Street, pleasant enough though with a strong smell of olives and cheese hanging in the air from the lunchtime stint. Nobody asked what we were doing in a food hall. The joke was obvious enough once you arrived. Class and Thompson is sand-wiched (appropriately) between two of the major art dealers in the city: Bourke Fine Art to the left, and the Edinburgh Gallery to the right. One look into the window of either will tell you what kind of art they prefer to trade in – traditional, as in very traditional, watercolours of the Castle's profile (appropriately) against a setting sun sort of thing. In fact, this corner of the New Town hosts a number of key galleries; further down the hill you will find Collective Forty-one – at number 41 (very appropriately) – and the Denoit Gallery, both of these being perhaps a little more liberal in their tastes. The point was, however, that by hosting his impromptu conference amongst the bagels and broccoli at number 21, Dexter obviously thought he was making some sort of two-fingered salute to the established order. The circus had pitched its tent in enemy territory.

I made my way to the counter where Dexter stood next to a young woman in an evening dress. She was heavily made up; more appealing from a distance than close up, like the girls behind the cosmetics counter in cheap department stores. Maybe she had more class than that. Blonde and tall, taller than Dexter with a high forehead and laughing wide eyes. She certainly looked as if she had the measure of him, drawing hard on a cigarette and blowing into his face. Something about her intimidated me: maybe it was that she was so obviously attractive – in a conventional sense – that she would have expected someone like me to flirt with her, or try to. And I wasn't going to do that. Would she think that odd of me? Would she think it rude? What might all the others think? Should I at least make some attempt, for the sake of keeping to the form of these things? No, I wouldn't, I didn't want to join a list of endless fawning admirers. Anyway, I'd already decided I wasn't going to like her.

All these thoughts flashed round in the half-second between arriving at Dexter's side and opening my mouth. Maybe it took longer than half a second and that's why she raised an eyebrow at me like I was some kind of stammering idiot. Maybe I was standing there for quite a few seconds with my mouth open like a dumb fool before I could start up on Dexter.

'Peter, what's the meaning of this . . . I thought we'd agreed all news management should come through me ... I can't announce the agreements we've got until I have clearance on an approved release.'

Dexter smiled benignly at my awkward interruption of whatever aura he was silently trying to cast. This was him in relaxed mode, father to his family of artists.

'Charles! Meet Claire, she's our new legal advisor. I've been telling her all about you and your young companion. Not with you today?'

He was talking in a preposterous new voice which involved splitting each word into two halves which could be strung out with long vowels – thus 'legal' became 'lee-gal' and 'Charles' 'Charr-elles'. I was mortified. The girl offered me her hand. Somehow her actions added to my embarrassment. I could feel a film of sweat form on my upper lip and my hair begin to stand on end. Earlier in the day I had been dispensing words of wisdom at Standard Mutual and was still wearing the grey pinstripe number I had thought to be most appropriate for my conservative client. It was a suit of the utmost sincerity. Now I began to feel the material give off all the wrong signals about me. Should I explain, try to justify? Why should it matter anyway?

I edged closer to Dexter. 'Listen, we can't go public on the backers yet. I don't have consent and don't want them thinking I'm a bloody cowboy who promises one thing and does another.'

He grinned again, turning first to me and then the girl. 'Look, I think we'd better get started, I don't think there's anything to really worry about, I'm only going to say a few words and won't mention your sponsors. If you think you need to, stop me, or join in. *Communicate!*'

Dexter reached inside his denim jacket pocket to pull out a pair of glasses and a piece of folded paper. He cleared his throat and began, in the same pompous tone he had used with me, talking as if addressing the floor of the House of Lords on a matter of national importance rather than a handful of confused reporters with hams hanging over them.

'Good day, members of the press. Thank you for your attendance at such short notice. I would like to thank those of you who have written about us following our previous gathering, and for the interest your outpourings generated. At that meeting our discussion centred around sponsorship, although questions were asked relating to the art of our exhibition. Today whilst I would like to notify you of the significant progress that has been made regarding patronage, the rest of our impromptu conference will be focusing on the exhibits in our show. Therefore, after I finish speaking, in two and a half minutes, my associate, Claire, will begin a spontaneous discussion on the likely works on show. This will last twelve minutes during which our associate, Charles, might also make spontaneous interjections and asides. We would certainly welcome any spontaneity from yourselves at any point at all. Could you please stand by for something unexpected in four minutes. The method will become clear in our actions. Any questions?'

Enn-nee qwess-chions? There were no takers, the only sound in response being the snorts and sighs of those fearing they had been brought here on a fool's errand. At this stage I was hoping they would all go quietly, once Dexter's thin joke wore thinner. Perhaps it was the realisation that the vultures of the press were losing patience that made him throw some bait.

'My associate here from K and F and C will be happy to inform you of the progress on support from the bankers and the Standards and the Mutuals and so forth in due course, but I am in the position to inform you all of a major sponsorship deal concluded today between ourselves at the Collective and a major beer manufacturer. This is the first time the said company have been involved in such a venture, and we thank them unreservedly.'

Dexter began his own spontaneous round of applause. Again there were no other takers. When he stopped, the inevitable question came.

'Who are they?'

'Who?'

'Your sponsors?'

Dexter looked to me, I shook my head.

'As I said, my colleague . . .'

'Your beer sponsor, the one you just said you would announce now?'

Dexter milked the moment, clasping his hands at his mouth as if struggling with a heaving inner turmoil.

'Our sponsor, in their stated aim, wish their product to be the choice of the elite, the cognoscenti, the chosen. Therefore, I cannot think that it would be in their wishes for me to tell you their name.'

The non-announcement was greeted with silence. Dexter was making this difficult, openly toying with the press. Did he really have a sponsor – did anyone really care? What kind of corporate sponsor demanded this kind of secrecy? The questions were thrown at Dexter in rapid succession. He must have been pleased with the furore he had provoked.

'I don't understand. Your sponsor wants no mention, no association with your exhibition?'

'That can't be a sponsorship at all, surely it's just an anonymous donation.'

'Ridiculous! How could this possibly work?'

'Is this some kind of spoof?'

He stroked his beard, waiting for it all to die down before beginning again. The last comment had come from right in front of him, from a balding librarian-type in green corduroy trousers, a man who was also wearing a lumpy cardigan underneath his jacket. I suspected that he was closest to the truth, and wondered how someone with such appalling dress sense could also possess such insight. It was noticeable that Dexter cast his eye well over him when responding to the crowd.

'My sponsor wants the best appreciation for his brew, and the best to appreciate it. It is my judgement that banding their name around would destroy the mystique they currently enjoy. Sophisticated brands call for sophisticated marketing. For example, we understand that this particular beer has had a major advertising campaign which was extremely successful in that it was not noticed by anyone other than the opinion formers who were targeted.'

'And they are in agreement with this?'

'The opinion formers?'

'The sponsors!'

'I don't know.'

'Who are the opinion formers?'

'They know who they are, perhaps there are some here today. Could any opinion formers make themselves known . . .'

I could hear the girl struggle to suppress a giggle as everyone scanned the room. The silence of the rest said it all. There were evidently no opinion formers present.

Dexter let his smile emerge again, bringing himself back into ugly focus, like some Cheshire cat in reverse. He didn't offer any further insight. For all the barely concealed frustration and resentment his shambolic conference was causing this was still, at this point, looking not so bad for me. Some of the scribes had started packing up. My mouth was shut. I wasn't going to be forced to divulge any sponsorship details and could concentrate on not looking stupid. I made a mental note to begin to distance myself from Dexter. KFC had achieved all it could with this man and his tendency for maverick antics was making him something of a liability. If he wanted to set up these kinds of stunts, then fine; the relationships with the business community were in place now and his involvement was becoming the lesser part of them. I began to think of the wording of the letter I would send him resigning the account. It would have to be tactful but firm. We had set up the deals as agreed, and now that these were finalised it was time to part. Yes, a tactful way of putting it all. With all due respect, fuck off. Then, just as it seemed to be breaking up, the press call got spontaneous. It was overwhelming.

'An exhibit . . . sculpture, perhaps an instrument of pleasure . . . we think it might raise the dead.'

Those who cared to look up, and there were more than a few who probably wished they hadn't, were greeted with the sight of Claire, our 'lee-gall' advisor, waving a dildo above her head. A stainless steel one, or maybe chrome. When she had started to speak it had been in a mild Scottish accent which had then mutated by the end of the sentence into a parody of an ancient Morningside whine – Miss Jean Brodie well past her prime. I wasn't the only one who was better with my mouth shut. And she had introduced herself like a schoolteacher too; voice gaining in volume and purpose as if bringing an unruly class to order, the rising inflection turning the statement into a question whilst also holding an I'm-keeping-pleasant-but-I-could-get-very-nasty threat underneath. Whatever, between that and her brandishing of the unspeakable device, the exodus had halted. The attention of the non-opinion formers was back on Dexter's merry crew.

She delicately pulled a lever out from the side of the thing at its base. This, it appeared, was some kind of attached wind-up key, folded into the mechanism as an opening fork might be to a tin of Spam.

'Beautiful, isn't it? Crafted with modern materials from original two-hundred-year-old drawings. An intricate device, designed here in Edinburgh by Dr Alexander Brodie, sometime around 1830. His plans have only recently been discovered in a city archive, and make fascinating reading. He was vilified during his lifetime, but history may be ready to recognise his genius. What do you think it was for?'

She began to turn the key over as she waited for an answer.

'Perhaps we jump to obvious conclusions with too much haste. This is a surgical instrument, made by the mind of the scientist, not the hedonist, although they could of course be one and the same.'

She laughed and released the device to unleash its energies. A whirring noise filled the air as it shook through a series of vibrations. It was offered round but few were willing to touch it, especially the women. I was curious myself; there was no doubting that the creation had a strange kind of beauty, gleaming with the reflections of the puzzled faces peering at it, looking both ancient and contemporary at once. You would have had it for the mantelpiece if you didn't realise what it was for. What it was for? That was what made it ugly, no one could see it without immediately thinking of its context, myself included. That was why nobody wanted to touch it. There had to be a point to this, something in this beauty in the eye of the beholder stuff, a point about art. Wrong again.

'We can guess what you think this might be for; it is obvious from your reaction. Perhaps you are correct, and this is nothing more than a vibrating dildo, one of the earliest of its kind, suitable for anus or vagina. Dr Brodie's sketches do not make it clear which might have been preferred. Think again, ladies and gentlemen of the press. Have one more look. Touch it, it is harmless. The inventor intended the instrument to house a dynamo-type mechanism that we have not included in this reconstruction. That is why when it is wound up it merely shakes violently. Originally it was intended to give off continual electric charges – shocks, ladies and gentlemen.

It is our contention that this is no dildo made for pleasure. This is a tool specifically devised to raise the dead.'

The notebooks were out again. A bout of furious writing had begun, even if the questions betrayed a lingering scepticism.

'When were the original drawings for this discovered?'

'What became of Dr Brodie?'

'Can we have access to the draft sketches?'

'What evidence is there that this was ever meant or used for such a purpose?'

Every enquiry was greeted with an enigmatic smile that must have been copied from Dexter. But no answers were really needed: everybody knew that. They might get in the way of the story, and that was what these people had suddenly been given on a plate, a story their editors would thank them for.

And if it wasn't quite enough, Dexter intervened and opened his mouth one last time.

'We intend to test our theory and to arrange a full trial. You will hear of our results, and some will even witness them.'

'You seriously propose some kind of experiment involving the dead?'

'This must be a stunt to publicise your exhibition, surely?'

The smile returned, a smile of the utmost sincerity, and stood next to me. I could not bring myself to share it.

THE CAPTAIN studied the figure of the man clambering onto the gang plank. Although he seemed in imminent danger of falling overboard as he struggled to balance his weight against that of his suitcase, and the leather on the soles of his shoes slipped on the greasy dew under them, the captain did not move to help him. Instead he preferred to remain passive, taking in as much of the newcomer's aspect as was possible in the dull light of the quayside lamps. So many had come to him on mornings like this, desperate to be spirited away, but this one was a strange character. In half an hour the ship would slip moorings and begin to make its way down the coast, south, to England. Felixstowe the first port of call, there to unload its filthy coal cargo. What would make any man eager to join them? Because someone needed to be away from here, anywhere but here.

The man made his way across deck, gingerly striding over the ropes and pools of black tar that lay in his path.

'Good morning, captain. I asked at the dock gates and they tell me you are heading south on the hour. They advised that you may be agreeable to taking a passenger. Is this the case, sir?'

The captain sucked on his pipe. How much might such a journey be worth to this man? How keen was he to leave Edinburgh?

'Might be.'

'Well . . . if I may ask, would you be agreeable if I were to pay a fare?'

The captain nodded.

'Are you at liberty to tell me what that might be?'

The man had smiled nervously as he spoke. As they all

did, thought the captain, the gamblers and the cheats always anxious to please and to know that escape is possible. This one had something else to him though: there was an arrogance simmering below the surface. This civility wasn't coming easily to him. This was a vain and proud man. And then there was the leather case he held tightly to his chest. Most of the men who had lost at the gaming tables lost everything except the boots they stood in. This man held something precious and kept it close.

The captain grunted and lifted his cap, scratching his scalp with his other hand. He looked up into the mist and haar, and took a deep breath, stepping closer to the other as he did so. He let his gaze fall onto the stranger again. Yes, it was there, obvious as he moved closer. He had not been mistaken – the bloodstain on the left sleeve, and another he had not noticed before on the right. There was more than a whiff of smoke about him too, together with a more telling odour – kerosene, the same paraffin oil they used to fire the stove in the galley below.

'Three pounds.'

The man's hand reached inside his waistcoat to his wallet. The notes were handed over without a word. The captain placed them in his coat pocket without counting them.

'You got a name, sir? I need one for the ship's log.'

The stranger made as if to speak and then paused. For the first time a look of exhaustion came into his eyes.

'Rennie . . . James Rennie . . .'

'You been in a fire, sir? Had an accident? Anything you'd like to report to the port authority before we embark?'

Another pause, then a smile, then a sigh.

'No fire, no accident . . . My name is James Rennie, traveller . . . Here.' He withdrew his wallet once more and lifted more notes from it. 'Will that get us going, and get me a clean shirt?'

The captain took the money and pretended to count, his eye sneaking a glance at the monogrammed initials on the passenger's case. 'A.B.' they read. Again he had not been mistaken.

'A clean shirt? At least a different shirt, Mr . . . Rennie. We cast off at six, Felixstowe by tomorrow evening. I suggest you travel in the galley below deck.'

The man nodded in agreement; they had understood each other. It was important they understood each other.

FILE NOTE: OUR UNIQUE PARTNERSHIP, COMPANY HISTORY OF

We decided, unanimously, to investigate the background of the individual concerned, to find out if
there was any previous history to this man which
might indicate his future actions, or indeed how seriously we should take his attack. It was decided to
employ all resources available to us in search of an
answer. We would accept that many might find some of
these unusual, perhaps questionable, and maybe even
incredible. Those who would have such a reaction
would certainly, however, lack a full insight into
the unique partnership that is Roberts, Begby &
Lawrie.

We were formed in 1768, the founding partners having
served apprenticeships in the city's finest solici-
tors' practices. The goals that we adhere to today
are those that made up the founding partners' original vision; goals of the highest levels of service,
loyalty and faith in the establishment. Ours is a
democratic partnership and all relevant issues subject to debate with individual power of veto. All
decisions are therefore unanimous. No other partnership could be as democratic as ours. It is inconceiv-
able, and this, it must be admitted, makes us unique.
The strength of our desire to make a lasting contribution is another factor that distinguishes us from
our legal colleagues, although it is not the strength
of the desire per se that is the differentiator, more
the rather extraordinary procedures we have developed
in order to fulfil it.

145

Some years ago, it was decided, unanimously, that to be truly democratic there must be no bar to a partner's voice being heard on any issue confronting our practice. Such bars could have been foreseen as seniority, gender, social standing and age. It was decided that none of these should ever prevent an opinion or view being aired and appreciated as valid. Age had, at the time, become a particularly contentious issue, since members of the original founding partnership had reached the age of retirement, departure and indeed, death. It was decided that none should be a bar to any contribution being accepted in good faith. None, since we are truly democratic. Physical presence therefore, or indeed lack of it, is not accepted as an argument against those who would wish to be heard. Instead, those who do enjoy a physical presence are merely obliged to be the executors of the will of those who do not. Communication is maintained, and our founding partners continue to partake of an active role in the governance of the practice. Communication is maintained through mutual faith. We can put it no simpler than that.

Our methods of investigation then, without embarking on a detailed explanation of complicated matters, are somewhat wider in scope than others might be able to employ. Through the good offices of all our partners, and their associates, we have been able to ascertain much of the tawdry record that makes up our Mr Dexter's past.

THE DEXTER THEORY of public relations. Chapter one, news management. First, summon a group of journalists to your chosen venue, any venue, although the more ludicrous the better for making them ill-at-ease and hostile. Second, before you begin, rubbish them, but in an obtuse fashion, one that insults them by somehow communicating that you do not judge them to have enough intelligence to realise that they are in fact being rubbished. If the finer aspects of this second point are too advanced for novice practitioners, just remember to rubbish them in the most basic fashion, perhaps issuing a schedule of events that no one will stick to, or maybe wave a sex toy at them. Third, and perhaps most important, give them a story that is so beguiling that they will be powerless to resist, eagerly scribbling down every detail with a vision of front page glory glowing hot in their minds. The story should be wild, captivating, just the right side of impossible. Four? Step four of course is to rubbish the story you have just given. In an obtuse fashion. Step five is to return to step one. Repeat ad nauseam, literally.

Let's think about steps one to four and what kind of comment they are likely to generate. Discreet coverage perhaps, and maybe that was what was wanted. *The Herald* ran a diary piece, tongue-in-cheek style, gently chiding pretentious arts types for hosting their press event in a cheese shop and introducing a contraption that defied description but could almost certainly have grated cheese if granted a bit more friction – except that it had been unveiled as a work of art. Two columns in total. No quotes, no photographs; not necessarily harmful. Likewise *The Scotsman*, whose Festival preview slot also featured a gossipy-witty paragraph or two, again in the context of pseudo-intellectual artists letting it all hang out – 'The Dexterus Collective Gallery Group (sic) again indulged their taste for the bizarre and exotic news conference . . .' etc, etc. Not harmful, or as harmful as it could have been, as it was meant to have been. Nothing set to print about the threat to excavate some of Edinburgh's deadest citizens. No one had taken up Dexter's hint or pieced it together with what had gone before, at least, not yet. This didn't mean I was no longer frightened by the prospect. Every day now started with a systematic trawl in search of signs that this thing really was falling out of my control, a search usually interrupted by calls from sponsors wanting to know when they would see their coverage, receive the works they had been promised, when my plan to promote both would click into action. And every day I would ask myself how I was going to emerge with any kind of credit from an exercise now sabotaged from within. Should I just tell them all it had been a mistake and hope they wouldn't hold it against me or KFC?

Thursday morning came and it was Nick Kennedy, interrupting everything with another corporate identity crisis. Jules had been in a panic, suddenly realising that the fax machine she had programmed to spread the news overnight of New Town Photocopiers' launch of their new Gold Sterling Maintenance Service two days ago had in fact sent the same release forty-nine times to an irate florist in Paisley, wherever that was. Poor Jules had begged for all hands on deck whilst we tried to get the message out to the relevant newshounds before her deadline elapsed at ten. 'Charles, please . . . I'm hanging on by my neck . . . couldn't you take these next door and ask if they will let you belt them out from there. Every other bastard machine is clogged and it's just so awful . . .' The sheer terror of what was happening managed to make her face appear simultaneously pale and flushed, cheeks and forehead alternately throbbing scarlet and grey. Poor Jules. I could only sympathise; I was in it up to my fingernails myself.

And suddenly here was Nick.

'Charlie, when you introduce yourself as a . . . KFC man, does anyone ever mention chicken?'

I felt my mouth chew over the notion of a smile; what kind of question was this? A wind-up, some kind of joke, like one of these 'knock-knock' efforts?

'Sorry, Nick. Can't quite make you out.'

'Chickens, Charlie. Fucking chickens! Kentucky fucking chickens!'

'As in, what . . . a new business lead?'

'No dick-wit, I mean us. *Us!* Being taken for them – KFC – it's what some people call them! Fried fucking chickens!'

At last I was beginning to stagger towards some kind of vague insight into what on earth it was he was so agitated about, although why this was the prime issue at nine-fifty on this particular Thursday morning was as much of a mystery as ever.

'I can't tell you it has been raised by anyone I've spoken to.'

'What – never?'

'As far as I'm aware.'

Nick scowled at me, radiating disgust and disbelief.

'Well, shit, Charlie. We're going to have to change it. I can't believe you missed it . . . Any ideas?'

'Not really, it just never really occurred to me that anyone would think of it in that way.'

'For a new name, for fuck's sake!'

I had been planning to get to that bit eventually, although everything was going blank with him rushing me like this. Over his shoulder I could see Jules emptying the frothing brown contents of her paper cup into the earth of a lilting pot plant, and surreptitiously lifting her pile of faxes from the corner of my desk before sloping off downstairs. Carole's orbit was also taking her further away from us with its barely discernible but wider loop. Nick's venomous energy had them all fluttering off like nervous birds before a storm. Somehow his impetuous challenge over our company name was going down as my disaster. Didn't I have debacles enough of my own without anyone else's being foisted upon me? The unfairness of it all was overwhelming. I sat impotent, as ever, as Nick heckled his straight man.

'I'm thinking of KFCC . . . Kennedy Financial Communication Consultants. Wouldn't have to pay for a new logo design . . . could just add a "C" to the existing one. What do you think?'

'Bit of a dead word, isn't it – "Consultants"?'

Nick's reply had come from an unlikely source and he turned to face its origin. Andy had strayed over, having obviously missed the earlier tirade, probably sorting out another fax catastrophe for Jules.

A potentially fatal error, sauntering into the scene of an ongoing atrocity, a mistake compounded by his assumption that Nick's hissed mutterings were for open debate.

'And what do you fucking know about it?'

I winced for Andy, but he stepped forward into the gunfire, regardless, determined to show his latin courage.

'I'm just saying . . . I think it's a redundant addition. "Consultants"? Goes without saying we are consultants, surely?'

'Listen, son, I'll tell you what goes without fucking saying. You keep your big snout out unless I fucking ask you . . . When I want your fucking opinion I'll . . .'

Etc. Etc. I can't remember what else was said by Nick at this point other than that he exhausted every possible combination of 'off', 'fuck', 'you' and 'out of it', including some truly innovative new ones that could only have come from a communications professional. Andy had a look that betrayed his alarm and hurt, together with his bewilderment at having managed to provoke such a response. A vulnerable look; one I had never seen before.

But the snake still had poison left to spare.

'You just stick to keeping an eye on Charlie like I told you. If this exhibition sponsorship goes down it'll be your fuck-up, son. You better have it under control, better have better press coverage planned than the shit I've seen. Better . . .'

Better better, fuck fuck. It just went on and on, the finger pointing, the rolling eyes, spray showers of spittle with every second consonant. So, any mess with the Resurrectionist Expression was Andy's fault, and the foul-up with our name mine. Kennedy Financial Fuck Fuck Better Better Communications. It had a ring to it, KFFFBBC. Quite. Had to be worth suggesting. Anything had to, I'd had enough.

'Nick . . . Nick! Will you fucking stop it? We get the message. Everything here is under control, I'm telling you. If it isn't, I promise you I'll take all the shit that's going. I promise. That good enough for you? Why don't you leave it to us and we'll work out something you'll be proud of? A new name? Sure, but give me time to consider a view instead of springing it on me. I don't think it's a priority right now, but if you want to discuss it then why don't we meet this afternoon. That will give me time to think it through. We tell our clients to be wary of instant solutions and we shouldn't be any different.'

Did I really say all that? I did. Did it shut him up? It did. Shut all of us up. No one had been more surprised to hear it come from me than me. I found myself talking again just to fill the stunned silence.

'What about late afternoon, about five-thirty? I've got things to do right now.'

Nick nodded, perhaps whispering something like 'Good' or 'Okay' but doing it so quietly and sheepishly that I couldn't be sure if he'd said anything at all. Andy pulled the same trick, mouthing 'thanks' or words to that effect, and fixing me a grim smile before following Nick's exit. That left me to blush on my own as I shuffled through a stack of papers, pretending to be immersed in my work.

I had stopped him, silenced him, sorted him. And promised to sort it all. I had been decisive and firm, been someone else, someone noble. I had been someone who did not move to protect himself when in danger but had intervened unthinkingly and unselfishly when Andy was under the same threat. An act of someone noble. Someone I was so ashamed of that I was still blushing three hours later.

FILE NOTE: PETER DEXTER, FULL HISTORY OF

We discover that Peter Dexter is a fantasist. Pablo
Dextrus also. Likewise Mr Trevor Blake, William De
Vries and Tony Spencer. Tony Spencer, or rather
<u>Anthony</u> Spencer, was convicted of fraud and served
over two years for his troubles, following an unfortunate mix-up over the level of veracity required in
an insurance claim. Perhaps that explains the later
indirect belligerence towards the city's insurance
broking firms. Anthony 'Wide Tony' Spencer had also
passed time at Her Majesty's pleasure following a
more youthful misdemeanour concerning the opposite
sex, namely, living off immoral earnings. Perhaps,
though, his activities here had been misinterpreted
by the court, and had been meant as an 'artistic
statement' on one, or even both sides of the trans-
actions involved. It could even have been an early
exercise in control, which we know to be of particular interest to the individual concerned.

We can be sure, however, that all of the previously
mentioned are fantasists, indeed certain, because
they are, of course, one and the same person. Peter
Dexter has enjoyed various incarnations during his
existence thus far - thirteen to be precise. Here we
have someone who changes name with more regularity
than others may change clothing or certain reptiles
shed their skins. Yet, if the obvious analogy can be
forgiven, like the leopard never changing its spots,
Mr Dexter, in his various guises, displays a consistency in his anti-social and reprehensible leanings
that would cause some to question the worth of the

effect involved in flitting from one title to another. There are those amongst us who believe that what we see now is merely the muddled consequence of a life-long habit, that Mr Dexter will sometimes simply forget who he is meant to be and will re-introduce himself in mid-meeting without recourse to earlier actions. There is, though, a more troubling explanation, that within a culture or establishment where one's name and word are one's bond this distracting custom of altering labels of personal identification is itself a form of subversive attack on that establishment.

And certainly Mr Dexter views himself as in permanent conflict with the establishment, whatever his view of that body might be. Might it be the establishment which has failed to understand him, to tolerate his tenuous relationship with the truth, or to appreciate his self-serving cod-psychology on the meaning and purpose of art?

Almost all of those we have received testimony from regarding this individual communicated an enduring disquiet. Indeed, our investigations have been no easy matter for the partnership; deciphering a past as deliberately obfuscated as this one has called upon almost all of our resources and energies. Nevertheless, it is the examination of motive that has caused the greater upset; any attempt at re-creating the thought-processes present in the perverse mentality of our unwanted enemy has forced an intimacy with this character's desires that has left us with a profound sensation of degradation and despoilment. There are those amongst us who suspect that the required investigation had been engineered in such a way as to force any pursuant to immerse themselves in the very ordure that he has made his home. The fact that the good offices of the law have been soiled in this way has not been lost on influential partners. The call for retribution grows louder; 'Dextrus' will one day have cause to hear it at his peril.

At one stage, as Paul Barron, he was briefly involved
in the communications industry, offering his services
as a Public Relations consultant. There were, we understand, few takers, and his involvement in this
industry ended with his arrest, petrol can in hand,
as his premises began to be consumed in a fateful
blaze. Again, this experience may explain the course
of the more recent future episodes in his life.

Episodes such as that recounted have made for an
eventful life, and may well have taught him much with
regard to impressing his will upon the gullible, as
well as the benefits of piety. Whatever, on the
whole, whilst _eventful_, it can be said that this was
a harmless, if irritating, existence, and that is the
essence of our findings against him. We are not,
however, unanimous in this judgement. There are those
of us who find Mr Dexter's growing predilection for
graveyards deeply unsettling, and feel he is seeking
to arm himself for a direct confrontation with the
establishment, _our_ establishment. We are agreed that
we must use all of our _considerable_ means to ensure
he does not find a suitable weapon.

OKAY, so I've never had a proper girlfriend. What's a 'proper' girlfriend anyway – someone you neck with at the cinema, someone you excitedly introduce to your friends, if you have any? It's someone you form some sort of item with, like salt with pepper, sugar and spice, cats and dogs. But that's not the essential bit. A 'proper' girlfriend is someone you have sex with, isn't it? That's what we mean.

I think that there are people who are not fated to have this sex thing, to never actually do it. I think of myself and the series of disasters that have stood between me and 'it' – drunkenness, misunderstandings, missed opportunities. I mean, how can you tell when a girl is too tipsy, if you're just about to pass the point where it's still possible? I think of my failures and I curse my luck. I was born into a virgin's caste. Fate, why fight it? Then again, if I'm honest, I would have to say that there but for the grace of God I probably wouldn't go anyway. Under intense interrogation I would have to concede that, yes, you make your own luck, and that I have conspired to make mine the very worst luck conceivable. You have got to want 'it' if you are going to get 'it'. To *really* want it and whilst there have been times when I've truly, really, wanted it, but not from the point of enjoying it in its own right but for the sake of not being left out any more, for finally making it as one of the gang, the gang of lads. Just so that I would finally be thrown out of the eunuchs' den.

My problem isn't luck. I remember the time when I was in London, working at Grevant Safety, when the whole sham was going down and I was discovering my professional vocation as a PR man. Working late, night after night, drafting releases, sculpting the day's disasters into believable lies. Desperate, adrenaline-charged, exciting days. And there would be Sarah at my side by the operating table, shadowing my every move, mopping my brow and handing me the PR tools as I strove to keep the patient alive with my new-found talent for post-rationalisation and empty platitudes. Sarah was next to me the whole way, sharing the excitement. Only that wasn't all she wanted to share. We would be leaving at ten, and then knocking back a bottle of house red at Dino's taverna, munching through a plate of garlic bread and discussing how wonderfully well we were doing and how awful everyone else was and how overwhelming the situation was becoming. Chicken fritters with fries. Garlic mushrooms. She would load up her fork and push it at my mouth. Go on, try some Charles, try anything you want of mine.

Poor Sarah. She was already a big girl and these cholesterol feasts wouldn't have helped much. A thin film of sweat accumulated on her top lip as she wolfed down her fill, and I always wondered where else the moisture was gathering in the dank cavities hidden under her clothes. She would wait until the plates were taken away and then suggest that we could take our coffee at her place, or here, it didn't matter really. What would I prefer, go on, what would I like?

It is more relevant to think about what I would not like. To be there in her private space as she lights low lamps, sets her favourite mellow music to play and sings along in a shy voice. What do I take in my cup – want something with it? Go on. And above our heads, like a dark swollen cloud, hangs the expectation that something will happen, that something should happen. The moment is crying out for it – a kiss, a tender, delicate kiss, our first kiss. A garlic kiss. Would it be so bad? Please, don't go on.

Say, she had said at the restaurant, wouldn't it be great if we had to work like this all the time? She wasn't joking; the twelve hour days, the doubt whether there would still be an office waiting to return to the next morning, the waiting to be paid, the writing of releases with one eye to the press and one to the auditors, threatening to expose everything if the gloss became so thick it was misleading – she would happily cope with it all if we could work 'like this' all the time. Her hands were on mine when she said it. Sticky hands, garlic hands. And, yes, we are at the point again when I am going to let someone down, hurt someone by squirming out from under the weight of expectations she has of me, hoping that if I do this now she will be less hurt than she would be later, if I had gone to her place for coffee and she had sat beside me and pressed close waiting for me to make something happen. And I would never make anything happen; I'd be too afraid that if I went along with it all – the kissing, the fumbling, the awkward intimacy – then I wouldn't enjoy it. And if I didn't enjoy it I couldn't give anything back, and I would be letting her down, letting everyone down.

I think of Jules reaching out to me in a smoky Stockbridge bar, reaching out emotionally, literally, desperately, her hand on my arm. And I know I'm hurting her by pretending not to notice and fixing another drink to escape, for both of us to escape. This is the best way for it to be, even though it hangs over me like a guilty secret. I can't explain why I'm so cold. Can't explain. You wouldn't understand. *I* don't understand. The worst kind of loneliness just the thickness of a silk blouse away, the loneliness you feel when you are in a kiss and you realise that you don't enjoy its taste even though you can feel your partner throwing everything into it in the hope that you are. The loneliness of knowing that you can't offer what the other is yearning for, that you can't give anything back.

Sex is like success: there is no point having it unless you are going to be comfortable with it, and you won't get it unless you expect it. Maybe the answer is to teach yourself to be ruthless in the pursuit of it, to teach yourself not to care so that you won't feel inadequate when you are on the receiving end of a kiss and find yourself not giving a damn. Boxers learn how to take a punch. Maybe there's a way to steel yourself against the worst of the other. Teach yourself not to notice the pain, not to flinch or show any weakness. Andy could show me how to be assured. He's so much better at it all than me. He could teach me how to show the *signs* of giving something back. Maybe with him I really would be giving something back.

AT NINE-THIRTY the house lights dimmed for the first time since the show had begun. The effect on the crowd was immediate, a hush descending so that the only sound that could now be heard other than the occasional cough or titter of nervous laughter was the hissing of the gas lamps in the darkened stalls. Rennie hadn't insisted on this kind of build-up; it had been the management's idea, eager to feed the growing atmosphere of sensation that had already attached itself to this latest addition to their repertoire. He steadied himself in preparation, taking in the stale backstage air, surrendering to a moment's silent contemplation of the ropes, pulleys and rods of the apparatus hanging above. There was nothing in any of this to make him anxious, he reassured himself, nothing he had not faced before. Still, he had noticed in previous shows how his own voice would become more strident and aggressive once he was out there in front of them. Obviously he was prone to succumb to whatever tension there was in the moment. It was, he thought, worthy of some wonder that this kind of audience could instill a hidden fear in him when the other, and markedly more intelligent, ones of his past did not. He took a deep breath and smoothed down the whiskers of his beard. It still felt new to him, hardly a part of him at all. On the other side of the curtain he could hear someone clearing his throat. The master of ceremonies had stepped into the half-light of the extreme left sweep of the stage. Rennie listened intently, stroking his beard once more. It was important to stay calm if the routine was to be performed well.

'Ladies and gentlemen, the Alhambra Thee-at-ter is proud to present the world's finest, most *mysterious*, most *modern* and *scientific* mind-reader and entertainer extra-orr-din-arry, here in Glasgow, for your entertainment too-night, the *ree*-markable, the *in*-credible, Doc-torr *Ren*-dini!'

The applause was spontaneous even if right on cue, most of the audience grateful for any outlet for their nervous energies. They had been forced to endure over two hours of assorted tremulous Irish tenors, inept jugglers, ageing acrobats and feeble strongmen to arrive at this point, the one star attraction they had paid to see. Rennie nodded to the stage-hand waiting for his signal. A flurry of turning and cranking commenced and slowly the heavy scarlet drapes began to part. Rennie strode out and the applause continued.

He reached the centre spot and stood motionless, barely acknowledging the welcome. Prolong the build-up, they had told him, lengthen the act; anticipation is all. Rennie wondered how he could make himself appear more mysterious: perhaps a moody silence would be an option. Then there was his dress; he could not be persuaded to don the silk robes that others would have worn to provide a tantalising hint of the Orient. Rennie instead wore the same suit he had travelled in for the last six months, his one concession being the black deep-pocketed smock he had seen the magicians wearing; an eminently sensible notion, it was important to keep his jacket reasonably clean, and some subjects had shown an alarming tendency to drench his sleeves with saliva when yielding control. Not all the suggestions merited immediate rejection though; he had been tempted to explore the use of powder and paint to make up his face and perhaps he would try some dark eye shade next week to add a little intensity to his visual appeal. Rennie's hand moved slowly from his chin to the side pocket, gently patting the device hidden there. He closed his eyes for a second; it was there, it would work tonight like it always did, the one thing that had never let him down.

He was ready to begin.

'Thank you . . . Thank you! Ladies and gentlemen, you are very kind. This evening we have a very special show for your pleasure, a very special show to celebrate the coming of the new year. In three days' time it will be 1830. Are we ready for that?'

The response was muted: they hadn't expected to be addressed in such a manner. The attempt at jaunty good-humour had been strangled to a large extent by the stern authority he had learned to carry in his other life. The empathy of the performer didn't come naturally to Rennie, and he wondered what they made of him. Then there was the strange-ness of what he had actually said. He had meant to say 'Are you all looking forward to that?', but had let different words escape as he struggled with his lines. Now they didn't under-stand what he was getting at. He was being too mysterious.

'When the new year comes, ladies and gentlemen, we become new people. We make resolutions, promises, we become a year older. The world changes around us, and we change with it. Tonight, with the aid of science, we will give some of you the chance to become new, *different* people right now, days before the new year dawns. I can assure you that it will be a dazzling spectacle, a magical wonder . . . yes, truly, ladies and gentlemen . . . but to do this I will need volunteers. Now . . . who amongst you is willing to come forward and enjoy this unique experience?'

Rennie peered into the darkness ahead of him. There seemed little sign of any movement, and a mild panic set in. His instinct was to start up again, plead with them for co-operation straight away, but he had been warned not to do so; any obvious disappointment or worry on his part would make them even less likely to present themselves. Assume that they will, they had said, and they will. Yet could he believe that? Three weeks since the act had been unveiled, and the volunteers were drying up at the same rate as the show was selling out; it was becoming harder every night. Perhaps rumours of the condition of previous subjects had spread. Already, as a last resort, the stagehands had had to be primed and placed on stand-by to play the part if need be, though they were less than enthusiastic for the notion, having more reason than most to avoid active participation. Rennie turned to the side again, speaking to the wings.

'Can I have the chairs please. We will need six.' He pretended to be absorbed in the process as the chairs were brought on in pairs and were set to face the crowd from the centre of the stage. Still there was no one coming forward to fill them.

'Come now, ladies and gentlemen. We are looking for three brave fellows to come up and join me, the three bravest fellows in the Alhambra. Would they make themselves known?'

Rennie allowed himself a smile as the commotion at last stirred below. He had offered a challenge that few could resist, especially the foolhardy. The first of the aspirant performers appeared at the end of the stage, picking his way through the dazzling footlights to clamber up towards Rennie.

'And do we have three lovely lasses in the house to join these handsome fellows? Remember, ladies, you could meet the man of your dreams right up here, tonight. You might share something with one of these lads that will bond your hearts for eternity . . .'

He cupped his whiskery chin between forefinger and thumb, caressing himself with slow, indulgent strokes as he considered his words. '. . . because that's what I offer, ladies and gentlemen. *Eternity* . . .'

Two other men had just joined his first guest when Rennie heard a cheer from the back of the hall. He motioned for the combined group to sit together in one cluster to the left, and then turned back to see what had caused the latest stir. The sound of sporadic clapping was rippling through the rows towards the stage. Out of the darkness he could see two women gingerly making their way to the front; two young women possibly still in their teens, clinging on to each other lest they collapse in a fit of nervous cackling. Rennie's eye fixed on the straggly ringlets of hair, the dirty lace brocades, tatty shawls and clumsy gait of the pair as they gradually progressed forward. Cheap girls, he thought. Glasgow tarts. Still, they would do, the show could begin. It was important the show could begin.

FILE NOTE: DEXTER VS ESTABLISHMENT, BRODIE,
        ASSOCIATIONS WITH

When we learn that 'Dexter' is also 'Dextrus', and
that he considers himself to be an heir to Alexander
Brodie, and indeed, plans to rekindle the latter's
ruinous experimentation, our sense of alarm is
magnified to an unparalleled degree. Brodie is a
name we have known well. Brodie was once one of us,
but slipped into the other side. Brodie felt he had
been underestimated and sacrificed everything that
is precious in pursuit of immortality. Have we been
negligent in underestimating 'Dexter' likewise?
Questions were asked as to how the partners had
failed to spot the handiwork of Brodie's shadowy
genius in the device that had been brought to the
partnership's premises. It had been there for all to
see, but some of us had been blinded by the obscene,
and had failed to see beyond it. We take full responsibility and bow to the greater experience of the
previous partners in these matters. They tell us how
Brodie had threatened the establishment to its very
foundation. The measures taken to quell his actions
were in themselves the most extraordinary the
partners had ever conceived. We had hoped that they
would never have to be repeated. Sadly, we concluded,
that time might be approaching.

Brodie had sought immortality. Ironically, we had
had to surrender some of ours to silence him. Brodie
was a jewel within the highest profession of them
all, and who still casts a dark stain on the history
of medicine. Brodie was a fallen angel. Like the
devil himself.

'AND YOUR NAME, SIR? Alan? . . . Another Alan. Ladies and Gentlemen, a big hand for Alan from? Partick . . . Alan from Partick, yes. Pay attention, please, Alan from Partick. Try thinking of your favourite colour, please, whilst we . . .'

'Blue.'

'Sorry?'

'I said, blue.'

Rennie paused. Sometimes the volunteers had been drinking before the shows and this could affect the quality of their response. Sometimes nerves overcame them once they were up in front of everyone. Sometimes they were just plain stupid.

'Alan, I asked you to *think* about your favourite colour, not to *tell* me it. If you had been paying attention you would have noticed that, wouldn't you? Now the audience isn't going to think I'm the greatest mind-reader if I tell them your favourite colour is blue now, are they?'

Rennie's obvious sarcasm drew bursts of laughter from the crowd but this only seemed to encourage the antics of the errant guest who now stood up to take a bow as well, fooling to the delight of the audience who cheered their approval.

'Settle down . . .'

The instruction drew little response. Rennie found himself cast in the role of flustered schoolteacher, trying vainly to retain order in an unruly class. Worse, the contagion was spreading; the other subjects had begun to smirk and wave, peering into the gloom, searching for more encouragement. Rennie knew he lacked the stagecraft to bring them all back to order. This way of life had not been of his choosing; it was more a desperate means to an end, and a laboratory, of sorts, for his experiments. He looked to the grinning jester who continued to cavort in his moment of fame. A hand went inside Rennie's smock, seeking out the smooth shiny side of the tool hidden inside. Rennie's fingers found the wind-up arm and discreetly added a few extra turns, his growing sense of vexation telling him a strong dose was called for here.

The two girls still awaited their formal introduction, but Rennie chose to ignore them for the moment, fixing his last charge with a malign stare.

'Alan. Sir . . . Mr Alan of Partick, please sit, and *think* of your true love . . . *think*, if you will. Do not speak, think please . . . of her name.'

Rennie watched the wayward volunteer settle back into his chair. The boy closed his eyes in mock concentration, smiling leeringly with the pleasure the thought of his true love brought. Rennie walked over and squatted before him, side-on to the audience. He took the other's hands in his, clasping them together as if leading him to prayer.

'You are thinking of your true love's name, sir? Please nod . . .'

The young man nodded, mouth curved in a vacuous smile, eyes closed. Rennie smiled too, turning to face his audience and offering a comical impersonation of his subject's expression. Rennie was encouraged by the sound of laughter in the stalls to continue with his efforts, squeezing his face tighter from top to bottom, broadening the grin as far as he could. The laughter grew more raucous. He knew all eyes were on him. Deftly, shielding it from view, he quickly drew the device from his pocket. His facial contortions were proving an effective distraction; even the other volunteers sitting close by would have struggled to notice as he slipped it between the clasped hands of his unwitting accomplice.

'Alan from Partick, I want you to think of a kiss from your loved one. Can you do that? Please nod . . .'

Rennie didn't even wait for a response before releasing the catch at the base of the implement. The device began to buzz and vibrate at once, discharging waves that seemed to jolt through the subject from his hands up his arms to his chest and torso until his whole body was locked in spasm. Rennie strained to keep his hands wrapped around his volunteer's as the jerky motions threatened to throw the device to the other side of the theatre. It was as if the now barely conscious figure was making an instinctive attempt to escape it. Gradually, after almost half a minute, the powered motions of the device began to slow, and Rennie released his grip, tucking his instrument stealthily into his pouch as he stood back up. He felt exhausted and drained; almost as shocked as the audience whose shrieks he felt like adding to. The power of his invention was capable of surprising even himself, every extra turn on the wind-up capable of stunning a horse. Why had he let his temper dictate the dosage he had just given? How was he going to revive the figure now slumped on the chair?

'Ladies and gentlemen, when I asked Alan to think of his true love's kiss I did not imagine it would be quite as strong as that!' Rennie mopped his brow as the crowd howled in appreciation. He had them now, had their attention. They did not care about the state of those up on the stage although they might occasionally pretend to. They were just like the other crowds he had once performed for – they only cared about themselves, and they wanted to be entertained.

'Yes, ladies and gentlemen, what a kiss . . . shall we find out who gave it to him?'

Rennie smiled benignly at the two girls, sitting opposite the row of men. They stared at the prone body. Rennie waited until the audience's impatience communicated itself to them, and they returned his gaze.

'And you, dear, what is your name?'

The reply that came back was more a murmur than a proper response. Rennie found his patience snapping in exasperation. Why did these fools volunteer themselves if they couldn't speak clearly enough for the audience to hear them?

'No . . . No . . . you will have to be louder than that, my dear. Will you please tell us your name?'

'Jeannette Reilly.'

'Ahh . . . Jeannette . . . thank you!' The sarcasm had returned to Rennie's voice. He stared dispassionately at the girl. There was fear in her eyes. Rennie continued, enjoying the confident superiority he now had. It was important he took control. 'And where are you from, Jeannette?'

'. . . G . . . Gallowgate.'

'Gallowgate? How lovely! And is your friend from Gallowgate as well?'

The two nodded glumly.

'And what is she called?'

'Bernadette.'

'Jeannette and Bernadette – and you'll be sisters, won't you?'

They nodded again, wary, timorous, like two abandoned animals waking in the wolf's lair. The thin smile that formed on Rennie's lips was real enough, though the audience could have been forgiven for thinking it was part of the act, a pantomime villain conducting the trial of the innocents. The truth was Rennie relished the display of such cartoon cruelties: it meant he did not have to hide his contempt for those around him, both on and off the stage. The ill-informed, the illiterate, the sentimental and avaricious, all here in search of cheap thrills, eager to pass the responsibility of amusing themselves onto others. What had they done to deserve *him*? No matter that the earnings he was on the verge of making here would comfortably exceed any he would ever have made in medicine, no matter that the popular acclaim he would enjoy as an entertainer would far surpass any measure of fame he would ever have gained as a pioneering surgeon, no matter that here he had total control over an audience that *wanted* to believe in his magic rather than bay sceptically at his bold theories; no matter for any of this, this was the wrong arena for a man of his talents, strictly second-best, a mockery of all he had hoped to achieve. How many of them had any notion of the real depth of his skills? How many of them had a notion as to who he *really* was? Rennie gently fingered the bristle of his chin, the tips finding the corners of his smile. If, he thought, some of these unfortunates, from time to time, paid a price for their ignorance then it could only be a balancing of dues and slight revenge for the travesty that meant he had to be there. Besides, it wasn't even him who was perpetrating these acts – it was the great *Doctor* Rendini.

The girls waited anxiously for his next move.

'So, tell me, Jean-*ette* and Berna-*dette* from Gallow-*get*, do you ever frequent the Partick area?'

The shaking of heads told Rennie this was not the case. He raised a dictatorial arm to quell the derisive laughter that he himself had instigated with his mock inquisition.

'So you have never visited that fine part of the city or met young Alan before?'

Again the pair shook their heads as if their questioner were accusing them of some heinous crime. The audience snorted and wheezed its delight.

'So you can tell us *nothing* of young Alan?'

Rennie paused, extending his reach towards the girls so it seemed that he was almost re-introducing them to the crowd. The gesture combined with his impassive stare to communicate something deeper, almost disturbing; there they are ladies and gentlemen, tonight's feast, quivering and helpless just as you wanted them.

'Who shall we start with, ladies and gentlemen? Which of these two lovely young lassies will surprise us by telling us all about Alan?'

Rennie let his arm drift so that it moved from pointing at Jeannette, the brown-haired girl who had spoken for both of them, to the one who had not spoken at all, the redhead, Bernadette. He lingered when the latter was in his sights, raising an eyebrow in a subtle acknowledgement of the audience's choice. He let his arm fall and took three short strides towards her, kneeling down and studying her freckled young face in fascination.

'You have nothing to be frightened of, my dear, nothing at all. Why so shy all of a sudden? We are hoping you can talk to us about Alan. Do you think you can do that?'

The girl sunk into her shoulders, avoiding Rennie's unwavering eye. He continued the chase regardless.

'I think you might astonish us. I think you might astonish us if you can think of Alan, and Partick . . . can you *think*?'

167

Rennie was pleased his provocative, double-edged question met with noisy appreciation from the floor. Once more he had found the necessary distraction as he withdrew the device from its pocket again. He had it wedged between the girl's tight, clammy hands before anyone could notice. This time the procedure would be more difficult; the discharge would have to be regulated and controlled if it were not to overwhelm the recipient. Ideally, he would do this manually, winding the toy clockwise whilst the guard was set to 'off'. Yes, he thought, a gentle stirring of the soul. But that was not what anyone had paid to see; they wanted fireworks, sparks and all. At least the girl was callow and bowed, with green eyes flashing under blinking red lashes that spoke of the powerful foreboding she felt as he bore down on her. Negative emotions were more powerful than positive ones, he had learned. She would be all the more ready to receive the dry taste of fear on her tongue.

'Are you thinking of him then, lassie? . . . Eh?'

Rennie was able to hold both her hands together with just one of his, leaving the other free to stroke the wind-up arm in a slow circular motion. The girl's head slumped forward as he did so, drooling and thrusting towards Rennie, and into the audience's direct view. She looked as if she had passed out, issuing a sound somewhere between a sigh and a retch. Rennie felt a rush of irritation coursing through his veins. It was better when they stayed upright so that the audience could see the subject's eyes, even if they were tightly closed. Then they would know it was no illusion. He quickly cranked the winding arm round and round, snapping his heels together as he jumped back onto his feet. He flicked the catch free at the base of the device and turned to the audience.

He was thinking of what to say, what cutting remark with which to open the next round of questioning, when the sudden wailing interrupted his concentration. The girl was standing, teetering comically on unsteady heels, but standing all the same. Her mouth was half-closed, chewing on an unspoken word like a drunk. It was her sister who was making the noise on her behalf, screeching in horror at the state her beloved had found herself in. Rennie sensed an abrupt stillness in the audience. None of them dared move in case they missed anything or drew attention to themselves. They knew they were witnessing something extraordinary. Rennie let himself savour the triumph. Yes, ladies and gentlemen, he thought, something *in*-credible, something *ree*-markable, something *extra-orr-din-arry*. The man of mystery had arrived.

HENRY HUGHES of Standard Mutual was quite forthright when he spoke to me. 'Art?' he said. 'This isn't art. It's a pile of shit.'

He'd called me over so that I could see for myself. Unfortunately, he was absolutely right – it *was* a pile of shit, literally.

He'd called me over so that I could see for myself, so that he could tell me he was sending me the bill for its uplift and disposal, face to face. And so that he could fire me. Face to face. This was bad enough but it wasn't the cruellest part, the cruellest and most ironic part.

'I've got an MD wondering why I agreed to the company displaying a piece of modern art I had never seen, this unknown work that you had told me would be so innovative, so distinct. What do I tell him? Do I tell him that I agreed because I trusted you, Charles, that I trusted KFC? Or do I just tell him I was stupid? Come on! What do I tell him? You are the communications people. What do you say?'

What did I say? What could I say? I could not speak, it was so overwhelming – the smell, the affront, the sheer crap-shade colour of it all. Henry Hughes was angry. He wasn't enjoying this. Behind him, through the plate-glass doors to Standard Mutual's reception I could see the gaggle peering out. Every grade of clerical class, from secretary to security man, manager to mail boy, all united in their disbelief. And behind me, though I hardly dared look, the passing pedestrians and street traffic who had stopped in their masses to enjoy the show – The Resurrectionist Show, as produced by Peter Dexter.

And, ladies and gentlemen, what a show it was. Starring Henry Hughes as the Marketing Manager whose career was on the line for his ill-advised decision to display an unseen work of art on his company's doorstep. Also starring Charles 'Charlie' Kidd as the

Public Relations professional whose career wasn't so much on the line as deeply immured in the six-foot-high dung heap he found himself now staring at in a silent mesmeric trance. And introducing Andy Adriano as the quasi-romantic lead brought here by his inferior superior to lend smouldering gravitas to the otherwise surreal scene.

Act one. Aforementioned Public Relations professional fixes deal with aforementioned Marketing Manager for aforementioned company to exhibit an unseen (by either) exhibit from eponymous exhibition. Gentlemen's agreement agreed, including six-figure sponsorship deal by which the aforementioned exhibit will be leased to aforementioned sponsor for permanent display. Act two. Ten-thirty a.m., three weeks later. Uncredited extras arrive at aforementioned company headquarters, citing aforementioned agreement to exhibit aforementioned exhibit on steps leading to aforementioned HQ on Lothian Road. Extras spend next two hours building platform on aforementioned steps. Act three. Dumper truck appears to deposit fifteen tonnes (approx) of animal manure (uncredited) on aforementioned platform. Aforementioned 'pile of shit', however, is no ordinary dung heap, being instead *'Nastiness '98'*, the bold new work created for aforementioned sponsor by 'The Dexter Collective Art Collective' (sic) as part of aforementioned deal. Act four. Aforementioned Marketing Manager calls aforementioned Public Relations professional. Requests urgent presence to discuss urgent problem. Act five. The arrival and slow death (professional, literal) of aforementioned Public Relations professional.

'Well, what *do* you fucking say? What do your KFC have to say about this?'

I didn't have anything to say. Dexter had never shown me the script.

But Henry Hughes was still angry. He wanted words. Not necessarily an apology, just words that he could chew up and spit back at me, just to prove how angry he was. He was wearing a dark green suit, the same one he always wore. It was probably very expensive but had creased terribly, unlike his hair which was dead straight, held in place by some sort of gel, or wax stuff, perhaps axle grease, so that not a single strand was out of place. His head hair seemed a tint or two darker, more hennaed than that on his top lip, which had a distinctly ginger hue. As I watched the moustache twitch in anger, I found myself absently pondering why the two should be shades apart. He was using everything to articulate his rage. To show everyone how angry he was. Right now, that was important to him.

And I was letting him down with my silence. It was taking all my effort just to stand upright without burying my head in my hands. Andy stepped in, bewildered, but trying valiantly to be discreet, voice low and contrite.

'Look, err . . . Mr Hughes. Want us to arrange anything? Have you got this lot being taken away?'

Words to chew and spit.

'*You?* Organise anything? Think I'd let you near Standard Mutual ever again? Don't you bother, mister . . .' Henry Hughes took a few steps to get himself sufficiently close to me in case I'd somehow missed him. 'DON'T YOU *DARE* BOTHER!'

Andy came over, too, stepping between myself and the aforementioned shouting bastard. I wasn't aware there was a space but was grateful all the same. The moustache had drawn dangerously close and I'd begun to wonder if it had a life of its own. That at least would account for the difference in colour. Andy's voice carried a shaky authority, like a policeman going down in the middle of a riot. '. . . Steady . . .'

Act six, the cruelly ironic part.

'I've got someone else sorting out this mess,' offered Henry Hughes. 'A *real* P R agency. Clarke-Scott at Rutland Square, on a crisis management contract to keep this fiasco out of the press. *You'll* be paying for them as well, invoiced directly to your lot. All I want *you* to organise is getting your financial compensation ready, *understand*?'

All that effort, all that networking, all those calls. Just to create a golden opportunity for *another* agency. Andy gently steered me away. I felt like I would cry.

Act seven, the *epilogue*: As I was led from the scene and caught the appreciative glances of the enthralled onlookers I felt my first moment of insight into what this might have all been about. Performance art. Acts one to six, of course. The mound of excrement was a sideshow, a mere prop, it was always meant to be. *We*, the aforementioned Marketing Manager, PR man and his colleague, were the exhibits. It had all been set up to create a situation whereby we would be the show.

And I would be the punchline.

Perhaps Henry Hughes at Standard Mutual should have been grateful – at least his exhibit didn't set off a security alarm. That was the fate of Scottish Provincial whose 'set of contemporary erotic/neurotic sculptures' which had been left overnight in the foyer pending the return to the office of the marketing executive whose career was also about to be on the line for authorising their display without seeing them, began, inexplicably, to vibrate and hum ominously, thus triggering the sensitive infra-red alarm system; and further thus a full-scale emergency drill. Irate fire and police chiefs were to subsequently ask just why a respected Edinburgh financial giant had deemed it necessary to store such a collection of tacky plastic, made-in-Taiwan, battery-powered and time-set dildos on their premises. Sheila Clements, the relevant marketing executive, subsequently declined to offer such an answer, preferring instead to take a prolonged period of sick-leave to recover from the stress of that particular morning's alarm call, coming as it did from the Chairman and Chief Executive of the Scottish Provincial Group. Ms Clements had further added to the confusion of the situation by failing to recognise the urgency and sincerity behind this initial call, telling the (what she took to be) crank caller to 'Piss Off', and was only subsequently persuaded of the now even more irate inquisitor's authenticity by a series of follow-up calls. Once his identity had been established, however, she was able to take decisive action, faxing an immediate personal apology to the Chief Exec's private office, cancelling all appointments for the next two weeks, and throwing first an epic tantrum and then the best part of thirty valium pills down her throat before withdrawing to a darkened room in tear-stained nightie with a thumb in her mouth. Explicit instructions were left that the protective cocoon would only be left once the whole ghastly episode was dealt with. Erotic/Neurotic, quite.

I heard all this from one of the team at Barr Associates, the PR company Scottish Provincial had hired to sort them out of their mess. They had called me, like any professional communications consultancy, to gloat over their new account win, and to ensure I appreciated just how good they were. They also took the opportunity to brief me as to what my 'line' was to be should any journalists contact me in the hunt for more facts. My 'line', it subsequently transpired, was to refer all enquiries to Barr Associates who were on a lucrative damage limitation contract. Although I did have the option of entertaining such questions myself should I feel sufficiently confident of the outcome of the legal proceedings Scottish Provincial would invoke against KFC in the event that I supplied any information regarding the exhibition sponsorship to the press.

Barr Associates sounded very competent, committed and capable, totally focused on their client's case. I wondered if they might help sort me out. What should my line be on everything else? On Henry Hughes' mysterious moustache, on the whole Charles Kidd issue? Was it too late for damage limitation? Was there anything left worth redeeming?

Barr Associates, though, had a tough enough brief without me. After Dexter's press conference in the delicatessen – the one which had ended with another dildo display – newspaper interest had finally been aroused in the dealings of the Dexter/Dextrus gang. A gang of which I, presumably, was now a suspected member. The calls had been flowing into KFC for over two weeks, and increasing now that rumours of the Standard Mutual debacle were spreading. Were we really going to resurrect the dead with this device? Were our sponsors happy to be associated with this kind of activity? Didn't we appreciate that some would see the joke – assuming it was all a joke – as being in the poorest of taste? My line on such enquiries, pre-Barr Associates marking their client's territory by pissing on me, had been to deny everything and anything – no, nothing of the kind was being considered. Now, a different strategy was required, one where I would cunningly use non-communication as a form of communication. One where I would hope that the media would get the message by not getting the message. Perhaps such a strategy is difficult for the non-professional to understand, but basically, in purely *technical* terms, I diverted all calls to Andy who would say I was in a meeting, and then I wouldn't return them.

Perhaps it sounds deceptively simple, though it wasn't simple at all. A strategy like this is the product of a trained mind with years of experience. When it comes to non-communication, to hiding behind silence and marching under the white flag of surrender, some of us are in a league quite of our own.

So the battle lines, if you chose to call them that, were drawn. On one side the screaming hordes of the press, ever on the attack, and on the other, the dogs of war, the mercenary forces parachuted in at short notice to repel them – the Clarke-Scotts and Barr Associates. Irresistible force meets movable object.

The war was being fought on three fronts: the search for the true identity and motivation of Peter Dexter/Pablo Dextrus; the search for the true legacy of the 'Resurrectionist' years of Edinburgh's past; and the search for the truth about the dark genius of the shamed Alexander Brodie, inventor of the shiny vibrator Dexter had buzzed the crowd with. It was the latter aspect that had added a new dynamic to the reportage of the whole affair. I could tell by the tone and type of enquiry being made that the portrayal of Dexter's group was changing from one of harmless mavericks to dangerous renegades up to something fraudulent or sinister. Or both. A threat to us all. Did they, the educated and informed ranks of journalists, really believe this, or did it just make for a better story to chase? Whatever, the muscle used by Standard Mutual and Scottish Provincial to 'kill' coverage (Andy told me third-hand of the threats to pull all future advertising from any title publishing anything that might cause embarrassment in this regard) only seemed to drive the reporters' interest deeper underground. Graverobbing was suddenly a hot news item again. I was walking along the street and I saw the tacky hoarding outside the newsagent's advertising the evening paper's screaming lead story – *Sick Exhibition Stunt Slammed by Outraged City Leaders*. I didn't bother buying it to satisfy the brief pang of curiosity I felt with regard to whether the city leaders were outraged before the paper goaded them about the exhibition, or merely after it. I wondered whether 'Outraged City Leader' was an elected title like Lord Mayor or Provost, and if so just how outraged did you have to be to stand a chance of winning it? No, I didn't buy the *Evening* bloody *Bugle*, I just wanted to run away from it all, all this coverage we had generated. Already the *Scottish Sunday Review* (without naming corporate names) ran a full two-page feature on the artistic community's fascination with the notorious (although no one had heard of him before) Archibald Brodie, he of a suspected murderous past. One collective had even proposed repeating one of his experiments with the dead as an 'artistic statement'. What next?, it asked, and wasn't the most troubling element the involvement of big business in bankrolling this macabre activity? The fabulously named *Glasgow International Herald* – just thinking about the contradictions inherent in the title used to give me a migraine each morning before all this shit hit the fan – took the opportunity to remind its readers that this kind of thing is liable to happen when 'the arts get out of hand', which of course gave them the opportunity to revisit – in words and glorious pictures – previous incidents which had also presumably left city leaders outraged; dead sheep in formaldehyde as sculpture, excremental canvasses as portraiture, plastic surgery as a statement. Here was a lesson in having your cake and gorging on it. An opinion former in *The Scottish Citizen* managed to file a fierce piece criticising the other titles for rewarding 'this warped and deranged masquerade of a spectacle posing as an exhibition' with the 'oxygen of publicity they obviously sought' whilst at the same time padding out his feature with five columns worth of his theories on graverobbing and whether our show went anywhere towards proving any of them. This was a dangerous article, the first to tap into the dark underside of Dexter's studied theatrics. Edinburgh, it argued, has spent a hundred and fifty years reassuring itself that the graverobbing epidemic of its past was fuelled only by a need for bodies in the medical lecture theatres. But there had been a point where demand became so large that it eventually led to widespread murder. Burke and Hare were just two of many who eventually bypassed the cemeteries in order to fulfil that demand. What if the bodies had been used for something else? What if there was an even more macabre secret still hiding in the city's shadows? Was it conceivable that so many corpses had been required for simple teaching purposes?

The *Citizen* piece appeared in mid-August. Ironically enough, its author – a chronic alcoholic – died three days later in hospital, after a failed liver transplant.

Hostilities immediately intensified, and my phone would not stop ringing. They all wanted to know about Dexter, the who, the why, the when. He was a wanted man – I hoped he would be happy. For me, all I could do was watch from the sidelines, powerless to intervene. For me, the only pleasure was to watch the fighting take place on a battlefield I had, unwittingly, helped design. For me, the war was over.

Of the remaining sponsors, two notified their withdrawal by fax and one by a solicitor's letter sent registered post that I actually had to sign for in front of the rest of the office. Nobody asked any questions or offered words of condolence. KFC were in for a heavy hit; all the would-be contributors wanted their money back, and threatened to sue for its return. Dexter was predictably uncontactable, the cash predictably untraceable. I, no longer even a drowning man, more a ghost amongst living beings, visible only to himself. The days went by in quiet contemplation, watching them all busy themselves like bees in an empty hive, empty and deprived of its queen, with Nick strangely absent. 'Down south, in the big smoke . . .' I heard Jules explain. 'Chasing something big, a deal . . . a buy-out . . . maybe a buy-in . . . something big.'

The word was he was pulling off something to save his skin and was negotiating with a multinational consultancy who were presumably keen to own a share of a dwindling Edinburgh agency. 'Network, stupid,' said Jules, explaining how we might become one more dot on a mega-corp's map. 'They all want a world network in order to offer a full service to their global-thinking American and Japanese clients.' Hmmm. It was too complicated for me. I was puzzled as to why such clients would feel comforted to know they had access to a failing concern in Scotland. In my own small way I had contributed to this – not the fact that we were a dying company, although some credit is undoubtably due – no, the fact that we might have appeared a worthwhile outpost in someone else's empire. Clearing out my desk, I'd noticed that my cuttings collection had already gone, spirited away as ammunition in Nick's crusade to persuade down in the smoke. 'Of course KFC are extremely well connected,' he would be telling the would-be buyers. 'Plugged into the financial groups, banks and fund operators, together of course with the journalist lobby who report on them. Plugged into all Edinburgh's vibrant industries and, indeed, its artistic community. I will leave a copy of recent coverage for your perusal . . .' And, *of course*, he would have been right. We *were* well connected, at least we *had been* up until the point when he had left. Now it was history. How was I going to be able to tell him?

But this wasn't the important part, the vital consideration. It wasn't the thought of how I could break the news, or even whether I should resign before being fired that was preoccupying me as I sat at my desk, vainly trying to think globally. It was more fundamental. I watched in increasing detachment, wondering why anybody bothered. What did it mean, the phone calls, the pleading, the faxing of releases heralding the arrival of xxx Copiers super-gold-ruby-platinum-teflon-formica-topped photocopy machine service. What purpose did any of it really have? I thought of Dexter and how he had fatally punctured any faith I might have had in this way of life; and I thought of my own overwhelming sense of failure at having ever been so stupid as to believe that I had found somewhere where I belonged. That I could make any sort of worthwhile impression in a world inhabited by the Nick Kennedy's, Henry Hughes's, Sheila Clements's. Peter Dexter too – whoever he was. What was his plan, they all wanted to know? I didn't know. I only knew what he was doing to me, and how close he was to success. He was teasing. Teasing me. Teasing me into suicide.

Jules was chirpy again. I suspected some kind of change, another man in her life promising everything, offering to be the part of the equation that would make her whole – a 'proper' boyfriend. I feared for the worst, another shit gently squeezing her clammy hand at the appropriate moment in their lovemaking, saying nothing but promising everything with a look in his eyes. Promising everything with his silence. Promising, what? Nothing, Jules. Can't you see it's all an assumption on your part. You are setting yourself up to be hurt again; they all offer nothing. That's what we mean by a 'proper' boyfriend, isn't it, Jules – one that hurts you.

It was festival time. Jules was excited, reading the *Fringe Guide* over and over, seeking out the hidden gems of the programme. Her diary was full, tickets bought and bookings booked for almost every night of the three-week binge. 'Comedy stuff, drama stuff, dance stuff, music and some stuff I don't know what it is!' She was even more excited about this than the proposed buy-out/buy-in/ buy-in-out-up-down that Nick was still negotiating down south. 'Gonna be big, Charlie. It's gonna be bloody big.'

And who was I to argue? What did I know of how these things worked, how anything worked? Jules was heading to a secret show. She didn't seem to mind that she couldn't keep it a secret. 'You respond to this personal ad thing and they send you some stuff and if they like your stuff you get an invite to somewhere nobody knows. Bloody exciting!'

Someone had liked Jules's stuff. That was more than could be said for me. Even I didn't like my stuff, any of it. I hated it and everything it stood for. There were parts of me that I loathed more than anything or anyone I'd ever known, including almost every aspect of my loathsome character. I despised the face in front of me in the mirror every morning. The things its sleep pallor betrayed. My indecision. My willingness to be led. My stubborn refusal to ever assert myself. My inability to share anything other than my low esteem.

I hated myself as if I were another person, someone I could arrange to meet in a darkened alley and then beat senseless. I would have kicked that apology for a man as he was flat on the floor, kicked him for his lack of backbone. His indecision. I was ready to cut my own throat just to spite my own indecision, to prove it wrong for once just to laugh at it, face to face, in my final moments. See?, I would say, I've done it. Done for both of us.

'**W**HERE ARE YOU FROM?'

'Partick.'

The audience gasped.

'What is your favourite bar?'

'The Old Smiddy Inn.'

There was another audible intake of breath in the crowd. One voice, isolated from the rest, began to sob.

'Who is your true love? Who do you dream of kissing?'

'Agnes Calder.'

This time there was a mixture of shock and laughter, the latter being the minority force.

'... and ... what is your name, dear child?'

'Alan ... Alan Dalziel.'

The words had barely escaped her lips as the applause began, followed by a stamping of feet on the Alhambra's wooden floor. Then the cheering – Rennie liked the cheering – and then the laughter again as elements in the crowd shouted their own ribald suggestions.

'Ask her what she keeps in her breeks?'

'Tell us whit a guid man like her can offer a lassie!'

'An whit *she* wants frae a wummin!'

Rennie was happy to let the suggestions fly. Prolong the act, they had said. Besides, they would be all the more likely to listen attentively once this steam had been let off. And that's what it was, he thought. Steam, or hot air – a shallow refuge for those that were frightened or unwilling to acknowledge what they had just seen, the transference of one person's soul to another. But played for laughs, they hoped.

The girl's sister was beginning to be overwhelmed with

hysteria, tugging at her sibling's sleeve, struggling to find a voice with which to scream.

'Bernadette . . . please, Bernadette . . . ohh my lord! Bernadette . . . ohh poor Jesus! . . . Bernadette . . .'

The words went round and round in a soft and rapidly hoarse whisper, like the incantation of the rosary. Hail Bernadette, mother of grace. Rennie made no effort to stop it, or to comfort its author. No; prolong the act, this was part of the show.

There was, of course, a way in which he could have calmed the distraught sister – he held it in his pocket. One charge would be enough if she could be persuaded to hold the device for a few moments, and his experience of the previous nights had taught him that she probably could. Yes, she could, if she were told that by doing so she would bring back her loved one, which, in a way, she would. But Rennie had barely started with Bernadette; there was still enjoyment to be had with her.

'Is there a Bernadette Reilly here?'

Rennie faced the audience as he asked his question. There was no reply.

'Is there an Alan Dalziel, from Partick?'

He still faced the hall. The reply came from behind him, to the renewed amusement of those who watched.

'Then would he come forward and make himself known?'

'I'm here, here!'

Rennie turned and found the young red-haired girl had walked from her chair to stand by his side.

'I'm pleased to meet you, Mr Dalziel.' Rennie offered his hand. The girl shook it with hers. 'Tell me, see that girl over there that you were sitting beside. What do you think of her – is she bonny?'

'Och . . . She's alright, I suppose.'

'Not as fancy as Agnes Calder?'

The redhead was a picture of embarrassment as she mumbled and looked to her feet. There was no hint of confusion that her own footwear was similar to that of the 'lassie' she was judging. Rennie continued.

'. . . Because Agnes Calder is your true love?'

'Aye . . .'

The one-word reply sent the crowd's clamour to new heights. Rennie let it run its course as his subject shifted awkwardly, disturbed that her innermost feelings seemed to be the cause of such hilarity.

'Tell me then, Alan. Are you a strong lad?'

The girl was more guarded now, wary that the audience seemed to find it so easy to laugh at her.

'Maybe.'

'Oh come now, Alan. Surely you Partick lads have iron in your bones? I'd have thought that you were a hardy soul?'

'Maybe.'

'Well, I tell you, why don't we see how strong you really are then?'

Rennie turned to the two male volunteers who were still sitting on either side of the prone figure of the original 'Alan from Partick'. Their expressions of ashen terror made it clear they were beginning to regret forwarding themselves as Dr Rendini's raw material. Of the two men, the one to the right was the heavier-built, a portly gentleman with a ruddy face, sweating in a tweed jacket, black trousers and scuffed boots. He must have been about twenty-eight, thought Rennie. Twenty-eight and sixteen stone. How could the poor afford to indulge their stomachs like this? Rennie wagged a finger to usher him forward. He was reluctant to leave the relative safety of his chair, but stepped forward tentatively all the same. The weight of the crowd's expectations meant it had to be so.

Rennie laid an arm around his shoulder and turned him towards the girl.

'Well then, Alan. Do you think that a fine strong lad such as yourself would have the brawn to lift a full-figured man like this? I will be surprised if you can, and I will tell you, all the people here will think that you are a real mighty fellow if you can.'

This was another challenge that Rennie knew his subject would find hard to refuse, even without the encouragement of the crowd who were now bellowing for an attempt to be made.

The girl stepped forward to face her load, her face barely reaching his chest – a comical sight as she earnestly sized up the task. The audience hushed as she squatted, bending her knees to go lower, and then wrapped her thin arms around the man's generous buttocks. A sharp intake of breath and she moved up again, straining audibly as the man's feet were lifted from the stage and her own took his full weight. Even Rennie found himself surprised at the sight. It was a marvel; the mighty atom lifting an impossible haul, like an ant carrying a leaf many times its size. He watched the two tottering on the spindly heels of the shy, young Gallowgate hussy who had taken to the stage but half an hour ago, spinning round in proud achievement. Yes, he reflected, not hiding his amusement. This was truly a strong lad with iron in his bones.

I SIT THERE killing time. There is nowhere left to go. I'm slipping down, deep down, and there is nowhere left to go. I'm killing time and the effort overwhelms me.

Edinburgh was going to be where I was meant to make it all happen. After London. Where I'd failed to make anything happen. It was meant to be an easier place, less competitive. Maybe that was the crucial mistake I had made, not dropping far enough down in the Public Relations league in order to find a standard where I would excel by comparison with my contemporaries. Where might someone at my level of competence expect to play? Perhaps in Eastern Europe there would be agencies keen to sign me so that I could handle local media work in their less sophisticated environments. Maybe working on the marketing strategy of the Murmansk Festival of Screechy Tuneless Music; or perhaps further afield in, say, Mongolia, sorting out press packs at Ulan Bator's Yak of the Year Show. And if that was still too demanding perhaps there was some undiscovered Amazon tribe still living in the Stone Age who would appreciate my professional input at the launch of that season's designer collection of penis gourds.

I must have looked ready to explode. The one person who had done more than anyone else in my entire life to cause me such grief had gone to ground, disappeared before I could get him to explain why – 'why' for any of the humiliations or 'why' he had orchestrated things to scupper my Edinburgh dream. So I was left ready and waiting, to spontaneously combust with the disappointment and frustration of it all. Scary stuff. Even Andy Adriano was worried about me, dropping by every morning – 'Hey, Charlie, how's it hanging?' – even if he never waited for a reply. 'Catch you later, man.' If only he would. I would watch him stalk away with a purposeful stride that seemed to speak of his intelligence and vitality; a beauty in him and in everything he did, like the way he would run his fingers through his dark, dark hair, or kiss the knuckles of his hand when lost in boyish concentration. I would watch him glide around the office and brood on these thoughts. I wasn't going to fight them any more. No, these were harmless thoughts. 'Catch' *me*? Never. It wasn't ever going to happen. What would he want with a loser like me?

And Jules must have been worried too, trying to tell me that my luck was about to change, reading out my horoscope from the trash pages of *Vixen* magazine, or whatever it was called, 'Today's foxy reading for today's go-getting girls.' Quite. Or perhaps it was more today's essential reading for today's overwrought slappers – one hundred glossy pages of fashion advertising, slimming and sex advice. Jules, of course, swore by it. She eagerly translated the predictions from woman-speak to man-speak so that they might appear more appropriate. I could have told her to spare the effort.

'Listen, Charlie. Listen: "You have been under stress at work or in a social setting where an acquaintance has been making life difficult. Now is the time to confront the source of your troubles if your ambitions are to be realised. Six for luck, and blue for tranquillity. Key letters – *D* for danger and *R* for Romance."'

Despite Jules's enthusiasm I found myself unmoved. '. . . And *B* is for bullshit I suppose.'

'Hang on . . . I read somewhere – what was it? "O is for Orgasm but it is also for Opium." Is that a proverb or something, Charlie? I got the feeling it's supposed to mean something.'

'Means fuck all to me. Where did you read it?'

'Part of the blurb for my show. You know – the "secret" show. In the letter this morning, telling me where to go for it. It said, "We will entertain you at the house and then move on somewhere sacred. O is for Orange but it is also for Opium. Be prepared for something Ex-Tra-Or-Din-Arry." It's a bit bloody daunting. Wish you were coming with me, Charlie, but I suppose you can't. It's secret, you see.'

And there was suddenly some new thoughts for me to brood on. Two new thoughts. The first was that I knew someone who talked just like that. The second was one worth brooding on in its own glorious right.

That it shouldn't just be time I was killing.

INTERMISSION; and behind the curtain, Rennie found himself working harder than ever. He was trying to revive the prone figure of the original Alan from Partick, now a slumped wreck, lying inert on the same chair he had been happy to perform on less than an hour beforehand. Rennie knew he had the medicinal means to bring him round – a shot of the cocaine sulphate compound he used in his experiments would probably revive even one as inanimate as this – but the problem was, what exactly would be there when he did? Rennie thought back to the flash of rage that had caused him to charge the device so highly before releasing it on this subject. Why had this fool insisted on pandering to the crowd like that? Why had he gone out of his way to provoke Dr Rendini into using his full force? Still, at least Rennie was finding a method of testing the machine's parameters.

Then there was the other subject – the girl who was a young man, the confused and increasingly irascible Bernadette Reilly who had found herself reincarnated as a strongman. A sedative was required here: one for herself and her hysterical sister – 'What have you done to her? Put her back . . . you hear . . . put her back . . . right now!'

A sedative – a strong one – like a cup of the sweet tea Rennie had them prepare for moments like this, sweet tea with a dram to help them over the shock. They were usually happy to swallow it; in fact, they would swallow anything. The 'dram' was laudanum, and with any luck, once they woke after imbibing it, they would scarcely remember its taste, let alone being at the theatre. Rennie saw to it that the cups were on their way. It was important to calm the situation; the second half of the show was almost due. He had to get started again.

What would be on the bill for this next part of the performance? More of the same, thought Rennie. He still had two
untouched volunteers from his earlier appeal, including the
fat one whom the girl had somehow managed to lift. Another
volunteer, a skinny one, could work well in conjunction with
him. There were possibilities. Rennie walked to the area off-
stage to ask them to resume their places, rehearsing his welcome back address in his mind as he did so. His silent
run-through came to a sudden end when he looked up and
realised they were gone. Rennie looked left and right. Had
they run away? How dare they do this to him?

He turned his furious glare to the stagehand sitting idly by
the exit corridor. Had he been there when they fled? Surely
he should have had the wit to prevent their escape? The boy
realised he was under Rennie's icy scrutiny, and jumped to
attention, turning the levers for the curtain pulleys in the
mistaken belief that Rennie wanted to start the second half
immediately. As the curtains opened, so the applause began
to ring out anew. The crowd's appetite had been whetted and
now appeared insatiable.

Rennie stood before them, suddenly exposed.

'. . . Apologies . . . ladies and gentlemen. As you can see, I
am alone . . . It would appear our brave lads have deserted us,
as their courage would appear to have deserted them. I am
willing to continue, ladies and gentlemen. I have scarcely
begun to show to you the wonders of telepathic science, but
I will need volunteers . . . We need more stars, ladies and
gentlemen, to continue the show. We have seen what fun we
can have . . . Now, where are the two brave lads, the real brave
lads who will earn our admiration . . .'

Rennie halted, distracted by the presence at the foot of the
stage of two elderly men. They stood, peering forward, looking almost lost, blocking the view of those seated behind them.

Rennie searched for a steward who might remove the
annoyance. None seemed immediately forthcoming, he would
have to deal with them himself.

'Excuse me, sirs. Do I take it that you wish to respond to
my challenge?'

Rennie's sneering tone had the audience convulsed. He had asked for two 'lads' to come and share the fun, and here they were, a pair of spindly old gargoyles, gaping at him with stern expectancy. They were completely out of place in the bear-pit atmosphere of the Alhambra, more obviously so as they edged forward into the lights. These were gentlemen, of sorts, Rennie observed. Besuited and behatted, collared and cravatted, and from a different world to the rest of the low-life audience. Yes, dressed to distinction, albeit the distinction of at least twenty years ago; when did anyone last wear knee-length breeches and white stockings like that? What did these two have against trousers? Rennie shook his head in puzzlement, aware that this exchange was now part of the performance. He cupped a hand behind his ear as if to demonstrate his impatience for a reply. One came soon enough.

'Correct, sir. You may take it that this is our intention.'

Rennie was taken aback. Were they serious? The firmness of the response would seem to suggest that they were. He began to wish he had not addressed them. Now he would have no choice but to accept them on the stage. Rennie's hand sought the comforting presence of the device in his pocket. He would rely on the usual method – the tried and tested method – to subdue the strange newcomers if he had to.

'Very well. Come and join us Mr . . . ?' Rennie put his hand behind his ear again as the pair were led up to the stage.

'Mr Begby and Mr Roberts.'

'And where are you from, sirs?'

Rennie pointed to the chairs as they entered stage left. They ignored his direction and stood immediately before him, but when the reply to his last question came, it was in a different voice, and came from the mouth of the elder of the two. A cultivated voice, a *professional's* voice.

'We are from Edinburgh, sir. A city we believe you know well.'

The growing sense of disquiet inside Rennie was not helped by this remark, which he chose to ignore, preferring instead to ready himself for what he was sure would be the final performance of the night.

Urgency was required. What else would these buffoons say that might alarm the audience, who drew comfort and reassurance in his persona as Dr Rendini, 'Man of Mystery'. Yes, *his* audience. He would have to do whatever was needed to protect them.

The first step involved turning his back to shield them from view of his mysterious device. He thrust both hands deep into his pocket – one to hold, the other to crank the precious machine. Rennie's conscience stirred as he did so; had he not already been troubled this night for loading the piece with too much power, and yet here he was about to do the same? He raced through the options in his mind. Would the crowd not expect the mighty Dr Rendini to quell the tongues of any scurrilous rumour-mongers, especially ones intent on defaming him, right here, on his own stage! Rennie turned the mechanism's arm round and round, unable to stop himself. What kind of act would he have the two perform? Transferring one's mind to the other was not really a possibility. The audience could not be impressed, assuming that the pair were known to each other before they presented themselves, and so there would be no surprise if one could be made to talk of the other's intimacies. Rennie thought back to the freckled face of his last subject. His previous over-enthusiasm had meant that he had caused the machine to absorb far more of the unwitting donor's soul than he would have planned. He had only had to give the mildest of charges to the girl before she took possession of another's being. There had to be more of the original spirit still left in the device. One hefty discharge of its power and there could be yet another 'Alan from Partick' gallivanting on the boards tonight. Although it might not be as amusing a spectacle as the young girl cavorting as a 'lad' there was comic potential, surely, in the skeletal old man performing similar antics. Perhaps he should have him carouse to the ladies in the stalls, or down a yard of ale, or perhaps pick a fight with his elderly companion and rival in love for the heart of Agnes Calder. Yes, of course, there was no fool funnier than an old fool. The older the better.

'Give me your hands if you would, sir, and I would ask you

to remember the last kiss you enjoyed, sir, the last *passionate* kiss . . .'

Rennie turned a leering face to the audience and relaxed the catch of his invention, its whirrings and rattling motions seemingly vibrating through the knuckles and bones of the ancient hands holding it. He looked for signs that the machine had had its usual effect, holding back from any action until its rumblings had subsided.

The old man's eyes were closed, though not especially tightly. To those close enough to see them, it might have appeared he had nodded off to sleep. Rennie hoped otherwise.

'Can you hear me, sir?'

The eyes opened at once, startling Rennie with their mixture of ivory-white polish and luminous cyan blue. How could a relic like this have such vitality in his eyes?

'Aye.'

'And who are you, sir?'

'I told you. I'm Mr Begby from Edinburgh.'

The voice hadn't changed at all, except it had more of an archness to its tone. Here was someone who truly wished to rise to the Man of Mystery's challenge after all. Rennie's first thoughts were that his invention had been faulty, or rather that this strange individual had found some way of blocking its action. He glanced furtively down at it in his hands for any apparent signs of fracture. Perhaps there just hadn't been good enough contact with the papery-thin translucent skin of the recipient. The device had never been designed for the kind of external use he had to perform on the stage. Full contact along all the gleaming surface; that was how it had been meant to work for maximum efficiency. If he had managed to insert it inside the anus, or if appropriate, the vagina, the outcome could never be in doubt, nor indeed inside a manmade cavity such as an open and deep incision. Any of these were preferable, if unrealistic in the present circumstances. It was hard enough getting volunteers as it was. What a *show* I could give them, mused Rennie, if they could only conquer their pious squeamishness. Why was it that he was always the only one prepared to make sacrifices for science? The irony was that *he* should be the one reviled for having the strength of will to carry out such an act, and how he would relish using that mighty will right then and there. Yes, that would prove to this old impostor that he wasn't a man to be toyed with. He pictured himself plunging the tool deep into the body of the musty laggard, and then letting loose a surge of energy that would lift him clean out of his seat. But for the meantime, lamented Rennie, with the entire theatre still looking on, the more normal methods would have to apply.

'I must ask you, sir. Please surrender to my mysterious powers . . . we will try again, sir, if you will . . .'

Rennie had the device out of his pocket, shielding it only partially under an arm as he turned and turned the handle. He was still concerned that the machine not be fully seen, but imposing his resolve was the priority of the moment. Thin hands, he quietly cursed, such gaunt hands. It meant losing too much power to the air; precious material that it had taken his every reserve of application, sacrifice and tenacity to mine, only to be lost here in the haze of lights onstage. All he could do was compensate for the wasteful evaporation with an extra load of energy, or was it?

'This time, sir, I wonder . . . could you let me see your tongue before we proceed?'

The clear blue eyes of the waiting accomplice looked back at Rennie with some incredulity, and he refrained from any movement, obviously unwilling to subject himself to any such undignified examination. However, the jeering whistles from the crowd soon communicated their impatience and their sympathy with the mysterious Rendini. Eventually the old man yielded, slowly opening his mouth.

'Yes . . .' mused Rennie aloud whilst tilting his guest's chin up with a single finger. '. . . A gift horse alright, but a real elderly nag!'

The roar of laughter from the stalls was Rennie's cue to pounce, thrusting the device down the gullet of the mouth facing him. He flicked the catch at the base of the machine and clamped an arm round the back of the old man's head, holding it close to him so that there could be no escape. This time it was the skull that seemed to carry the rattling of the device's inner rotations. Rennie looked at the mossy down of white hair blurring into one thick coat as it throbbed with the rapid twitches the invention produced. A full transfer, it had to be, he thought. See how you cope with that, you ancient bastard.

The buzzing was gradually becalmed and Rennie released his grip, taking a step back as he realised that the earlier sounds of glee from the audience had lapsed into silence. Perhaps it had made a disconcerting sight, the way he had manhandled an elderly person in front of them. Still, he had had no choice, and soon enough everyone watching would be enthralled by the results of the action.

'Can you hear me, sir?'

Rennie drew his hand across his forehead to clear the sweat that was accumulating, and noticed for a moment how cold it felt. The same hand that had held his subject's head still was suddenly cold and numb, as if it had been clawing snow.

'Aye . . .'

The old man's eyes remained closed, an encouraging sign.

'Then *who* are you?'

Rennie felt confident enough to turn away from his subject and face his audience, an arm outstretched in triumph as he waited for the answer.

'I'm Jamie, Dr Brodie. Do you remember me?'

Rennie blinked, swallowing hard to suppress the nausea surging upwards from his boots on its way to crash into the roof. A pounding giddiness took immediate possession of him, making it difficult for him to focus on anything; every image, including the old man and his mute partner now as blurred again as they were during the mighty tremblings of the device.

'. . . I . . . I am afraid I do not know what you mean, sir. Are you not a lad from Partick . . .'

Rennie was reeling, desperate for any respite. The reply was immediate.

'You must remember "Daft Jamie", sir, the lad you murdered in Edinburgh last year in your first experiment with your scientific machine.'

The gasps from the floor were an unwelcome disturbance as Rennie sought the clarity of mind he needed to work through the possibilities. Could this really be the voice of 'Daft Jamie' coming back to haunt him? Despite the terror that the notion brought with it, part of him wished it was – what would it say about the power of his glorious invention if it were true? Incredible. It was so strong that part of his first subject's soul was still trapped within its metal walls a year after its traumatic debut. And what did it say of the inventor? That he was a genius, a genius whose only fault was that he had ever doubted the depth of his own talent. The same failing as before, when he was still a *real* doctor, Dr Alexander Brodie.

But should he admit to this? Absolutely not. The mobs had gathered outside Surgeon's Hall only days after 'Daft Jamie' vanished, determined to show him the charity and succour in death that they had manifestly failed to demonstrate when he was alive. There would be those still willing to lynch any they thought responsible for the poor laddie's demise. Brodie or Rennie, it would make no difference as long as someone was held to blame.

'Do you deny my friend's assertion, sir, that you are the Dr Brodie who murdered "Daft Jamie", the bodysnatcher Tam Rennie and his accomplice young Alex, and the unidentified man whose charred remains were found in your workshop in the fire that preceded your disappearance from Edinburgh?'

This was the voice of the other wastrel who had sat silently throughout the proceedings. He, too, was on his feet, an unexpectedly animated figure with a cultured voice that spoke of time in the courts, as did his manner and posture – a hand to hold his heart for sincerity, the other marking the air with each point for clarity. How did they know this? wondered Rennie. Where had they received such information when his had been the perfect escape? Had he not read his own obituary in *The Scotsman*?

'Of course, I reject your preposterous allegation, and I would remind you that there are witnesses to this slanderous attack.' Rennie waved an impetuous arm in the direction of the floor, mustering as much wounded indignation as he could. Unfortunately, the appreciative hoots that greeted his last comment did nothing to intimate his interrogator.

'Then who *are* you, sir?'

'I . . . I have made it clear . . . I am Dr Rendini . . . Man of Mystery.'

'Then I am afraid it is you who are being preposterous, sir. May I put it to you, and those watching, that my friend's allegation is either true or it is false. Would you care to agree with that assessment, sir?'

'I have told you and tell you that it is false!'

The inquisitor raised his flat palm to silence Rennie as he slowly turned to the crowd.

'And you, ladies and gentlemen, do you all understand that the claim can only be true, or false, that there is no other possibility?'

The old gentleman waited until the cries of 'Aye' died down.

'Then it seems clear that if the claim is true, then you are a murderer, sir, and should stand trial for that crime. If it is false then you are a fraud and a charlatan, since your "science" of mind reading has succeeded only in awaking a fantasy in the mind of a vulnerable citizen who deserved care and respect rather than the assault you visited upon him.'

He stopped and took three slow paces across the creaking stage to stand head to head with Rennie.

'I ask you again. Which is it to be – true or false?'

Rennie faltered, staring deep into the eyes that scrutinised him, knowing that somehow these eyes did not want for an answer, that they already knew all there was to know of Steven Rennie, the mysterious Dr Rendini, and the infamous Alexander Brodie. Yet that wasn't the point of the outburst against him; it had all been for those watching a show, his farewell performance.

The jeers of the crowd now ringing in his ears, Rennie patted the outside of his pocket, instinctively seeking to reassure himself with the proof of his genius. He felt the terror grip him instantly: the invention wasn't there. He ran to confront the man on whom it had last been used.

'Where is it? What have you done with my mechanism? Where? Where is it, you old bastard?'

Rennie made to grab his original tormentor and shake him for its return, but found himself thrown to the floor. Several men had stormed the stage and now set upon him, kicking him as he fell.

'Leave me alone, you imbeciles. They have stolen my invention. Let me go!'

Rennie made one last vain attempt to stand as more legs closed in around him. Through a gap in the forest of knees and boots he saw the chairs where his two accusers had been sitting.

They were empty.

TRANSCRIPT: TAPE 6

Interviewer:
When did you realise that you were all being led to a graveyard?

Lowes:
Not until the very last. We'd been heading up Lothian Road, straight in towards town, the West End, and I'd begun to think we were going to gatecrash someone else's performance. It was about three. It must have taken about half an hour to get everyone dressed up in our new outfits, get us out of the house and all the way there through the Grassmarket.

Interviewer:
'New' outfits?

Lowes:
We ... had these sort of sheets draped around us like togas. We weren't allowed to put our clothes back on. I guess we looked like a fancy dress party out on the loose, a posse of Roman Emperors ... ghostly emperors ... Pablo had his white face and a garland of gilded leaves as his crown, and his magic wand of course. The girls had a few little harps made out of cardboard and cooking foil ... Angels and devils ...

Interviewer:
Did anyone see you all?

Lowes:
Yes, I guess plenty did. There were lots of people about, but whether they noticed us, or thought us unusual in any way, I would be doubtful.

Interviewer:

For the benefit of the tape, could you state which graveyard you entered?

Lowes:

St Cuthbert's.

Interviewer:

Had you been there before?

Lowes:

Never knew it existed. I'm not 'up' on graveyards, and it's tucked away, isn't it? Right under the Castle, a missing part of Edinburgh that no one ever sees because they are either staring at the Castle or the gardens or Princes Street . . . And you go down the steps, and you follow the paths and the next thing you realise you have left them all behind and you've come down into this underworld. At least that's how it felt that night.

Interviewer:

Did you know whose grave you were going into?

Lowes:

Well . . . Eddie had been babbling some shit as we progressed, giving us a lecture about Thomas De Quincey, about his talents as a writer and his life and trials and how *Confessions of an English Opium Eater* was a landmark of literature. He was going on and on . . . De Quincey was an *artist*, he said. He didn't have to live by the petty rules of the day; he transcended them. A man of genius, a scholar, a man of appetites. By the time he was thirty, he was taking 230 grains of opium a day. This wasn't an addiction, this was an artistic statement. He was reaching for something higher, a different plane of consciousness. He looked for others to fund his journeys so that he could pursue his artistic destiny. Married an eighteen-year-old farmer's daughter so that she could whore for him. Tough peasant stock you see . . .

Interviewer:

You didn't realise De Quincey is buried in St Cuthbert's?

Lowes:

(drily) Not until we were stood round his fucking grave, no.

Interviewer:

So this was who you had all been brought to 'rescue'?

Lowes:

It seemed so, yeah.

Interviewer:

What was the purpose of this activity? Did Dexter say what he hoped to achieve by exhuming De Quincey?

Lowes:

(bitterly) Sure. He outlined his plan and we took a fucking vote on it . . . (pause) . . . I guess he wanted to see if we would do it, if we *would* dig up anybody – so why not De Quincey, who he'd said was his idol. Maybe De Quincey came to mind because of this thing about clubs. I'm sure Eddie had said that De Quincey founded the Resurrection Club in Edinburgh sometime in the eighteenth century . . . Started it as a joke, to annoy the other clubs. The Resurrection Club gave people new names and identities, new everything, so that they could reinvent themselves . . . so maybe Pablo thought he should resurrect the resurrectionist . . . That was his kind of joke. Then Pablo was saying at the graveside that he had something up his sleeve which could bring *Dear Thomas* back to life so that we could learn the secrets of his age, find out how degenerate *his* Resurrection Club was. Did they really have a means of transplanting minds from one man to another? De Quincey was a tall man, but the word was they had buried a much shorter one. We could find out. De Quincey had been a sick man, with an opium habit that would have killed most within days, yet we could see from his headstone that he was over seventy when he finally died . . . an *extraordinary* age . . . How had he done it – how had he cheated the grave for so long? We had to know . . . Pablo had to know.

Interviewer:
So there *was* a plan?

Lowes:
This wasn't *explained*. Understand? Like all of this, it's in my head but I'm not sure how it got there. All I can remember for sure is that Pablo asked us to start digging and we did.

Interviewer:
With your hands?

Lowes:
(wearily) With spades and shovels . . . the usual shit. It had been set up; the tools were already there . . . and the music and the smells. Pablo's party was ready to roll once more. Boys to do the digging, girls to mop their sweaty brows.

Interviewer:
Everyone took the task on willingly?

Lowes:
(aggressively) Well, fucking why not? What was the harm in it? (long pause) Were the dead going to rise up in protest?

ROBERTS, BEGBY & LAWRIE W.S.,

MARY KING'S CLOSE, EDINBURGH.

The partnership has always made strenuous efforts to keep discreet whatever interventions were deemed to be required. That is to say, limited, both in scope and overt influence. We would always prefer to allow miscreants the opportunity to repent of their own volition, or failing this, to learn the error of their ways through circumstance rather than confrontation. We are never comfortable with the notion of making our powers known to more than the select few who have graced our boardroom, or indeed those isolated reprobates whose corrupt ways have necessitated the physical action we execrate. Nevertheless, after lengthy debate and consideration, we are unanimous that we have no choice but to intercede, and that regrettably, the successful clandestine nature of previous operations of this ilk may not be repeated in this case.

This is a cause of some not inconsiderable consternation amongst the partners, and there have been opinions expressed which hold sympathy with the view that if our proceedings are to be witnessed by a wider public than those hitherto exposed, then our justice must be seen to be firm, decisive and merciless. If we are to be seen then let us be seen to make an example of those who would test us, runs the argument.

However, it has never been the partnership's method to allow a desire for vengeance to hold sway over the choice of punishment for those who intrude in the domain of our jurisprudence, and there have been those of us who have pleaded for tolerance and a contemplation of the facts involved in this instance, free from the emotionally charged remembrance that the mention of Alexander Brodie always prompts. That this view is at odds with those set out earlier means that there has been friction within the partnership, and the emergence of a factionalism in our chambers which is as new as it is abhorrent to us. We progress therefore with a cautious consensus in the interests of avoiding a split which would be the ruination of Roberts, Begby & Lawrie. In this spirit we are agreed:

That a covert operation can only be implemented when dealing with a solitary individual, and that this is not appropriate here where a network of deviants dance to the tune of our antagonist, and do so willingly.

That we shall make our rendezvous with the said degenerate and persistent offender. A meeting that is perhaps overdue.

That this shall take place at a juncture opportune to us.

That 'Peter Dexter' will be dealt with in a fitting manner.

That any other who has sought him out in appreciation and approval of his manifesto shall be dealt with likewise.

That anyone who has helped him in his mission to debase will be judged accordingly.

That 'Daniel Lowes' will be brought to face judgement.

That Charles Kidd be dealt with accordingly.

We can put it no simpler than that.

GREYFRIARS CEMETERY. August 21st. I had come to say goodbye to a favourite place. Of all the many graveyards Dexter had taken me to, this was the one I had loved the most, thinking it the most beautiful spot in Edinburgh, returning over and over. Today it didn't move me like it usually did; not even the late sunlight stretching lazily across mossy lawns, or the weathered granite headstones absorbing the last of the day's heat, had any effect on me. I would normally gaze out to the back of them and beyond where the landscape falls into the hollow of the Grassmarket, and then beyond that across to the Castle, hovering majestically way above. A view that would gently overwhelm with its tranquillity. Today I had come to say goodbye and to feel that calm for the last time. But there was no calm. Someone was calling me.

There are more buried in Greyfriars than the number of tombstones might indicate. As one of the city's oldest burial places, space here has always been in demand. The old have had to give way to the new, literally. Many of the dead now lie displaced in unmarked graves, forced out by the pressure of new arrivals. Forced out by other forces; as one of the city's oldest cemeteries it is also one of the most plundered, an early magnet for the resurrectionist's trade. Several plots near the Kirk still have their mort-slates standing astride them, the iron casings built into the burial plots to deter graverobbers. Dexter had told me about these, and how the thieves would have set about their work. There was, he said, an *art* to resurrection. It would have been performed with guile and craft. I can remember his voice bleating in admiration as he told of it. They would come by night trying to work fast under the cover of darkness, usually in winter, when the guards were least likely to venture out into the cold to patrol their territory. They would have tools, artist's tools – a canvas sheet to receive the earth and to prevent any of it spoiling the smooth uniformity of the grass. Then the hole itself would be dug, at the head end of the grave, using special wooden, dagger-shaped blades to prevent the clinking of an iron spade hitting any stones. Then the technique; they would go down as far as the coffin itself, stopping once this was reached. Then the top would be wrenched off using two hooks pulled up by rope. It would not be necessary to lift all of the lid, only a large enough portion to allow the body to be pulled through to the surface. Sacking was thrown over the grave at this point to cover the sound of the wood cracking. Any sound now escaping would be at once muffled and distant, belonging to another world. Once retrieved, the body would be stripped of its burial clothes. These would be scrupulously buried again. The corpse could now be taken for sale, once the earth had been replaced and the surface of the grave restored to its original condition, leaving a perfect fake, an empty space for generations to venerate in the years to come.

The whole process was a task that could take a team of professionals less than an hour. The rewards for such quick work were substantial: five to ten pounds for a body in good condition – the equivalent of a year's rent for the average working man in the early 1800s. And here, in this very graveyard, lay two of the men generating this extraordinary demand, Alexander Munro *Primus*, and his son Alexander Munro *Secundus*, Professors of Anatomy at the University, lauded heroes of the medical age. The bodies they bought for experiment made way for their own in the very same graveyard. The ironic part, the almost cruelly ironic part.

Was it them or their victims who were calling me? I couldn't tell. I was confused. The voices were screaming in my head, different tones, wails and clamours – a cacophony I couldn't hear clearly enough. Some might have been calling for justice, others perhaps to mock; all were somehow aimed at me. I knew this without question although not what I had done to harm them. I looked again at the mort-slates. It was the Resurrectionist exhibition I had tried to instigate that was to blame. I felt a rush of guilt at my attempted collusion to assault these people's dignity. I scanned a furtive glance around the headstones and the grass. I'm sorry. I wouldn't have let it happen, I swear. I hoped they could hear me and recognise the sincerity. But the voices continued their onslaught, becoming louder as they sensed I was making to leave. They were not merely saying goodbye.

I began to run towards the exit, pausing for the last time at the pink gravel that marks the grave of John Gray. John Gray, not a distinguished man of science like Munro, but a decent man, an honest man who had diligently cared for his family until he had died from tuberculosis at the age of forty-three in 1858. Never a wealthy man, he had nevertheless had the heart to take in a stray dog and care for this beast too, a Skye terrier called Bobby. And it was this dog that gave Gray his posthumous fame by its display of love and devotion, living as a stray once more but staying at the side of his master's grave for the next thirteen years. An extraordinary act of devotion. 'Extra-orr-din-arry' as Dexter had said. I thought of him now, and the voices calling to me were suddenly quiet. A sudden sense of calm at last. They had communicated their message by their silence. I knew what I had to do.

Lowes:
(agitated) The *scene*? What is it about you and the fucking 'scene'? The scene . . . (calmer) Who talks like that? (snorts) How would I describe the scene? A weird scene . . . that good enough? A very fucking weird scene. Five lads trying to dig down without crashing into each other, five noble lads in shoes and boots but precious little else aside from the robes we had draped around us, toiling in the sweaty summer moonlight, drifting with the music and luscious scent of dreams, distracted by the sound of Pablo hooping it up with the chicks . . . frolicking away like Nero as Rome fucking burns with its own craziness . . . and the girls have to dance around like nymphs, hopping around the tombstones and candlelight, letting go of their own shadows, letting go of everything and going round and around, hand in hand in one long chain, unpaid extras in someone else's movie fantasy . . . laughing and getting high on the delirium they'd unleashed . . . That would be the 'scene', I suppose . . .

Interviewer:
Did Dextrus speak at this time?

Lowes:
Only to make us dig faster. Maybe that was a sign he was losing his nerve . . . wanted us to have it all over before we were discovered . . . (adopts high-pitched whine) Come on my friends. The professionals would have reached the body in half an hour!

Interviewer:
Weren't you worried about being caught?

Lowes:
Not particularly.

Interviewer:
Why not?

Lowes:
You seem to think we were all thinking logically at this point . . .
Like we hadn't been stoned . . . drunk . . . abused . . . humiliated
. . . liberated . . . 'Caught?' What the fuck does that mean? Who
was going to catch us? None of this was real any more. Don't you
understand? At that point we were starring in a dream . . .

Interviewer:
'Starring'?

Lowes:
. . . Playing a role . . . a role that wasn't *us* . . .

Interviewer:
A role that involved digging up a grave?

Lowes:
(nonchalant) Hey, I didn't write the part, you know? I just followed
the lines.

Interviewer:
So how did the script develop from there?

Lowes:
Blistered hands . . . slow progress . . . De Quincey's headstone had
toppled forward some time ago. Heavy granite thing. Pablo didn't
want us to move it, so to get at the body we had to dig alongside
and then cut diagonally inwards after about four feet. In the dark
it was impossible to see what you were doing. I kept on at it – we
all did – but it must have been a shambles. Pablo was getting
annoyed.

Interviewer:
How could you tell?

Lowes:
Just the little things, the tell-tale remarks that gave it away . . . (loud, high-pitched shout) MOVE YOUR LAZY ARSES! CAN'T YOU LAGGARDS GO ANY FASTER? HASN'T OUR DEAR FRIEND WAITED LONG ENOUGH? (laughs).

Interviewer:
So he was agitated. Were there any obvious reasons why he should become anxious at this point?

Lowes:
None especially. It was cool now . . . temperature-wise I mean. I'm not sure if St Cuthbert's ever really heats up, being in the shade all the time. Maybe it was cool enough to give him a chill . . . And all this physical effort had kind of sobered me up a little, sharpened my senses if not my actual 'sense' of normality. Maybe Pablo was worried he was about to lose his grip on us. I think that must have been why we had the music and the burning joss-sticks there . . . (intones rhythmically) *Pablo Pablo Dextrus Dextrus Pablo Pablo Dextrus Likus . . .*

Interviewer:
But there was nothing else?

Lowes:
I think he really just thought his moment was about to arrive, the one he'd built this whole thing for.

Interviewer:
Which was?

Lowes:
Which was when we came across De Quincey's bones.

Interviewer:
And when was that?

Lowes:
I've no fucking idea . . . Ten minutes . . . Ten hours. Who could tell? I'm not even sure we really did unearth them . . .

Interviewer:
How do you mean?

Lowes:
Well, it was a bit of hysteria again. Pablo is becoming more and more impatient and haranguing us to try harder, and then he pulls Claire over to stand at the foot of the hole we've made and he says, 'Look. Claire is waiting to reward whoever reaches the spot first, he who reaches deepest will reach deepest . . .' And he stands behind her, hands on her shoulders and pushes the gown she's wearing so the thing slips from her shoulders. She laughs and she's there in front of us with nothing but the smile on her lips and toy harp in her hands . . . She was so pale, so beautiful. I could only think of when I had first seen her in the sunshine all those hours ago and how she had struck me then, like a vision right out of this world, and here she had done it again only more so . . . soft, creamy white skin, slender neck and lithe limbs . . . She had some kind of silver paint on her nipples and a stud pierced into her navel that glistened like a jewel in the half-light. Maybe her nipples were pierced as well and that was why they had a lustre . . . but the point is that there was a symmetry to her that was beguiling, absolutely beguiling . . . and it led the eye down, slowly down from her eyes through her breasts to the tiny matt triangle Pablo pointed at with his device. 'He who reaches deepest reaches deepest as his reward.'

Interviewer:
What effect did this promise have on proceedings?

Lowes:
Well, it made Steve dig like a fucking lunatic for one!

Interviewer:
And you?

Lowes:
I was taken by it ... the picture ... the 'scene' (laughs softly). I had never seen beauty like that before, or been moved by it like this. I wanted to possess it but knew that this was the point – it ... she was beautiful because you couldn't possess it. I was confused ... I ploughed on but without too much conviction.

Interviewer:
And the girl, Claire?

Lowes:
She rejoined the dance. They were swirling round us. I looked up again, they were all naked and going faster than I could follow.

Interviewer:
Watching them made you dizzy?

Lowes:
Everything made me dizzy. I was about to chop my feet off when Andy struck gold. Thank Christ for that, I thought, thank Christ.

I KNEW WHERE TO GET HIM. Once Jules had said what she had, it was a giveaway. Poor Jules, she couldn't be discreet if she tried. Poor Jules. What did Dexter have planned for her? I was intrigued rather than worried by the question. What would he want with someone like that? Hadn't he poured enough humiliation onto the weary foot soldiers of PR? It had to be time to stem the flow, to set the tide travelling in the other direction, the only issue being whether I had the nerve to be the one to do it.

A giveaway then, a *dead* giveaway. Dexter had taken me to every graveyard in the city centre bar one, and there had to be a reason for its exclusion. Was it that this one was precious to him, that it couldn't be soiled by my presence, or did it have a particular history that would expose Dexter's method?

When they built the original church of St Cuthbert's in 1578 it would have stood alone on the shore of the Nor' Loch. It would have made a pretty sight, if one could ignore the smell of the shit and debris floating in the gentle waters. A pleasing cameo indeed, the proud and erect little kirk nestling in the shadow of the castle towering above. The reality though was that it would have been a truly isolated building, far removed from the bustle and com-motions of the Old Town, and too far removed from the safety of the city walls. The result? The most pilfered graveyard in Edin-burgh's history, a free-for-all body depot, perhaps the first example of self-service shopping long before the retail paradise of Princes Street was ever conceived. The authorities tried to combat these activities of course: the cemetery walls are the highest in Scotland and were eventually joined by a watchtower that stands to this day, the only such security measure in the western world. The criminal fraternity continued to rise to these challenges, however, and by the eighteenth century only the city's paupers would be buried here, the rest preferring to lie in a more secure berth for the afterlife. So the graveyard duly became a final resting place only for the poor, and stricken visitors who knew no better or had no choice. Yet Dexter had made this place his choice, I knew it. Why? Was it to resurrect the dead as he had threatened at the press conference? Possibly. Very possibly. I did not know how he might hope to achieve this feat but I felt somehow that this wasn't the important part, that the *vital* part would be putting on a show. Dexter loved a show, as long as he was ringmaster, as long as he was cracking the whip above the performing animals.

O is for *orgasm* but also for *opium*. An extraordinary statement, but what does it mean? I set myself the task of finding out; it had to be another clue. St Cuthbert's gave the answer in the grave of the famous opium eater, Thomas De Quincey. How had he come to be buried here? He was a visitor, a long-term visitor to the city which he found very accommodating, throwing up a variety of fools who were willing to fund his lifestyle. That did not stop him from dying a pauper: his addictions to opium and alcohol saw to that. A man after Dexter's heart, another who viewed his life as a canvas for his artistic status, a status which made those who surrounded him, the patrons of his art, and they would pay for the privilege of his company accordingly. De Quincey was a scoundrel who cheated a living out of Edinburgh's gullible middle classes. A raconteur, thief and fantasist forever one step away from immortality. Perhaps he would enjoy tonight's show. I felt sure he would be close enough to appreciate it. Yes, he would be where the action was. His tomb would set the scene.

Going along that night was a dare I dared myself, to prove if I ever could see anything through. I was thinking in terms of my own epitaph, and the problem some kind of decisive action at the last would pose for its author. I knew how it would read without it, carved in solemn stone: *'Here lies Charles Kidd. In death he found the certainty that had been missing in his adult life. May he rest in peace, but it doesn't have to be here. He could move if you want. What do you think?'*

I set myself the dare and surprised myself by meeting it. I was there that night, there to tackle Dexter once and for all. I was there before midnight, and I wasn't alone. For company I had the tramps looking to bed down at the side of the church, and the teenage drunks loading up on cheap cider. And there were others as well, long before Dexter's cast arrived. They were waiting too. The dead were calling, as they had at Greyfriars. They knew that I meant to join them.

I remember reading the inscription on the plinth that marked a family grave to the left of the raised ground where De Quincey lay, a message dating back over a hundred years and still shining in its sincerity: 'Death is a debt to nature due, which I have paid and so must you.' Quite. The message spoke so clearly to me in the evening gloom; it spoke to me of destiny. I had reached the end of the line. I thought of the goodbyes that would be left unsaid; I thought of writing one last letter to Andy, apologising for loving him and any embarrassment that this may have caused. Hopefully he would forget about me and pursue his career with a vigour mine had lacked. I would wish him well. Perhaps. But the letter remained unwritten. Did I really love him or just envy him? Could there be a point where these are one and the same? No letter. I decided to leave it for him to figure out for himself. I had every confidence he would make more sense of it than I. Then Jules, poor Jules – what should I say to her? Would she be mortified at my presence here when she was meant to be enjoying the company of the elite band of sophisticates she desperately wanted to join? Would I cramp her style so much? I would have to apologise again and thank her in passing for all her efforts to lift me out of myself. However much in vain her attempts were, at least she had tried. I couldn't deny that. And Dexter, I would thank him in a different way – I would take him with me.

I sat down to wait, leaning against a post in the grass, De Quincey's plot to my right. Dexter would come, and when he did we would pay our debt together. He might even be grateful; after all, he was the one who loved graveyards.

'What have you done wi' the rest o' them?'

The voice from behind startled me. I had not heard anyone approaching. I was even more surprised when I turned and stood to find myself facing not one but two men. How had they moved so stealthily?

'Well? What time is your appointment with your debauched companions?'

I peered at the pair through the darkness, unable to discern exactly who was speaking, and not entirely sure who it was they had taken me for. As for me, I could not remember seeing either of them before and was sure if I had that I would have remembered. An anxiety seeped into me as the moments passed. Was this an apparition I had wished upon myself or were these weirdos for real? That was the question.

'Am I mad?'

I said it aloud because it was all I could think to say, and because whoever of the two had spoken had done so with such conviction and abrupt forcefulness that he had to know the answer. In that respect the reply was as disappointing as it was confusing.

'That is no excuse, sir. We cannot accept that as any kind of extenuation. You have come here of your own free will and shall be judged accordingly.'

I heard the same tone, leaving me in no doubt as to who had the position of moral authority. This had to be a dream, I told myself, a dream of sorts where two whey-faced pensioners from the past in authentic ancient costumes would pounce and pronounce their sentence on me, like Scrooge waking to find the ghosts of Christmas past at his bed. Yes, pounce and pronounce; and misunderstand. Even the characters in my own dreams misunderstood me, how typical.

'I'm sorry . . . I didn't mean it like that, not as an excuse; I meant it as a question. I'm mad, aren't I?'

'We asked you the question, sir, and we still await an answer! Where are your companions?'

It seemed even the characters in my dreams lost patience with me.

'I'm not sure who you think I . . . Who do you mean?'

'You are never sure of anything, are you, sir?'

The figure saying this stepped forward to demonstrate that he could intimidate me with his presence. His partner joined him.

'You seek certitude and guidance from everyone you meet, never considering that it should come from within. That is why you fall under the influence of blackguards like Dexter. Yet if you had offered direction to others, you may have found it in yourself. *Service*, sir! Ask yourself how you may have served those who may have needed you.'

I had their faces close to mine as they made their point. I could feel no breath on my skin, but was near enough to study them in detail. Incredibly old, incredibly thin. A pair of performing lizards. I felt the cold as they drew closer, the chill that told me this was no dream, that they were sincere in their own way. They had taken me for one of Dexter's gang. These were the debt collectors come to take what was nature's due. I had thought I was ready but now when I looked death in the eye I turned and ran. I ran for my life.

TRANSCRIPT: TAPE 6 (continued)

Interviewer:
'Struck gold'?

Lowes:
Gold or ivory . . . bones . . . whatever . . . He went through the soil and he came up with something white. Could have been a stone or a piece of glass or anything, but in that atmosphere it must have appeared good enough for him to claim his prize from Pablo. And for Pablo to go even more rabid.

Interviewer:
In what way?

Lowes:
Steve wanted out, just to jump out and I guess . . . get it on with Claire as had been advertised. But Pablo screamed at him to stay where he was and to watch where he puts his spade. Careful! Can't you be careful? You'll ruin everything and we've waited too long to let that happen!

Interviewer:
Did he do as he was told?

Lowes:
Yeah. We were all to take our time now, to not disturb the remains too much and to look for the skull. That was the important part . . . the *vital* part. After all his wild abandon, Pablo was suddenly fussing over us like a pernickety schoolteacher on a field trip. Goodbye, Mr fucking Chips. (Laughs quietly) We were to continue and he would prepare . . . what was about to take place would be simply

extraordinary . . . we would see . . . *ex-tra-orr-din-arry* . . . He wasn't wrong either.

Interviewer:
How did he 'prepare'? What did this involve?

Lowes:
He . . . (hesitant pause) He slowed the girls down, I think. The five of them in a circle, although he himself was talking faster and faster, a man possessed, talking total gibberish. I couldn't make all of it out, maybe the others could hear it clearer, like Colin, ogling at the bits on view. I suppose he wasn't used to so much flesh on parade . . . Hell, he wouldn't be the only one. I think Eddie was lying flat out at this stage, like he'd corpsed, unconscious or asleep. Peaked too early, I guess . . . There would have been three of us digging in the grave, me and Andy; the other must have been Ciaran. I really don't know where the others have gone, just drifted away at various points . . . Anyway, Pablo was bleating his garbled commands. 'Remember we are a club, united, by our own rules . . . we have bonded. Think of your favourite dead relative. Do not be afraid to feel sad. Negative emotions are strong! I want you all to give me something to help our dear friend Mr De Quincey escape. He needs your energy . . . just a loan . . . spare it and we will triumph . . . an extraordinary triumph of science awaits! We can prove them all wrong . . . all of them . . .'

Interviewer:
And the digging continued as he spoke? Did you find the skull?

Lowes:
We had all slowed more or less to a standstill. You couldn't help notice what Pablo was doing . . . would have put anyone off . . .

Interviewer:
What was that?

Lowes:

He had the vibrator in his hand. He'd been waving it around all night, only now he was closing in with it. (Adopts warbling tone) 'I want your energies . . . dear Thomas is waiting for your energy to lift him.' (Resumes normal voice) He was waving it in their faces, then he was rubbing them with it. It wasn't switched on, or it wasn't making any kind of sound if it was . . . And he was stroking their buttocks with it as he went up to them, then closer, under the chin, gliding it down their arms and getting more and more intimate . . . He stopped with Claire, had her leaning against a headstone, facing him, and he let the thing wander all over her. We were all watching by then. All over her; calves and thighs, and then parting her knees with it and stepping nearer, pushing her right back against the stone. He must have slipped it inside her. A sad smile came on her face and she let out a moan, softly at first, then louder . . . He's still doing his own commentary . . . 'Think of your favourite dead relative . . . *concentrate* . . .' There had to be a manual control on the tool because he was fumbling with it, both hands, and I could see there was some kind of winding or stroking going on. And then she was louder and louder, wailing and flapping her arms . . .

Interviewer:

Approaching orgasm?

Lowes:

(long pause) I don't think so . . . that wasn't it. The sound owed more to distress than pleasure . . . and her movements . . . eyes so tightly closed, legs twitching and kicking into the earth . . . it was as if she were trying to escape the thing rather than embrace it . . . I've heard lots . . . heard a few women come and I'm sure I would know whether they were into it or not. And even if there can be a thin line between ecstasy and pain I felt that this was . . . neither . . . but deeply unsettling all the same. There was a spell on that place. That's what I was thinking, a spell on the whole fucking place because it was getting colder and colder and colder.

Interviewer:
When did Dexter stop manipulating the device?

Lowes:
When Colin pulled him off.

Interviewer:
Literally?

Lowes:
Yes. He went up and barged right between the pair of them, pushed Pablo to one side, and when he turned he had the thing in his hands. They were shouting at each other, Pablo outraged and Colin saying 'Enough!' Pablo wanted to reclaim the dildo. 'Let me have it, you fool, before you ruin everything!' And the music was still playing with its urgent pulse even if proceedings were off course. The loop going round endlessly . . . (shakes head) What a spectacle, what a *scene* . . . scandalous . . . Colin could fend him off quite easily. He's bigger – a rugby player's brawn against Pablo's squat little monster. So he was holding the thing in one hand and staring at it like it's a blood-stained dagger pulled straight out of someone's heart . . . 'Disgusting,' he muttered. 'Vile and unnatural.' Pablo still makes the odd snatch for it, but Colin is mesmerised, fidgeting with the switches, won't let him anywhere near . . . He must have been jolted into hitting one of the wrong buttons because suddenly he's wailing just like Claire had been, spinning on the spot, wrapped around the thing, as if committing hari-kari with the piece. He collapsed in a heap eventually, right where he had been standing, and then he didn't make a sound.

Interviewer:
Did anyone rush to help revive him, and what had happened to Claire?

Lowes:
(sighs) No one rushed to help anyone . . . Claire was left to shiver in the cold. She didn't seem to want to move any more than Colin.

No one rushed to help anyone. That was when the guests arrived
... or materialised.

Interviewer:
Who do you mean?

Lowes:
The guest stars, the character actors. The two old codgers in period
costume straight from the set of a Sir Walter Scott novel. In all
the gear – top hats, cravats, stockings and breeches. Proper Regency
gentlemen they were. I was impressed. The full works, and right
on cue ... completely dead-pan, not a trace of shock or surprise
at what they had walked in on. They made straight for Pablo.

Interviewer:
Did he seem to know them?

Lowes:
Maybe he didn't know them, but he acted as if he might have
expected some kind of interruption and here it was ... He had a
resigned attitude. The opportunity to do whatever it was seemed
to be falling away even before this happened, and now another
problem. This pair though – I don't know where they got them from
but I have to say they were magnificent ... caricatures hamming it
up with total commitment.

Interviewer:
Commitment to what?

Lowes:
To their given roles as interlopers, or providers of comic relief ...
Whatever it was that Pablo's production team had devised for them
so they could take the heat out of that particular moment. And
they gave this their all ... Imperious glares, snooty noses in the
air. They stood leaning on their walking sticks, another hand on
hip or tucked into a waistcoat pocket like fucking Napoleon. I
warmed to them, I really did. I just couldn't take them seriously. I
might have been in the minority there, of course ...

Interviewer:
Why, were the others more fearful of them?

Lowes:
They must have been . . . perhaps there was something sinister about their presence. They were whited-up as well, like Pablo . . . but thin men, bony men, almost skeletal and so very old. I presumed they had cultivated the ghostly glow like Pablo had, only theirs was the more convincing. They had managed some trick with their footwear so that their legs didn't appear to touch the ground but faded into the grass. An illusion, a clever one for outdoors . . . You had to admire the craft and effort that had been put into it all, although this was let down somewhat when they spoke. Their voices were not authentic at all; too much Scots and not enough Edinburgh plums and marbles in the mouth. 'I'm Mister Begby and this is ma associate Muster Roberts . . . Whit yuse urr doin here, sur, is an abomination, and we urr here tae pit an end tae it.'

Interviewer:
If that was what was said, how did Dexter respond?

Lowes:
We waited and waited for a reply. Again, I wasn't perturbed by this but some must have let the build-up in tension get to them. Some started cowering a bit. Steve and Ciaran were beside me in the grave and they shrunk down so that their heads weren't visible to those above. I also saw that Eddie had woken up and had begun to crawl away whilst the rest had their backs to him. That was the last I saw of him . . . I waited for Pablo to respond. I couldn't understand why he didn't. These guys had to be his men, there to make some point that would pull us all back into line and get the boys digging harder, and the girls to give . . . give their energy in a different way, I suppose.

Interviewer:
But this might not have actually been the case?

Lowes:

Well, looking back, I suppose things were starting that maybe weren't part of the original script . . . like people sneaking off for good and some of those left behind starting to try and hide themselves. Pablo himself could have been losing his grip on things . . . all his clever words from earlier had dried up, and all he would say to these characters was, 'Be off! Be off! We are trying to make history and will not be bound by your petty rules and hypocrisies.' The newcomers stood and looked at him, probably waiting for more. They didn't get any. That was when Colin found his way back onto his feet and started acting seriously mad . . . And I *do* mean mad.

Interviewer:

In what way?

Lowes:

Mad? Mad as in barking mad, mad as a fucking hatter.

Interviewer:

Can you explain?

Lowes:

Squawking like a deranged chicken. Or like a damsel in distress, shouting from the top of her prison tower. (High-pitched whine) 'Pablo! Pablo! Help me, please. What have you done to me? I'm *scared*, Pablo. What's going on?' (Normal voice resumes) You've got this big hairy bloke suddenly acting like a fairy . . . pantomime stuff . . . wringing his hands and fighting back the tears. Another great performance . . . or so I thought. He's never been the same, you say? A woman trapped in a man's body . . . Rather him than me, Colin. Rather you than fucking me.

Interviewer:

You are sceptical that the events of that night were the cause of his breakdown?

Lowes:
I didn't say that. I'm sure there must have been something that happened which maybe didn't exactly help, but as I said, he was wired pretty tightly before we began. And it was him that pulled Pablo off Claire, him that took so much exception to it.

Interviewer:
Although you yourself also said that it was a disturbing sight when Dextrus penetrated her with the device, and that you thought she had been trying to fight him off at that time . . .

Lowes:
And I don't deny it. What's your point?

Interviewer:
That shouldn't *you* have tried to intervene if you thought she was in distress, that any decent person should have tried?

Lowes:
(sourly) What kind of fucking interview do you want? Want to hear what happened, or what should have happened, according to you? I've tried to tell you all along . . . things were not real . . . This wasn't me as I'm talking to you right now watching all of this. It was somebody else, somebody deliberately . . . I don't know . . . Someone brainwashed . . . I've tried to tell you but you haven't understood, have you?

Interviewer:
(pause) So you have no regrets?

Lowes:
(impatiently, agitated) Of course I've got fucking regrets. What do you take me for? I've got to live with all this, you know? I think about that girl a lot . . . She was so bright and vibrant when we first met . . . now a zombie, a fucking vegetable. I even think about Colin. But I have to say – a policeman! What was he doing there? Had he thought he would enjoy it, or was he undercover, expecting to unearth some art world crime ring? These people had sought

Pablo out; we all had. We all wanted a bit of danger and then complain if it gets out of hand. And another thing, all this damage is meant to have been caused by the vibrator thing . . . really? I mean, where is it now – this deadly weapon? I saw it – just a normal fucking sex toy. Yet it can rob a girl of her mind, drive another one insane and kill someone. (Sourly, slowing down) Sure it can . . . Sure, it wasn't a magic trick at all. (Sarcastically) Of course, these people were sound and well-balanced before *any* of this tragic stuff happened.

Interviewer:
Did Dextrus manage to calm Colin down at all at this point?

Lowes:
It wasn't really a matter of 'calming down'. He had gone . . .

Interviewer:
So we have the two new arrivals in their costumes. We have Claire, standing naked in a vacant silence. We have Colin becoming more hysterical, and some of those that are as yet unscathed are trying to make their escape. And you. You stayed?

Lowes:
Are you disappointed? Would you rather the story ends here?

Interviewer:
It doesn't, though?

Lowes:
No. The finale was on its way, the icing was about to go on the cake . . . the pièce de fucking resistance had still to happen.

Interviewer:
Which was?

Lowes:
The final arrival, the last guest star, the final act.

I DRANK A LOT OF WHISKY at Mather's Bar at the top of Queensferry Street, a five-minute walk from St Cuthbert's that I had made in less than sixty seconds. Mather's was open until four in the morning during the festival. That allowed for a lot of whisky indeed, though not enough to numb the fear and self-loathing that gripped me like a cheese wire g-string. I had set myself the dare. I had tried to see it through. I had been scared off. Where was the shame in that? None. At least, none out of the ordinary by my standards.

What would Andy have done? Would he have laughed them off? Or bloody Jules – what would she find to say if . . . Jules would face them, wouldn't she? I ordered another dram.

What if I'd been had? What if they, too, had been actors brought in for a specific role, maybe to ward off trespassers for the main event? What if they were laughing at me now, checking their make-up in a mirror and relishing how easy it had been?

And what was it they had said – didn't that give it away? 'You are not sure of anything, sir. Give service to those who may need you and you may find the certainty you seek in yourself.'

Cheeky bastards. I swallowed hard. Jules might need me. I would take them at their word. For once I would surprise myself. I was going back. I would overwhelm them all.

TRANSCRIPT: TAPE 7

Interviewer:
Someone else joined at this stage?

Lowes:
A youngish bloke, about twenty-five or thirtyish, hard to be precise in the dark. Modern clothes, normal clothes, shirt and tie and linen jacket. He made straight for Pablo as well, goes straight by everyone and nothing fazes him. I wondered if he was stoned as well . . . Doesn't seem put out by the girls hanging round with everything on show, or by these people in white sheets up to their necks in a freshly excavated grave, or even the fact that there are already two bizarre men ahead of him in the queue to have a pop at Pablo who himself is distracted by another man tottering around screaming like a banshee . . . No, this man ignores it all; he means business, and his business is Pablo. 'You bastard . . . you have ruined me . . . ruined me and I want to know why. I demand to know why!'

Interviewer:
Do you think Dexter knew him?

Lowes:
Seemed to. Called him by name. 'Not now, Charlie. I'm a bit busy with one thing or another. Can't this wait? I'm sure you'd be better off elsewhere.' The stranger thing was that the other guys seemed to know him as well. 'Can ye no await yur turn, Muster Kidd, or huv ye no manners at all?' Like I said, there was a fucking queue wanting to sort out poor Pablo – Colin, the old guys, the new guy . . . Just a matter of who would do him first, I guess, who would push themselves to the front and get him.

Interviewer:
So was this another scene concocted by Dextrus? What would its purpose have been?

Lowes:
A *scene* . . . Everything a scene. I don't know. I had stayed with it all this long because I thought there would be a point to it all, that there was a grand fucking design that would teach us all something about ourselves. And for sure there *had* been moments up to then when we had been given a . . . mirror . . . on ourselves, on our souls. Then I think that maybe all that there was to it was Pablo trying to see how far he could push us and being surprised over and over that it was all the way . . . (pause) Yes, he could push us all the way and we would take it . . . (pause) So maybe we did learn something about ourselves after all, something really shit.

Interviewer:
So these final arrivals might have been included as some kind of finale?

Lowes:
(sighs) These are supposed to be the last moments of someone's life we are talking about here and here we go again . . . analysing it like it's some kind of event, or performance. Fuck, and maybe *that* tells us, *me* . . . something about ourselves – that I'll fall into it. I'll tell you what I think today, which is that I don't think this bit was staged. I think Pablo was scared shitless that everything was out of control; nobody was acting like they should have been. At the time I took it all to be part of the show because everything else had been part of the show. Everything.

Interviewer:
(softly) Could you just tell me what happened from this point then?

Lowes:
Well, the guy that had just arrived was worked up – maybe he'd had his own herbal tonic to set him up. Really agitated . . . wanted to fight everyone, or anyone who got in the way of him laying into

Pablo. And Pablo wanted rid of him more than he wanted rid of anyone else. (Mutters between clenched teeth) 'Charlie, for fuck's sake just piss off. This isn't for you.' (Resumes normal speaking tone) I think, I thought that Pablo actually liked this new man. I had a sense that he wanted him away because he was trying to protect him. The old gents . . . they had no time for him, wanted to just push him right out of the picture. (Adopts accent) 'You wull stand down, sir. We huv warned you already about yer conduct and its consequences for you.'

Interviewer:
Did the newcomer respond to either?

Lowes:
It just fired him up the more. He nodded his head as if this was exactly what he'd expected, but that he would have the final say. 'No way, no way bloody José. I won't be neglected. You two . . .' and he turned to give out some heavy finger wagging at the old-timers. 'You pair don't scare me at all. There's nothing you can take from me because I've got one hundred per cent, *one hundred per cent* . . . of fuck-all. Think I don't know who you are? Stooges, bloody stooges. You're more of his kind, aren't you?' and he jabs out towards Pablo. 'You get off on the same shit as he does, don't you? Well, not at my expense tonight, boys, and not at hers either.' He nods to Jules, who is gawping at him in wild amazement. Mind you, she's stark naked so it might have been wild embarrassment. 'The show,' he says, 'is fucking . . . *over!*' He says this and plucks the vibrator from out of Colin's limp grasp, and points it at Pablo . . . and he winds and winds and winds it, and he's snarling as he does this like he's having some sort of fit . . . and Pablo's saying, 'Put it down, Charlie. Be a good boy now. Don't be stupid, *Charlie* . . .' And the old boys are hovering around trying to halt the proceedings but reluctant to touch anyone . . . and the girls are crying, and Colin's wailing, and Claire's in her own little world. (Shakes head slowly) Our new man winds and winds and winds the thing and he stops and takes three steps forward and he says to Pablo, 'Want a taste of your own medicine?' and flicks the switch and shoves it right down his throat . . . (long pause) I've never seen

227

anything like it. Pablo's eyes flicker with electricity like the lights in a pinball machine about to go 'tilt' ... and then his arms ... flapping like broken wings, faster and more frantic by the second until ... (disbelievingly) ... until he is lifted clear off the ground. (Halts to sip from glass of water) Then there was the explosion, or the flash before the explosion, a split second of blinding light that came before the sound came and knocked me clean off my feet. I staggered back up and out of the grave to find everyone gone. Everyone was fleeing the scene as the sparks rained down on us. It was like World War Three in there. These firework displays can look fantastic, but take it from me, they are best admired from a distance, the one they do above the Castle during the Festival especially so ... All of St Cuthbert's would glow orange, then emerald, then be bleached a brilliant white as the crackers went off in their sequence, and every time I thought, this is it, a direct hit. I had to dodge my way out as if I was under sniper attack, using the headstones for cover, one after the other ... until I was out of there and I was free. And that's how I felt, free.

Interviewer:
Did Dexter himself explode?

Lowes:
I told you what I saw. You tell me.

Interviewer:
Tell you what?

Lowes:
Anything.

Interviewer:
I don't follow.

Lowes:
Tell me what all this is to you. Or are you part of the show as well? I mean, you ask your fucking questions, you are sure about what it is you want to know, but for all *I* know you are part of the

same thing, another set-up. I respond to *your* ad this time rather than Pablo's. I swear to God this whole thing will drive me insane ... Once you see *one* thing, *one* person, *one* episode in your life as a sham, as some kind of con or performance put up just to get a reaction from you, well, it gets hard to stop. You feel like some kind of creature in the laboratory and everyone is watching so they can dissect you. So I sit here, answering your questions and I get to the end of it and I start asking myself if you are just another one of them and if this is just the next fucking game. Are you part of Pablo's merry fucking team? Are you? Is he behind all this? Is he listening to this? (Reaches forward to grab microphone, screams into it) ARE YOU SATISFIED, PABLO? IS THIS WHAT YOU WANTED?
(Tape ends)

ROBERTS, BEGBY & LAWRIE W.S.,

MARY KING'S CLOSE, EDINBURGH.

FILE NOTE: CLAIRE LISTER, PETER DEXTRUS, DANIEL
         LOWES, CHARLES KIDD ET AL

Although it is not our normal practice to take any
pride, other than a professional one, in the efforts
of our partnership, we would concede that the outcome of our direct excursion into the matters of Mr
Peter Dexter are a source of not inconsiderable
gratification to us.

And when we read, as we do, of the announced engage-
ment between Mr Charles Kidd and Miss Julia Rigby,
our small sense of satisfaction grows with the earn-
est hope that here is an individual who has perhaps
seen the error of his former ways and has steeled
himself to serve, as we ourselves chose to do so
many years ago.

It is of but minor irritation that an atypical
clerical error led to the arrest and imprisonment
of the wrong Mr D. Lowes, that is to say Mr D. Lowes
primus, when our manifest intention was of course
originally to apprehend Mr D. Lowes secundus.
Nevertheless, we are given to understand that this
person's conduct has in itself been an appalling
example to youth in general and his own son in particular, and are therefore not minded to rectify the
initial error in the execution of our order. More-
over, we are further encouraged by the news that
Lowes junior has recommenced his psychiatric therapy
and has impressed all with the sincerity of his
desire to seek whatever help it takes to put the
demons of his past behind him. We trust the medical
profession will not let him down in this ambition.

Finally, whilst noting the almost pleasurable irony
that Mr Peter Dexter should meet his demise in such
a theatrical manner - exiting, as it were, in a puff
of smoke - we also note and concur with the stance
taken by the Evening News when reporting on the
desecration that was visited upon the grave of
Thomas De Quincey at St Cuthbert's. Commenting that
the damage done to the church grounds could only
have been the result of 'thoughtless vandalism',
the paper asked, somewhat rhetorically, what kind of
perverse minds could take pleasure in committing
such a disrespectful act. It was thankful that the
perpetrators seemed to have been disrupted in their
shameless endeavours and hoped that one day they
would have cause to rue their behaviour, that 'there
may be some ways in which their actions may come to
haunt them'. We find ourselves in total agreement.

Indeed, we can put it no simpler than that.

ACKNOWLEDGEMENTS

Chambers' *Traditions of Edinburgh*
Owen Dudley Edwards, *Burke and Hare* (Mercat Press)
The author is particularly indebted to Michael T.R. Turnbull's
  Edinburgh Graveyard Guide (Saint Andrew Press)